Whiskey Jack Lodge

By
Randall Probert

Whiskey Jack Lodge
by Randall Probert

www.randallprobertbooks.net

email: randentr@megalink.net

Photography credits:

Front cover sketch ~ Sarah Lane, Bethel, ME
Tractor photo, pg 200 ~ www.farmcollector.com
Mower photo, pg 200 ~ www.history.com
Author's photo, pg 278 ~ Patricia Gott

Disclaimer:
This book is a work of fiction, but it does contain some historical information.

ISBN: 978-1977782885

Printed in the United States of America

Published by
Randall Enterprises
P.O. Box 862
Bethel, Maine 04217

Acknowledgements

I would like to thank Amy Henley of Newry, Maine for her help typing this and the many revisions. I would like to thank Laura Ashton of Woodland, Georgia for her help formatting this book for printing. I would like to thank Sarah Lane of Bethel, Maine for the cover sketch, and Pat Gott of Norway, Maine for the author photo.

More Books by Randall Probert

Whiskey Jack Lodge

Chapter 1

Rascal, Jeters and Silvio were still drinking coffee in the cafeteria with Warden Jarvis Page and a new young game warden, Marcel Cyr, when Rascal's wife Emma came in and walked over to their table and put her arm around Rascal and kissed him. Everyone there except for Marcel Cyr was well aware of what had taken place there in Whiskey Jack in the last couple of weeks, with Rascal, Silvio, Jeters and Jeff being hauled off to jail for violating the new Volstead Law—manufacturing brandy— and Emma being arrested for shooting a deer in closed season, although the deer was in the garden and eating her lettuce.

No one except for Jarvis and Rascal had suspected that it had been Emma who had turned against the men making brandy, but everyone suspected that somehow Rascal had been responsible for his wife going to jail for shooting a deer. Even though at the time, Rascal and Jarvis were walking across the dam towards his cabin for some of Emma's fresh baked biscuits when they heard Emma shoot.

She kissed Rascal again and looked at each of the men and smiled. As if she knew something they didn't. Jarvis, Silvio and Jeters all thought Emma would be angry for having to spend a night in jail. And more especially towards Jarvis for making the arrest, and Rascal, for they all figured that somehow he was responsible for bringing all of this down on Emma. They just didn't know how he had accomplished it.

"My, why are all of you men suddenly so quiet?" she asked with a happy smile. "I have a few minutes, would it be alright if I joined you for a cup of coffee?"

Silvio spoke first, "Darling, you can join us men anytime you wish for a cup of coffee." They all nodded their heads and Rascal pulled up a chair from another table for her.

"Emma, I'd like you to meet my soon to be replacement, Marcel Cyr. Marcel, this is Emma Ambrose. Rascal's wife."

Marcel stood up and shook her hand and said, "My pleasure, ma'am."

They sat down and Emma asked, "What are you men talking about? The Prohibition law or Women's Right to Vote?"

Silvio spoke up again, "Both, actually, Emma. I guess no one can fault any woman for wanting the right to vote. But this Prohibition law ain't right. Anita even made me promise not to make any more wine or brandy."

"That's too bad, I would have liked to have tried some of that rhubarb wine. Rascal tells me it was quite good."

Silvio, Jeters and Jarvis almost choked on their coffee. Both Emma and Rascal were smiling. And young Marcel Cyr had no idea what was happening.

"When are you officially retiring, Jarvis?" Silvio asked.

"This coming Saturday will be my last day."

"We all, everyone in Whiskey Jack, will be sorry to see you leave, Jarvis," Silvio said.

"I'll come up to fish and hunt. If I had my way I'd move my family here. But my wife, Rita, put her foot down and said 'no way.' She's already busy cleaning out the barn. That's where we'll have our furrier shop."

The train whistle blew, signaling it would be leaving in five minutes for Lac St. Jean. "That's our signal, Marcel. We'd better get back aboard."

They stood up and Marcel said, "It was a pleasure to meet you, Mrs. Ambrose."

"Emma, it is always good to see you. I hope you don't hold any grudges."

"Not at all, Jarvis. Bring your wife up anytime and spend a weekend with us," Emma said.

"Where are you heading now, Jarvis?" Rascal asked.

"I want to show Marcel things to watch on the border. We won't be back through until tomorrow."

The train crew had set off four empty flatbed cars on a side track for the mill and now had recoupled to the tender and was ready to leave. Jarvis and Marcel boarded just in time. Silvio and Jeters stood on the hotel train platform watching Rascal and Emma walk across the dam holding hands like two teenagers.

"Something is going on there, Silvio, with those two. They should be mad as old hell at each other. But look at 'em. They both act like teenage lovers."

"I don't know any more than you do, Jeters. Or why Emma is suddenly so happy and pleasant. She deserves to be happy though. She's a good woman, Jeters."

"Do you think Rascal orchestrated Emma being arrested and going to jail, Silvio?"

"I honestly don't know. The thought has crossed my mind. I guessed about everyone in the village thinks he did. But how? How would he know the deer would be in the garden at the same time as Jarvis being in the village? I don't know, Jeters, but something has happened. Just look how they both are when they are together.

* * *

After they took their seats and the train was on the way, Marcel said, "Those men back there seemed like a motley group. Can you trust any of them, Jarvis?"

"I would trust them all with my life. But don't underestimate them either. If any one of them was hungry and needed meat, there isn't any one of them who would hesitate to go out and get a deer. For themselves or anyone else who was hungry. There'll be times when the train will hit a moose or deer and you'll have to come up and take care of it. And it would hurt none if you saw to it that the villagers got most of the meat."

"What about Rascal? Is he as bad as his name might imply?"

Jarvis didn't answer right off. He didn't want to tell any stories about Rascal he couldn't back up. "The only time I ever had him in court was a second limit of brook trout. And last fall I had him for selling deer to two Massachusetts hunters. He had a good excuse and the judge was easy on him." Then he told Marcel the rest of the story about the two whiskey-soaked hunters.

He laughed then and added, "But Emma, you'll have to keep a sharp eye on. Last week I arrested her for shooting a deer in closed season."

"Emma? Are you serious? She seemed so nice and friendly."

"She is." Then Jarvis told him the story about the deer eating her lettuce.

"It was just by happenstance that I was in the village." Then on another note he added, "I have never believed in anything being purely coincidental," and he left it at that.

He pointed out to Marcel where Ledge Swamp was and that the train was now pulling away from Jack Brook, ". . .the inlet to Whiskey Jack Lake."

"There never has been much hunting from the villagers or from the Canadians in through here. We're too far from the village and the Canadians hunt mostly along the cleared border. You'll see when we get there."

A half mile north of Ledge Swamp they could see where the beaver had dammed up a cast iron culvert. "When beaver plug a culvert or bridge the station master at the village, Greg, will hire Rascal to trap them out. And I have always let Rascal have the hides and sell 'em."

"I have never seen wilderness like this before, Jarvis. I hope I'm up to it," Marcel said.

"Ah, you'll be okay, Marcel, once you get used to it and begin to feel comfortable using your compass. Have your compass with you no matter where you go and learn to depend on it.

"The train always blasts the whistle as it approaches the village and the border crossing. And it can be heard for miles away. Learn to use it and it will help you get your bearings if you do get turned around."

"That's good to know. Will the engineer stop the train for me if I want to climb aboard or get off somewhere out here?"

"All you have to do is ask the conductor or wave the train down if you want to board. They are very obliging. I have already spoken to the conductor that we'll want to get off at the border crossing."

"How far from the village is the border?"

"I think about six miles. The village is at mile ten and the border, I think, is about mile sixteen. There have been a few times when I have missed the train and had to hike along the tracks back to the village.

"When we leave the border tomorrow I'll take you up to the farm. This is where the lumbering crews stay."

Just then the engineer blew the train whistle signaling it was approaching the border. Jarvis said, "We'd better get our packs and be ready to jump off."

The engineer was used to Jarvis getting off at the border and he only slowed the train just enough so they could jump off, then he pushed the throttle forward again and a black column of smoke rose. Once inside the building, he made introductions. "Alfons, this is—or will be—the new game warden here after this week, Marcel Cyr. Marcel, Alfons Dubois."

Marcel said hello in French and Alfons replied in French. "Ah, a good French man.

"You getting done the job of game warden, Jarvis?"

"Yes, I'm retiring after this week. The job needs a younger man."

"I do not know, me. You get around the woods pretty good."

They had a cup of coffee with Alfons and talked for a while before leaving. After two cups of black coffee, they were ready to leave. "We probably should keep to the cover of the trees on our side of the line. The daytime temperatures will be dropping soon and then that's when the moose hunting begins. The meat is not so apt to spoil in the cold and the Canadian hunters can take their time and not hurry."

They had hiked about a half of a mile when they came across a well-used trail, crossing the cleared borderline to the Maine side. "This trail leads back to a small village and this is where I have had most of the illegal hunting."

"The trail looks used recently, Jarvis," Marcel said.

"It does, doesn't it. Let's see what they have been up to. We'll walk beside the trail so not to leave any sign that we were here." They set over in the trees just far enough so they could still see the trail.

After twenty minutes Jarvis whispered, "We're getting close to some good moose habitat. We'll have to be quiet from here and go slow."

Adrenaline was flowing in Jarvis's blood and he was excited of the possibility of catching an illegal hunter just before he retired. He was also thinking he'd have to give this all up after the end of that week. Marcel was nervous and perspiring so much he had to keep wiping his face with his handkerchief.

Ten minutes later they came to a marshy area directly ahead of them. The trail angled off to the left. Jarvis stepped behind a large spruce tree and Marcel followed him. "There are the remains of two old hunting stands off to the right. I tore them down two years ago. I think someone has built a new one off to the left. Let's go see. We'll leave our packs behind this spruce tree," Jarvis whispered.

They followed the trail towards the north end of the marsh and saw boot tracks in some mud that were heading back. Jarvis pointed to the tracks and made a sign with his hands that whoever it was had gone out. They were still being careful not to leave any signs that someone had been there.

Jarvis was looking up ahead and Marcel tapped him on the shoulder and pointed to a huge bull moose across the marsh scraping its antlers on some alder bushes to remove the velvet.

They stood there patiently waiting to see if someone was going to shoot it. After fifteen minutes the bull wandered back into the trees and out of sight. "If someone is here, which I doubt, then they didn't see it. We need to get up close enough to see if anyone is here."

Ever so slowly they worked their way forward and listening. About fifty yards up ahead Jarvis spotted a hunting stand that had been built about ten feet off the ground in some spruce trees. As they crept closer it became obvious there was no one there.

There was fairly fresh sawdust on the ground beneath the stand. "This is new. Look at the sawdust. Let's climb up and have a look."

From the stand they could see most of the marsh and there was now a lone cow where the bull had been. "These guys sure do know what they're doing."

There were two wooden stools which one might believe were for two men hunting from the stand. "Looks like two men use this," Marcel said.

"That's usually how they hunt. After the moose is down and dressed, one goes back for help and one stays with the moose to keep predators away. And he will always start a fire."

Jarvis picked up an empty shell in one corner and after looking it over he said, "British .303. Now we know what caliber they're using."

"Do you think they have already killed something?" Marcel asked. "We didn't see any drag marks or hair."

"What if they shot a deer and packed out only the meat in pack baskets?" Jarvis asked.

"Then there would be remains in the marsh," Marcel said.

"Right, let's have a look."

Jarvis put the empty shell in his pocket and they climbed back down. "It looks like someone walked through here," Jarvis said. When they came to mud there were boot tracks and two different designs. "Now we know there are two men."

"Look, Marcel," and Jarvis pointed to several ravens that had just taken to flight about seventy-five yards ahead. "That'll be the remains of whatever they shot."

There wasn't much left, but enough to identify the remains as deer and not moose.

"From the presence of four leg bones I'd say they deboned the meat and packed it out. See if we can find a spent bullet. It looks like the deer died right here." A bear had carried off the hide and head, but under all the messy stomach contents Marcel found the bullet.

"Good job Marcel. It's bigger than a 30 caliber, and my guess would be a .303," Jarvis said.

"Okay, now what do we do? We can't legally march across the border and start searching homes," Marcel said.

"Think about it, Marcel, and you tell me."

Marcel was silent for a while thinking, and looking the deer remains over and then he said, "Well, this wasn't a mature buck, only a small spike horn. So there would have only been at most maybe forty pounds of meat. To be split up between two men and probably their families. This kill is at least a day old, which tells me whoever it is is hunting during the week. I think they will be back soon for another kill."

"That was a pretty good deduction. I put this kill no more than two days ago. I think we should wait for them to return."

Marcel was afraid Jarvis was going to say that. "How long do we stay?"

"This is Wednesday, if they don't come back this afternoon, maybe tomorrow. Tomorrow at dark we decide how much longer we stay. Right now we need to leave the marsh and go back for our packs."

Jarvis cut across the lower end of the marsh so not to use the same trail and leave more sign that someone else was about. Back at their packs Marcel asked, "Okay, now where do we wait?"

"I've waited before behind that little knoll," and he pointed behind them. "There's good cover there and we can still see this trail."

The backside of the knoll dropped off slightly forming a nice depression for the two men to wait. They were only about twenty yards away.

Jarvis raked off all the old dried leaves and branches that would make any noise. At first Marcel wasn't sure what he was doing, but he caught on quick and helped. Then Jarvis cut off the top two feet of a small fir tree and stuck it in the ground on top of the knoll. And again Marcel did the same. He understood without having to ask that the small fir trees would conceal their faces while allowing them to see through.

In a low voice Jarvis said, "We probably should eat a sandwich now and drink some water. Later tonight when we're sure they won't be coming in we'll start a small fire and heat some water for hot tea." Jarvis laid on his back and closed his eyes. He was so quiet Marcel didn't know if he was asleep or not. With Jarvis so quiet Marcel was beginning to feel all alone in the big wilderness.

He sat up watching the birds and a mouse that had come up to smell the bottom of Jarvis's boots. Then it scurried off. There was a red squirrel in an adjacent tree that was scolding them. And suddenly he could hear something walking about a hundred yards in front of them. And whatever it was was coming closer. He touched Jarvis's arm and he opened his eyes, looking where Marcel was pointing. "Something is coming this way," Marcel whispered.

Jarvis sat up and he could hear it now. The noise was coming from the wrong direction to be the hunters. It had to be either a moose or bear. It was still coming closer. Marcel had a difficult time understanding how Jarvis could remain so calm.

Then the noise changed. "Did you hear that?" Jarvis said.

"Yeah," Marcel whispered back.

"That's a bull racking his antlers on a tree. This is the beginning of their rut. A little early, but that's what he is doing. Moose don't have sharp vision. If we stay still he'll probably just walk on by. Don't move. He would see the movement and think you a challenging bull, and might come at you. And whatever you do, don't cough, clear your throat or grunt. He would mistake that for another bull challenging him and charge at us."

The noise changed again and they could hear him coming towards them again.

Jarvis pointed and all Marcel could see were huge antlers swaying back and forth as the bull walked. He was only about two hundred feet away now. What Jarvis had said about the bull had actually made him more nervous.

Jarvis whispered, "I hope they don't shoot that bull."

The bull was coming straight towards them now and looking straight ahead. When the bull was only fifty feet away he stopped looking straight ahead with his head held high. He was sniffing the air. Jarvis found a rock about the size of a baseball and threw it at the bull and hit him in the chest. The bull flinched but he stood his ground swinging his huge head from side to side; looking for something. Jarvis threw another rock and hit the bull in the front shoulder. He still stood his ground. "Marcel, throw that stick," and he pointed to a three foot broken limb.

The stick took the bull in both front legs near the knees. The bull had had enough. He still had not seen the two men, but he didn't like being hit by sticks and rocks. He turned to the right and headed back towards the marsh. Marcel breathed a deep sigh of relief. Jarvis only smiled.

They both relaxed once the bull was out of sight. Jarvis, he laid back where he had been and closed his eyes. Marcel, he stayed sitting upright, on watch for any more moose. He was impressed with Jarvis' confidence and knowledge of the wilderness. He was beginning to wonder if he would ever develop that same level of confidence, understanding—and just *knowing.*

* * *

That was the last they would see of the bull moose. The sun was now below the tree tops and darkness would soon be upon them. Just before total darkness, Jarvis said, "I guess they won't be coming in tonight. While there is still a little light take this tea kettle,"—a fire blackened gallon can with a chain for a bail—"and get us some water from the marsh. I'll get a small fire going."

Jarvis found some white birch bark and some snapping dry softwood limbs. This would make a nice, quick, hot, smokeless fire. He dug out a small hole in the ground for a fire pit. By the time Marcel was back with the water Jarvis had the fire going. Marcel set the kettle on the fire and Jarvis added the tea.

"Might as well warm up a sandwich or two while we have the fire."

"How often have you had to stay out like this, Jarvis?"

"A lot; I couldn't tell how many times. My wife Rita would often say, especially during the late summer months and all through the fall, that I spent more time sleeping in the woods than I did in her bed." They both laughed. "She wouldn't be angry. She'd say it jokingly—she was right you know.

"If you're going to be a game warden, Marcel, and do the best you can, you can't ever look at it as if it were a job. It's a way of life and someday you'll discover it's a great game. I'm not saying there'll never be any disappointments, 'cause there'll certainly be a few. And you'll come up against some hard cases sometimes. But you must remember you have to remain in charge of any situation completely. You'll also get caught between a rock and a hard spot at times, and before you think about using your gun—well, you'll have to learn to use your mouth and talk your way around a bad situation. If you can't do that then you don't deserve to wear the uniform."

They were both quiet then. Marcel thinking and taking to heart what Jarvis had said.

With the sun now long gone they each wrapped up in a wool blanket and went to sleep. There was still some tea left in the kettle and Jarvis had said that would be good for breakfast in the morning. *Good and strong,* Marcel was thinking.

He lay awake for a while thinking about Jarvis and how comfortable he always felt alone in the wilderness. He really enjoyed being a game warden and it was too bad age was saying it was time to hang it up. With those thoughts he finally went to sleep. But it was a long night for Marcel Cyr. His senses were on alert and he awoke at the littlest disturbance.

An hour before sunrise Jarvis woke up and awoke Marcel. "We'd better eat our last sandwich now. If I were looking to shoot something I'd want to be in the hunting stand at daylight," Jarvis whispered.

As they were eating their sandwich they stood and walked around to start the circulation and stretch muscles. Marcel discovered that during the night the cold had worked its way into his bones and now as blood was beginning to flow, he realized he was cold. Jarvis didn't seem to be affected by the cold.

They put everything back in their packs and ate their sandwich. Marcel was still hungry enough to eat the leg of a horse. "I would expect them to come in anytime now, so be alert." They stretched their muscles before crawling back behind their cover. Marcel started to say something and Jarvis put a finger to his lip and shook his head slightly, *no,* and then touched his ear. Marcel got the message.

It was only a few short minutes later when Jarvis tapped Marcel on the shoulder and he put a finger to his ear and then pointed at the trail coming from the border. Marcel was amazed at how acute Jarvis' senses were. It wasn't long and he could also hear something coming from the trail. Whoever it was was being very quiet. These men definitely knew what they were doing.

It seemed to take forever before the two men came into view. They were not talking and taking every precaution not to make any noise. How had Jarvis first heard them? They walked on by them and never looked their way. They each were wearing dark green clothing, each had a rifle, and they were about 5'10" tall and maybe 200 pounds. Jarvis waited until he figured they must be at their stand and he whispered, "The one in front is Fredk St. Pierre and the other one is Ralph Paquette. I arrested them five years ago for killing a moose right here. That was September, they must feel pretty safe now in August. Five years ago they gave me quite a bit of trouble and I had to work on 'em a little. My guess is if we have to arrest them today they'll be pretty meek. If one of them does try to cause problems, do not hit him with a closed fist. You'll only break your knuckles. Use the flat of your hand and hit him right on the chin or nose. You'll have no more problems with him."

Marcel nodded his head he understood. While they waited for the shot he couldn't help but think how cool and collected Jarvis was. He was actually enjoying this. It was nothing more than a game to him. Albeit a rough one.

They waited and waited and slowly darkness was beginning to turn to daylight, and just like Jarvis had expected there came a loud rifle shot. The report echoed back and forth in the mountains and then there was a second shot and the report was different. "A smaller caliber," Jarvis said, "I hope they have two deer and not two moose. I surely do."

"Now what?" Marcel asked in a whisper.

"We wait. We'll let them probably debone the meat and fill their packs. When they come by us with their heavy packs we'll jump 'em. I doubt if they'll run carrying pack baskets full of meat."

Marcel had to stifle a laugh. But what would they do with a moose?

There was no hooting and hollering from those two. In fact they were still being very quiet. An hour passed and Jarvis whispered, "They are coming now. They didn't have enough time to debone a moose.

"Don't let them know you can speak and understand French. Listen to what they are saying. They know I am very limited with my French. You go stand behind that thicket of fir trees. When they go by me I'll step in behind them. When you hear me speak that's your cue to step out in front of them. Are you okay?"

"Sure am, let's do it."

"Good, go take up your position."

Fredk and Ralph were stepping right along now, but still being quiet. Jarvis was excited and his pulse was rapid. So too was Marcel's.

Jarvis could see them now. Fredk was in the lead. They were hurrying so maybe they had planned to go to work afterwards. He waited patiently, excitedly, until Ralph walked by and then very quietly he stepped in behind Ralph and said, "Bonjour, mon ami." They both stopped and swung around and their first instinct was to raise their rifles at the man in uniform until they recognized Jarvis. They well remembered the outcome five years ago when they tried to overpower him. Marcel now was standing behind Fredk and he surprised him and secured his rifle. Ralph Paquette was still in shock and hollered, *"Maudit krist tabernac!"* And he threw his rifle to the ground. "You Jarvis! Always you Jarvis! Where you come from?" They both were very upset. Hell, they were mad, but they were not about to cause any problems. Especially not since this time there were two game wardens (*garde-chasse*).

Marcel emptied Fredk's .30-30 rifle and put the shells in his pocket. The empty was still in the chamber. Jarvis did the same.

"Marcel, handcuff these two together. Fredk's hand left, he's left handed, to Ralph's right. He's right handed."

Jarvis waited for him to finish and then said, "You watch these two, Marcel, I'll be right back." He took his axe from his pack. He came back in a few minutes with both packs and two walking staffs for Fredk and Ralph. "You boys will need something to keep you from falling."

"Are you all set, Marcel?"

"Yeah."

"Lead off, I'll bring up the rear."

St. Pierre and Paquette were having no problem at all following Marcel. They were an hour hiking down to the custom house.

"What have you, Jarvis? More moose hunters?" Alfons Dubois asked.

"No Al, only two early deer hunters. Would you fry us up a mess of this deer meat?"

"Why sure, I sure would. I'll have me an early lunch, I will."

As Al was frying up some meat he said, "The morning train has already gone north. Southbound should go through about 2:30 this afternoon."

"If you don't mind, after we have eaten, we'll wait outside."

"Ain't these the same two you have five years ago or so?"

"Same two, Al. Only not so troublesome this time."

"One hellava way to break-in a new man, Jarvis. Making him hike all over this Godforsaken wilderness and sleep out in the cold."

"It wasn't so bad, Mr. Dubois. I kinda enjoyed it," Marcel said.

There was plenty of meat and everyone ate their fill and instead of using up all of Al's coffee, Jarvis made a pot of hot tea for everyone. And he left ten pounds of deer meat on the sideboard for Al. "That'll be greatly appreciated, let me tell you," Al said.

They could hear the southbound train long before they could even see the telltale column of smoke.

"Thank you, Al," Jarvis said.

"Any time, and in about three weeks I could probably use some venison, if you should happen to have some."

There were only two other passengers on the train this morning and they would be going through to Beech Tree. During the ride to Whiskey Jack, Fredk and Ralph started talking in French. They knew Jarvis wouldn't be able to understand what was being said and they naturally assumed the young warden wouldn't be able to either.

Marcel was in the seat in front of them and he was having a difficult time to keep from laughing. Jarvis was in the seat behind them. And he wasn't thinking too much about Fredk and Ralph. He had to admit it, he was tired and just maybe he had made the right decision to retire. He was sixty years old and had had a good life as a game warden. But in all honesty, these long periods away from home and sleeping in a ground hollow with little to eat or drink was not now so appealing to him. Yes, he had made the right decision.

Jarvis had been so deep in thought he had not paid attention to Fredk and Ralph or that they had just passed Ledge Swamp. That is not until the train engineer blew the whistle a half mile out from Whiskey Jack.

The train was stopping only long enough for three more passengers going to Beech Tree. He might be home in time for supper yet.

Jarvis looked out his window at Rascal sitting on his porch. And he was beginning to envy him and his lifestyle, and if truth be known, Rascal probably made more money in the course of the year, with his guiding and trapping and the occasional deer he could sell. Yes this would be a good life here in Whiskey Jack. But he had his wife Rita to think about, too, and she had already said she would never live in the wilderness like Whiskey Jack. But he could dream.

The train lurched forward as the engineer opened the throttle and gave the pistons a little steam.

St. Pierre and Paquette remained quiet during the ride to Beech Tree. Marcel was finding it very difficult to stay awake and he was so hungry now he could eat two horse legs. Jarvis was remembering all of his cases he had worked at Whiskey Jack, the farm and at the border. There was only one that puzzled him. It was Rascal, before he went to war. At the head of the lake. He knew—somehow—Rascal had shot that deer, but he had never come ashore and there was no firearm of any sort when he searched Rascal's canoe. Someday maybe he would ask him about it.

The train came to a stop at the Beech Tree terminal and after the other passengers had left, Jarvis said, "Come on, it's a short walk to the jail. I'm sure you remember the way." Both Fredk and Ralph had a worried look on their faces.

"What have you here, Jarvis?" Sheriff Burlock asked.

"Both men were hunting in closed season on this side of the border."

Burlock removed the handcuffs and escorted them back to the cells.

"There's no way they'll get bailed this weekend, Lee. Marcel court will be Monday morning. You'll have to escort these two over to the courthouse. Tomorrow is my last day. I'll be in court to give testimony. You take the rifles and next time Inspector Bouchard comes to Beech Tree give them to him to take to Augusta for you. I guess that's it.

"Oh, one more thing, what were the two talking about after we left the border?"

"Apparently they had shot one deer three days earlier and that didn't last long. And it was St. Pierre's idea to come back this morning. Paquette didn't want to. Apparently his wife said that if he was arrested again she would leave him in jail.

She doesn't like Fredk St. Pierre, and if they were caught his association with St. Pierre would be over. Oh and there's one more thing. After five years ago they both are terrified of you. They think you live in the woods."

Jarvis started laughing then and said, "I have for a good part of my career. Now it's your turn, Marcel. I'll take this meat home and can it and then I'll bring you your share. See you Monday morning."

Chapter 2

"Hey, Em!" Rascal hollered from the porch.

She came out and asked, "What?"

"I just saw Jarvis and the new warden leave on the southbound."

"So?"

"They were sitting in separate seats and they looked pretty haggard, and there were two men sitting in the seat between them."

"And?"

"Well it just looked sort'a strange that's all. They've been gone for two days and suddenly show up with two men."

"Well maybe tomorrow at the cafeteria someone will know. Supper is almost ready."

"Oh boy, fresh biscuits and beans and salt pork. I don't know why your biscuits, Em, always taste better than anyone else's."

"I don't know. I was thinking, Rascal, about that new warden, Marcel. I think you would make a good game warden, Rascal."

"Yeah, I have thought about it, but I think my bad leg would hold me back."

"You know, Rascal, I would really enjoy a glass of wine. Maybe the next time we go to St. Jean we can bring back some."

Emma had certainly changed since spending a night in jail, but this surprised him. "I might try making some, but I'd really hate to be brought up in front of Judge Hulcurt again. He let us off pretty easy."

"Is the mill going to start on time on Monday?"

"I think so. I haven't heard anything different."

After supper and the kitchen was cleaned up, they sat out on the porch watching the sun reflect off the lake surface as it slowly settled below the treetops. "The nights are cooling off already. I think I'll go in," Em said.

* * *

The next morning at the cafeteria Rascal joined Silvio, Jeters and Elmo for coffee and donuts. "Elmo, will the mill start up Monday?" Silvio asked.

"Yes, all the work has been done."

"Did any of you see Jarvis and the new warden yesterday on the afternoon southbound?" Rascal asked.

"No, but I heard Tom Whelling talking with the station master and he said those two men were the same ones Jarvis caught five years ago with a moose. You know the ones who tried to give him some trouble. Except when they went through here it looked like Jarvis had given those two the trouble. You know, I've always liked ole Jarvis. I'll miss him not being around," Silvio said.

"I, for one, would never want to cross him. He may be too old to keep game wardening, but I think he can still take care of himself," Jeters said.

"Rascal, you met that new warden. What did you think of him?" Elmo asked.

"I'm not too sure. He seemed a little nervous, like he wasn't too sure of himself. But I'll give him the benefit of doubt. Who knows, maybe younger blood, he'll be around here more than Jarvis was."

"Yeah, but," Silvio chimed in, "Jarvis was never overbearing. He did his job and I think everyone in the village knew and accepted that."

"All I have to say," Jeters said, "he has an awful big pair

of boots to step into."

The four of them talked for a long while about the old warden retiring and the new warden who was taking his place, and eventually the talk turned to Prohibition—which no one was in favor of. "I wonder what the new warden's feelings are on that?" Silvio said.

"I wonder if Dubois at the border will be looking for alcohol coming back from Lac St. Jean?" Jeters asked.

"Maybe if too many from the village were all at once traveling across," Rascal said, "it might raise some suspicion."

"I would imagine the men in the village will be glad when the mill starts up Monday," Silvio said.

"I would imagine so, although some have worked straight ahead on maintenance during the shutdown," Jeters said.

When the men broke up after their coffee, donuts and conversations had ended, Rascal went back home and with his axe and saw, he went out back to start on his winter firewood. Right now he would drop the trees to the ground and limb them and later he'd hire one of the stable's work horses and twitch everything to the cabin before working it up. He didn't want firewood or anything getting in his way of fall trapping this year.

"I'll be back for lunch, Em."

"Be careful."

He worked most of the day on Sunday dropping hardwood trees for firewood. He even found a few dead and dry ones still standing. Monday he would hire the horse and bring everything down to the cabin and get those worked up before cutting any more.

* * *

"You know, Rita, I kinda like this sleeping in, I just might like retirement," Jarvis said. "It's been a long time since I have slept this late. What time is it?"

"A little before 7 o'clock. I'll get up and start breakfast," Rita said.

After breakfast he shaved and put on clean clothes and walked to the courthouse.

Marcel was already there with St. Pierre and Paquette. There were three other people in the courtroom also.

"Good morning, Marcel. Did the prisoners give you any trouble?"

"Not at all. In fact they seem to be very humble this morning."

"How does it feel, Jarvis, to be retired?"

"Well, these last two mornings I have been able to sleep late. I'm sure I'll miss the job some. The exploring and the excitement of catching someone. Like when we caught St. Pierre and Paquette."

"I understand what you're saying there. I have to admit I also felt the adrenaline rush."

The judge's door opened and Judge Hulcurt stepped into the courtroom. Everyone stood. "Be seated, please," Hulcurt said.

The courtroom was silent while Hulcurt reviewed the case reports in front of him. After several minutes, "I think I'll hear the case against Fredk St. Pierre and Ralph Paquette. Please stand."

Hulcurt looked over his glasses down at the two. "Five years I think it was— Yes, I'm sure of it now. Five years ago Warden Page brought you in for shooting a moose in closed season. I remember your names and you, Mister St. Pierre, spell your name Fred with a k at the end—Fredk. And I must say you two look different this time. Your faces are not all covered with bandages."

Jarvis said to Marcel, "Stand up and tell the judge you will translate for him to the two prisoners."

Marcel stood up beside Jarvis and said, "Your Honor, these two do not speak or understand English. I speak French and will translate for them."

In perfect French Marcel translated what Hulcurt had said so far. They each were surprised to hear Marcel address them in their own language.

"Warden Jarvis, is there any reason why you are not in uniform in my court?"

"Yes Your Honor, I'm retired. Friday was my last day."

"Congratulations. Did either of these two give you any trouble this time?"

Marcel translated.

"Marcel Cyr was with me, Your Honor, and no they did not give us any trouble."

"Tell the court about the case."

"I was showing Warden Cyr around the district. When we left Whiskey Jack we went by train to the border and we hiked up along the border. I wanted to show him places to watch and trails coming from the Canadian side across the border. We found a well-used trail and followed that to a marsh well inside the border on Maine's side."

Marcel was translating all this.

"We found a new hunting stand that had been erected in trees and on the floor of the stand was an empty .303 cartridge. When we saw a bunch of ravens take to flight out in the marsh we went to investigate and found the remains of a recently killed deer."

"But the two deer you have charged them with were not shot until the day next on Friday. What was there that made you think they would come."

"The first deer was small and would not have lasted two families for very long. And the fact that I usually didn't work the border until September when Canada has their annual moose hunt. So I thought whoever shot that first deer might know that I don't usually work the border until later and might take advantage of that."

Marcel was busy translating every word and Hulcurt

could see the expression on St. Pierre's and Paquette's face change with surprise.

"And you say they did not cause any trouble this time?"

"That's correct, Your Honor."

"Did you know who these two were before they were apprehended?"

"Yes, Your Honor, when they walked by us when they came in before sunrise I recognized them both."

"You know, this case is getting interesting. There are several questions I need to ask of these two, but before I do that I'm going to set this case aside for now and take care of these other three cases."

There was one case of public drinking of alcohol, and the judge fined him $25. Another case of fighting—two days in jail. And the third case was a speeding automobile through Main Street—$25.

"Now, back to the deer case. Mister St. Pierre and Mister Paquette, do you admit to shooting deer in closed season?"

Marcel translated this and waited for their reply. "They do, Your Honor."

"Before I sentence them—I just have to know why they went back to the same spot where Warden Jarvis caught them with a moose five years ago."

Marcel translated this and they each had much to say.

"Your Honor, Fredk St. Pierre has a small family farm and then in the winter he cuts some lumber on his own land. He has four children, the fourth being born this spring. Neither he nor his wife were wanting another child."

Hulcurt broke in there, "The doctors now know how women get pregnant."

Marcel translated and both St. Pierre and Paquette had to stifle a laugh. "To continue, Your Honor, the mill where Mister St. Pierre was selling his logs burned and there was no money coming in. He even had to sell his best milking cow. But after the money was gone there wasn't enough to buy meat for his family, so he felt he had no choice but to poach a deer or two.

"Mister Paquette's story is very similar, Your Honor, except his wife gave birth to their fourth child a year ago."

"I guess I can understand that. But they each have a small farm which should be conducive to deer. Why did they feel they had to come to Maine to poach deer?"

Again, the two men had a long explanation. "Your Honor, according to both men deer come to their winter wood operations for feed, but cross the border into Maine in the spring and they don't return until winter when the men are lumbering and the deer then have fresh tops to browse on. And since the sawmill burned they could not cut trees and the deer did not come."

"This is quite a story isn't it, Jarvis." Hulcurt said.

"It sure is, Your Honor."

"Do you believe them, Jarvis?" Hulcurt asked.

"I'm inclined to believe them, Your Honor."

"How about you, Warden Cyr. You have as much to say about this case."

"I have to agree with Jarvis. One cannot help but feel sorry for them."

Marcel translated everything that had been said.

"Jarvis, I understand that you brought them in Friday afternoon and they have been in jail since."

"That's correct, Your Honor."

"Then how do you feel about sentencing them to two days in jail and time served. No fine and you'll return their rifles?"

"How do you feel about this decision, Marcel?" Jarvis asked.

"Under the circumstances, I have to agree," Marcel said.

"So, we all agree then?"

"Yes, Your Honor."

"Explain that to St. Pierre and Paquette, Marcel."

"Yes, Your Honor." After Marcel had finished explaining

31

the decision, both Fredk and Ralph were shocked. They would never have thought the outcome would be like this.

When Marcel had finished Judge Hulcurt added, "I'm letting you two off easy this time on the recommendation of Warden Marcel Cyr and retired Game Warden Jarvis Page. A little advice. I don't want to ever see either of you in my court again."

Hulcurt hit his gavel on the stone and everyone jumped. "Case closed." And he stood up and reentered his chambers.

Marcel took the handcuffs off and said, "You are free to go."

Jarvis gave them their rifles. Fredk said something to Marcel. "Fredk wants to know if you would buy his rifle, so they can pay for train tickets."

"Tell him I'll give him $30.00 for the rifle."

"He said okay."

When Fredk gave his rifle back to Jarvis, Jarvis gave him the money.

Both Fredk and Ralph were talking to Marcel. "They want to thank us, Jarvis, for all we have done for them." Fredk extended his hand to shake Jarvis' and Marcel's. And then Ralph did the same.

"They promise we'll have no more problems with either of them."

They all left the courthouse and Fredk and Ralph headed for the train terminal. "How about lunch with Rita and me?"

On the walk to his house, Jarvis asked, "Now tell me the truth, Marcel. Did you agree with the sentencing?"

"Yes, I really felt sorry for them."

"You know I did, too."

"There's something else I want to tell you about Whiskey Jack Lake."

"What is it?"

"Last fall I arrested two of Earl Hitchcock's workers for using a set gun to kill deer. They had living quarters in the barn and were canning the deer meat and taking it home. They were using a 10 gauge Parker shotgun with buckshot. I had to sit on that for thirty six hours before they came to check it. When they got out of jail and returned to the farm, Earl fired them and told them never to come back. You won't have much trouble at the farm. And now I would rather doubt if you'll have much trouble at the border, least while for a year or two. But this winter if I were you, I would snowshoe back to the marsh and burn that stand and any other you might find on the Maine side of the border."

Chapter 3

Around midnight Sunday night a big cat started yowling not too far from the Ambrose cabin. It was across the twitch trail from the cabin and slightly uphill from the cabin. Both Rascal and Emma were awakened.

"What in the world is that, Rascal!"

"Sounds like a big cat. But I don't understand why it is making so much noise."

"Last year it was that damned bear, now it's a big cat. What kind of cat, Rascal?"

"I'm not sure, I'm just guessing, but I'd say a mountain lion. I don't think it's a bobcat or lynx. I'll check it out in the morning."

Just then the yowling changed and—"Now it sounds like two angry cats fighting."

"I'm going to want you to walk down with me in the morning when I go to work, Rascal."

Eventually Emma went back to sleep, but Rascal lay on his back until daylight wondering about the yowling and sounds of fighting.

As the sun was beginning to break the darkness, Rascal woke Emma and said, "Em, it isn't time to get up yet, but I'm going to see if I can find what was going on last night."

"Okay, take your gun, Rascal."

He dressed and strapped on his .45 handgun and eased the door closed quietly. First he checked up and down the twitch road for tracks. He went all the way to the dam crossing and then to the top of the hill. Nothing. From the top he started to circle back to the dam. Not far below the top of the hill and about seventy-five feet from the twitch trail, he found where two animals had been fighting. He picked up a clump of hair and looked at it. "It's definitely a mountain lion." He found small pieces of hide that had been clawed away. And ten feet beyond this he found the remains of a spotted deer. "So this is what they were fighting over."

He still wanted to find tracks and he could see a trail through the leaves. He followed that and found deer hair and bits and pieces of meat and dried blood. The trail went through a wet spot and there were several tracks. One big set, about four or five inch diameter, and two separate sets of small cub tracks.

He didn't want to come upon the mother lion with cubs so he circled back to the twitch trail and followed that out to his trap line trail. There in some soft sand he found another bigger cat track and no cub tracks. This bigger track probably was a male. The tracks turned onto his trap line trail and he noticed a bit of blood had been wiped onto the green leaves of a bush. "She hurt you, didn't she, big fella."

He had seen enough and he was hungry. He went back to the cabin. Emma had breakfast on the table.

"You're just in time, Rascal, I just set your plate on the table." As they ate he told her what he had found. "I wonder if that big male cat wanted the dead deer or the female," Emma said.

"I don't know, but he sure took a licking. I know male bear sometimes will kill a small cub so the mother will come into heat again. I imagine it might be the same for big cats."

"Wasn't she hunting awfully close to the village, Rascal?"

"I would have thought so, too. But that time of night the village is quiet and maybe one deer had run a long ways to get away."

"I think sometimes nature can be awfully cruel, Rascal."

"Yes, it surely can."

Rascal cleaned up before walking with Emma to work. As they were walking down the hill Jeters blew the steam whistle.

It was almost time to start work. "It seems good to see smoke coming out of the stacks again. Means we're back in business," Emma said.

Jeters shift ended at the start of the day shift and now he was sitting with Silvio at their corner table. "Sit yourself down, Rascal."

Elly brought a pot of coffee and a plate of fresh donuts. "Rascal, did you hear that awful screaming last night? You must have, it sounded like it was right behind your cabin," Elly said, all in one breath.

"I sure did, I didn't realize others could have heard."

"Hell, boy, the whole damned village heard it. It must have sounded to you like it was right at your door," Silvio said.

Rascal took a sip of coffee and a bite of fresh donut. Everyone was waiting for Rascal to explain. Even Elly.

"A mother mountain lion with two cubs had a spotted deer down and a larger male cat came along. I don't know if he wanted the dead deer or had intentions of killing the cubs so the female would come into heat again. Anyhow that ole she-cat literally tore the hide off the bigger male. The female and cubs carried the deer off and the male hightailed it up the twitch road to my trap line trail. I found a little blood where he turned."

"That must have been something. I mean the whole village was awakened with that yowling," Silvio said.

Elly went back to the kitchen and the train whistle blew. The three men finished the pot of coffee and asked for another, and another plate of donuts. "Elly, you're going to make us fat with your donuts."

"Well, don't eat so many," Elly answered.

"Can't help it, Elly, they're so good."

Four business-like people stepped off the train carrying briefcases. "Why don't one of you men go out to the platform and bring the cases of food in for me, and the newspapers."

Everything was taken inside and Silvio brought a newspaper to the table.

"Any idea, Silvio, who those four business-looking men are?" Rascal asked.

"Must have something to do with either the mill or railroad."

"Well I'd like to sit here all morning and drink coffee and eat donuts, but I have to work up firewood today. How is your wood holding up, Silvio?"

"Pretty good; I still have a tier and a half in the shed."

"I'll fill your woodshed before trapping."

Back at the cabin he took his saw and axe and went back out where he had been last week. There were no more dead trees standing so he started dropping beechnut, white maple and ash. He had filled up with coffee and donuts earlier, and he kept on working through noon.

By three o'clock he had a dozen trees down and limbed, ready to be twitched to the cabin. He was tired now and after a cold dip in the lake, he started supper—the last of the canned frog legs, canned peas and potatoes.

When Emma opened the door she was surprised, "You even took a bath."

"This is the last of the frog legs."

"Can you go up to the head of the lake for more?" she asked.

"Wednesday if it isn't raining. I want to twitch the trees down here tomorrow that I cut today."

"How many did you cut?"

"A dozen, give or take one or two."

"How much more wood will you have to get?"

"Maybe another day of cutting after I have this all worked up."

"Now let me tell you some news. Those four men that came in on the train today?"

"Yeah, who were they?"

"Two are government men from Washington and the other two are executives for AT&T phone company."

"AT&T?"

"Yes, and listen to this. The phone line is being run to the custom building at the border and Mr. Hitchcock will have a phone, the C&A station master will have one in his office also, and there will be one installed in the cafeteria that everyone can use. But the calls out won't be free. AT&T said they would have to charge 25 cents per call."

"When is all this going to happen?"

"The lines are being run on the telegraph poles now, from Beech Tree. They expect to have the line to the village on Thursday and at the border a week later."

"How did all this come about, Em?"

"In light of the World War in Europe, President Wilson wanted immediate contact with all border crossings and Congress okayed the bill. Isn't that great, Rascal? Now we'll have contact with the outside world from Whiskey Jack. We're finally catching up with the rest of the world . . . sort of," she added.

"Things are changing, they surely are. I never thought Jarvis would stop game wardening. I kinda always figured he'd always be here."

"You sound like you have lost a playmate."

"In a way, maybe I have. I knew Jarvis and what to expect from him. This new guy will be different. And being new, I suppose he'll have to prove to everyone that he can do the job."

As they were getting ready for bed, Emma said, "I hope those mountain lions don't start fighting tonight."

"Yeah, me too. I guess everyone in the village could hear them last night."

* * *

The next morning in the cafeteria, Rascal told his friends all about the telephone lines being strung now from Beech Tree and the telephone, ". . . right here in the cafeteria that everyone can use. 25 cents a call."

When the train came in, Fredk St. Pierre and Ralph Paquette were on board. St. Pierre was sitting in the window seat on the village side of the car. Jeters had gone out to bring the newspapers in and he recognized St. Pierre.

"Hey you guys, I just saw St. Pierre, one of the guys Jarvis and that new warden hauled out of here."

"Maybe they have been to court already and paid the fine," Silvio said.

While Jeters and Rascal were talking, Silvio looked at the front page.

"No wonder that ole crowbait retired," Silvio said, "he's getting too soft for the job."

"What are you talking about, Silvio?"

"Well, it's right here in this article on the front page. All about Jarvis Page retiring and Marcel Cyr replacing him. And you know what he did? He let 'em go."

"Who did he let go, Silvio?"

"Those two he and Cyr hauled out of here in handcuffs Friday afternoon. They had to stay in jail over the weekend cause there ain't no court on Saturday or Sunday. The judge, he sentenced them to two days and time served. No fine and Jarvis gave them their rifles back and then he bought one rifle so the two of them could buy train tickets home. I tell you, Jarvis has gone soft in his old age."

"Maybe he had a reason, Silvio."

"And it would have to be a good one for the judge to go along with it," Jeters said.

"Was this the same judge that gave us a break?" Rascal asked.

"Hulcurt, yes."

"Well, I'd like to sit here and argue the point fellas, but I have wood to work up. See ya tomorrow."

From the cafeteria Rascal walked over to the stables and asked Owen Haskel, "Owen, can I hire another horse today?"

"Sure you can, Rascal."

The day was hazy and humid and by noon Rascal was soaking wet from his own sweat. He was tired but he wanted to get everything hauled down to the cabin. When he had finished he wasn't as tired as the day before. But he still had to take the horse back.

"Will you be needing a horse tomorrow, Rascal?" Owen asked.

"I'll need one again, Owen, but not for a few days."

He had just time enough to wash up before Emma was home from work. "What no surprise ready tonight. Only kidding. That's a lot of wood out there. Is that enough to see us through the winter?"

"With what we have in the shed, probably. But I want to get some more, just in case."

"How is your leg? You've been on it a lot this last week."

"Tonight it is a little sore. But come morning it'll be fine."

"I just don't want you overdoing it."

* * *

After coffee and donuts the next morning, Rascal loaded his canoe and pushed off and headed for the head of the lake. The weather was early fall and no humidity. There was a little chop on the water, but not bad.

Like always, he sat still for five minutes before fishing. The only fly he ever used was a royal coachman or a red wolf. With his first cast he caught and landed one—about a pound. No bigger than this and he would need a couple more for a good lunch.

The sun was overhead and he had his three trout, so he went ashore to start a fire and roast all three fish. He thought about going back out and catching a few more brook trout, but instead he lay back and waited for lunch to cook. The smell of roasting fish was making him real hungry.

Finally the fish were done and he ate two real fast, and with the third he took his time. Then he put the fire out and lay back on the ground again. But as comfortable as he was, he had to get back to fishing and frogging.

Now that the sun was high in the sky and the temperature had risen, many, hundreds of frogs had come to the surface in amongst the lily pads. Some were even sunning themselves while lying on the lily pad. When he had depleted one area, he had only to move the canoe over slightly and start again.

He wasn't long before he had a gunnysack full of frogs. He had planned to catch more brook trout, but he would have enough work taking care of the frogs. So he packed up and headed for home.

The afternoon had turned off warmer than he would have liked. It was difficult enough pulling the skin off the legs, let alone having sweat run down his face and in his eyes. Every time he'd wipe the sweat from his face he'd get the slime from the frog's skin on his face. When Emma saw him she began to laugh. "If you'll wait, I'll change my clothes and help you."

"No sense with both of us getting dirty. I shouldn't be much longer."

"Okay, I'll start heating some water for you for a bath." He didn't object.

A half hour later he had finished and he brought in a two gallon container full of frog legs, and a few besides for supper. "We'll have to can these tonight, Rascal, so they don't spoil. The water is hot and I filled the tub already. You take a bath and I'll start supper. You better take your clothes off outside though. They are filthy."

The hot water felt good on his tired muscles and especially his bad leg. While he was soaking, Emma fixed a garden salad with lettuce the deer hadn't eaten, corn on the cob, cucumbers and fresh boiled potatoes with the frog legs.

"You better hurry up, Rascal; supper is almost ready."

"Okay, I'm just getting out of the tub."

"I wanted to bring home some brook trout but I figured there would be enough work with what I had."

"This is all so delicious Em."

"Well, what didn't come from the garden, nature provided. Yes it is all good. I wonder what rich people are eating?"

"Can't be any better than this."

After supper Rascal cleaned up the kitchen while Emma began canning all the frog legs. "Why don't you go to bed, Em. I'll stay up and watch the canner."

* * *

The next day Rascal spent sawing the tree length wood into blocks and splitting them. He worked tirelessly and by the time Emma was home from work he had every block cut, split and piled in the shed.

He didn't want to overdo it and have problems with his bad leg so he decided to wait for the weekend to work up more firewood.

"If you aren't going to work on firewood, Rascal, we could sure use some brook trout to can."

"I'll go up after coffee this morning."

"Only your own limit. You remember what happened last year."

At coffee and donuts Friday morning, Rascal said, "I'll get to your wood next week, Silvio, if that'll be okay."

"Do you like pea soup? Anita is planning on making one in the middle of the week."

"That would be good."

After coffee, Rascal went home and loaded his canoe and put his .45 handgun in the pack. Just in case.

The sun had disappeared behind some thin puffy white clouds. This would make for better fishing and he paddled for the head of the lake with a single purpose in mind.

The first thing he did was to go ashore and get a small fire going, so there would be only hot glowing coals when he was ready to roast a trout or two.

He eased the canoe off shore being careful not to make any unnecessary noise. And even then he waited before he cast his line up towards the inlet. He had only started to strip the line in when a huge brookie took the fly and cleared the water by four feet. The belly was a deep orange color. When it hit the water again, it dove straight for the bottom. Rascal's fly rod was almost doubled over. Just as he would bring it to the surface the trout would dive for the bottom again. This went on for a half hour before the trout wore itself out and Rascal was able to bring it in close enough to grab it by the gills. And then the trout started to fight again. But Rascal had a tight hold on it. He took the fly out and held the brook trout up. It was the largest brookie he had ever caught. He guessed it was probably more than twenty inches long and probably would weigh more than four pounds. He would save this one to show Emma. He would have to catch a couple of smaller ones for lunch. And he wasn't long doing that. But when he went ashore there wasn't much of a fire left and he had to add some more wood.

While he waited for the fish to cook he took out his .45 and fired a shot across the cove at a dead log on the ground and then he put the .45 back in his pack. He then stood back away from the fire and listened, with a smile on his face. He was simply testing the new game warden.

He eventually had a hot enough fire and roasted the two trout. Then he went back to fishing and in no time at all he had his twenty-five trout to take home. Before the end of the season he'd like to bring Emma up here and make a day of it.

He put enough green grass in the gunnysack with the trout to keep them from spoiling. The wind was at his back and he let it push him down the lake.

Once at home he cleaned the fish down by the wharf and then took them inside. Except for the big one. He wanted Emma to see this one. She would be home from work soon and he began fixing supper. More garden vegetables and fried brook trout.

Emma opened the door and said, "I could smell the fish frying as I crossed the dam."

"Look at this one Em," and he held it by the gills."

"You caught that in the same place?"

"Yeah, right up close to the mouth of Jack Brook. Have you a tape measure?"

"Yes, it's in my sewing basket. I'll get it. "

Rascal laid it flat on the sink counter and Emma measured, "Twenty two and a half inches. I wonder how much it weighs."

"Do you have a small bag of sugar?"

"I have a ten pound bag."

"Well let's see. Well it surely doesn't weigh ten pounds, but I'd bet at least five."

"This would be a good fish to bake in the oven this weekend."

* * *

The crew stringing the new telephone line arrived in Whiskey Jack at mid-morning that Friday. They were using a motorized handcar to carry the coil of wire and spool it out, to be connected to the telegraph poles. They continued on up the line to the border while another crew was busy running lines to Hitchcock's office, the station master and the hotel cafeteria. Everyone knew what a telephone was, but the crews attracted the attention of several onlookers.

The crew in the village stayed on Friday night and finished in time the next day to catch the train north to the custom building.

"Ain't this something," Silvio said, "bringing the whole world right to Whiskey Jack on one spindly little wire. If there's ever a road that comes to Whiskey Jack—well that's too much. I'll leave. That's what I'll do. Me and Anita live here because we don't like the populated towns and cities."

"It might be a good thing," Jeters said. "Times is changing, Silvio."

"I'm too old to change. That's fine for you young people."

There just was no convincing Silvio. He hated to see change, and in a way Rascal could sympathize with him.

Rascal worked tirelessly for another week finishing firewood for his cabin and seeing that Silvio and Anita had plenty of wood. For Silvio he hauled several wagonloads of dried wood slabs from the mill and piled them up beside the cabin. Jeters had said he would help Silvio saw them up for stove wood length.

He hauled a load for himself also before returning the horse and wagon.

"It sure is good of Mr. Hitchcock to let us get our firewood from his land. I would hate to think we would have to pay for it," Emma said.

In between days of firewood, Rascal and Emma were able to take an afternoon and go fishing. It was a cool day and overcast. Just right for good fishing. While Emma fished up close to the mouth of the inlet, Rascal held the canoe in one spot. With her second cast she hooked into one that bent her fly rod almost as much as the big one had double up Rascal's. With patience and a true fisherman's competence she eventually brought it in close enough for Rascal to pick it up by its gills.

"It sure is a brute, Em. There probably is another one up there just like this one."

She worked her rod back and forth, spooling out the line, and landed the fly with a soft touch. And Rascal was right, another took the fly and came out of the water like his had done and then like Rascal's big trout, this one also dove for the bottom. Rascal knew he didn't have to tell Emma to play the fish softly. She knew exactly what to do. Besides, Rascal knew Emma would be offended if he started telling her how to land a fish. So he sat there and watched. And being happy to see his wife so happy.

They had several trout but Rascal knew the fishing would

be better after 6 o'clock. So they caught a few frogs, to have frog legs and trout for an early supper. They went ashore and Emma started a fire while Rascal cleaned three trout and cut the hind legs off the frogs and peeled the skin.

The frog legs were too small to put on a stick like the fish, so he looked for a flat rock along the shore. Emma had the fish roasting and asked, "What are you looking for?"

"A flat rock we can put on the fire to cook the frog legs."

He found a piece of slate rock in Jack Brook. He waded out for it.

"Have you ever cooked this way before?"

"No, but we need a way to cook the frog legs." He put some skin from the trout belly on the rock, for the oil in the skin to cook the frog legs in, so the meat would not stick to it.

The slate rock wasn't long before it was hot enough to fry the fish skin. When there was enough fish oil, Emma put the frog legs on to cook. "This is as good as using a cast iron fry pan. I would never have imagined that a rock could be used to cook on," Emma said.

It wasn't long before the frog legs were a golden brown and they ate them while waiting for the fish to finish cooking.

"I hope the smell of this fish and frog legs cooking won't attract any bear."

She would have to mention bear. And this started the old images of the bear on the tracks a year ago and—probably—the same bear that buried all his traps around Ledge Swamp. He was on alert now and he couldn't relax.

When they had finished eating, Emma asked, "Do we have enough so we can make love right here before we go back to fishing?"

"I think we should probably finish out our limits and get back. We'll still have to clean them," he said.

This really puzzled Emma. But maybe he was right. They went back to fishing and the brook trout were running bigger now that the afternoon sun was not overhead. "This makes a big difference doesn't it, Rascal. The sun is almost gone."

"Yes, it sure does."

Emma noticed that while they were catching the last few to make two limits, Rascal kept looking ashore where they had eaten.

They had their two limits of twenty-five trout apiece and now were on their way home.

The air was cooling off already. "You know, Rascal, I'm glad we left when we did. The air has cooled and I'm a little cold."

"I think it's going to be a cold night. But probably not a freeze."

They stopped at Antony's before going home, and Silvio and Anita met them at the wharf.

"Would you like some brook trout?" Rascal asked.

"Surely would. How many do you have?"

"We have two limits and we'll give one limit to you and Anita. They aren't cleaned though."

"That won't be a problem."

Emma handed a gunny sack to Silvio.

"Won't you come in for a while?"

"Thanks, Silvio, but we have to clean ours too. I'll talk with you in the morning."

It was almost dark when they pulled up to their own wharf. Emma was glad now they had not taken the time for love-making. They would have been even later.

"I think I'll clean these here on the wharf so the cabin doesn't get all fishy smelling."

"I'll go up and start a fire so we'll have warm water to wash up with, and I'll bring down a pan to put the fish in and a lantern," Emma said.

When she returned with the pan and lantern she also had a knife to help Rascal clean the rest.

"You know these big trout—I'd like to smoke cure them."

"But we don't have a smoker. How would you do it?"

"Tomorrow I'll build a rack to put the fish on over a small fire. That's how the natives used to do it. I think," he added.

"We have twelve really big ones. Fourteen if we smoke these two also."

"Okay, fourteen. We'll soak these in a salt brine tonight. The rest I'll put in the root cellar."

The fish heads they had cut off the smaller ones and the innards went into the lake. Probably before daylight the next morning a mink or otter will have eaten everything.

Emma took the fish to smoke inside to put them in a brine and Rascal took the others out to the root cellar.

When he returned Emma had taken off all of her clothes and was washing up. "I put my smelly clothes out on the porch, you'd better do the same, so the cabin won't smell like fish."

While Rascal was washing up Emma made two sandwiches and coffee—parading around in her birthday suit. While they were eating Rascal asked, "Is that offer to make love still open?"

"How fast can you finish eating?"

* * *

At breakfast the next morning, Emma said, "Remember I have to work a half day today to make up for yesterday."

"Okay, after coffee with the men, I'm going to buck up the log slabs I hauled in."

Rascal walked with his wife to work and went over to the cafeteria.

Elmo had joined Jeters and Silvio, "Thank you again, Rascal, for the trout, but Anita and I were almost to midnight cleaning and taking care of them."

"We fished until it was too late to think about cleaning them."

"Before I forget it, Rascal, the station master, Greg, would like to see you," Elmo said.

Rascal finished his coffee and walked over to Greg's office. "Come in, Rascal."

"You wanted to see me?"

"Yes, I have a beaver problem I'd like you to work on at mile twelve, a half mile north of Ledge Swamp."

The first thing he thought about was another encounter with that bear. But maybe a half mile north might be far enough away from the swamp.

"I'd like you to get started tomorrow. There will be no trains through at all tomorrow. Oh, you can have Elmo help you again. Our blacksmith has made a couple of beaver rakes to pull the dam apart when you have all the beaver. The rakes look like oversized potato rakes."

"Elmo is in the cafeteria now. I'll talk with him."

"Elmo will be on overtime for the railroad and I'll give you $50 this time if you'll open up the dam or dams.

Back at the cafeteria Elmo was just leaving. "Elmo, come back." Rascal waited until he had sat back down. "Greg has another beaver problem he wants gone. This time he wants us to open the dams after we have all the beaver."

"Sure, when?"

"We have all day tomorrow. There won't be any trains through on Sunday. And I think we should get an early start. Maybe we can finish up in one day."

"What time?"

"Why don't we meet here at 6 o'clock."

"Okay. Where we going?"

"Mile twelve and a half, north of Ledge Swamp."

"The Swamp? Hell no! No way, Rascal! Have you lost your mind? That's where that damned bear chased us. No, I don't want anything to do with him again."

Jeters said, "I'll go with you, Rascal."

"Let's go see Greg and make sure it's okay with him."

"Come in, Rascal. What's the problem?"

"Because of what happened last year with that bear that

chased us, Elmo doesn't want anything to do with work around Ledge Swamp. Jeters said he would go."

"Okay, then I'll give you $80 to split between you."

"Tomorrow morning at 6 o'clock, Jeters. I'm assuming we can use the handcar?"

"Yes of course."

Once outside, Jeters asked, "Rascal, are you telling me everything about this bear?"

"How do you mean?"

"I don't understand Elmo turning down a chance to earn a little more money. What's he so afraid of?"

"He gets nervous any time he is in the woods. I think that's why he doesn't hunt." He wasn't about to tell Jeters the whole story. He would tell the entire village.

Rascal went home and put what traps he would be needing in his pack basket, a pair of pliers and some wire and a little castor.

"Why isn't Elmo going with you, Rascal?" Emma asked.

"I think he's afraid of that bear that chased us last year. He chased us all the way to Ledge Swamp when we came across that other bear and the two fought. The beaver problem is a half mile beyond there."

Emma didn't say anymore but then she started thinking about yesterday when she wanted to make love after they had eaten, and Rascal had turned her down and this was right after she had made the remark about a bear smelling the fish and frog legs cooking. *I wonder if there is more to the bear story than Rascal is saying?*

* * *

Rascal didn't sleep good that night. Images of that bear kept flashing across his inner vision. Sometimes he would wake up sweating. He kept trying to tell himself they probably wouldn't even see the bear. Then just before sunrise he had the same dream that he had had a year ago—of the bear laughing at him. This time when he awoke he got out of bed and started the fire and fixed a pot of coffee.

Emma could smell the coffee brewing and she got up and dressed. She had to work a half day today to make up for Friday. "Are you taking a lunch?"

"No, I hope to eat beaver. I'll take a pot to boil water for the tea though."

"Are you taking your .45?"

"That might be a good idea." He strapped that on, kissed his wife and walked down to meet Jeters.

Jeters was there waiting for him with the handcar already on the rails. Rascal put his pack on the handcar and said, "Greg said Smitty had made two rakes for us to use to open the dams." They both walked over to the blacksmith shop. It was too early for Smitty to be working so they looked around his shop. They were leaning up against the wall.

"I notice you're wearing your gun, Rascal. Are you expecting trouble?"

"Not expecting—just in case."

Jeters wasn't sure if that made him feel any better or not.

The day was promising to be nice. There was just enough coolness in the air to know fall would soon be here. The bugs—or most of them—had died off in the summer heat and there was no humidity. They moved up the tracks at an even pace. There was no need to hurry today. There would not be any trains through.

"When are you going to help Silvio cut up his slabs, Jeters?"

"I'll work on it a little each day next week. Remember I work at night and have to sleep in the daylight."

They were coming close to the twelve mile marker and Ledge Swamp. "Jeters, try to be quiet from here to twelve and half," Rascal said in almost a whisper.

Jeters replied in a low voice. "Okay, but is there something you aren't telling me, Rascal?"

Rascal didn't answer him and both were silent. The only noise now was the handcar wheels on the iron tracks. As they rolled beyond Ledge Swamp, Rascal had a knot in his throat and his heart was beating so heavy he could hear it. No sign of the bear. Maybe he had moved on.

Fifteen minutes later they rolled to a stop at twelve and a half and Jeters set the brake. There was only a small dam on the west side of the tracks. "Probably only a coffer dam," Rascal said still talking in a low voice.

"On this side the water is up and over the culvert by two feet or more."

"We'll set one trap on the coffer dam first, in case while we are working down below we spook the beaver and they head upstream. If they do we'll catch one, at least, when it goes over this dam."

Rascal showed him how to dig out a trough on the top of the dam and Jeters made another trough over to the left side. "Why so far over there, Jeters?"

"Looks like they have been going around using this trail. The dam isn't as high here."

"Good point."

He then watched how Rascal was setting his trap and anchoring the chain, "Why so much chain, Rascal?"

"To give the beaver room enough to swim to deep water where it'll drown. You wouldn't want to try and pull in a live beaver. Trust me, I tried it once. Big mistake. It was like fighting with an angry bear."

Rascal watched him finish setting the trap and securing the chain and then they both were back on the tracks. "Oh my gawd, Rascal! Bear!" Jeters let the screeches out of him.

This was Rascal's worst fear coming true. The bear was between the rails walking up towards them. "Walking and not running," Rascal said. "This is a good sign."

"Are you crazy, Rascal? A bear walking towards you is a good sign? You brought a gun didn't you?"

"Yes, a .45 Colt handgun. But to do any good, he'll have to be much closer." The bear now was about two hundred feet away. Head down and walking—still towards them. "I doubt if he can even see us. Bear don't have a keen eyesight. But they can small a pine needle a mile away."

"Well, what are we going to do, just stand here? "Do something, Rascal!" The bear was now only about a hundred feet away. "The top of his back, Rascal, is about waist high to me. What are you waiting for! Shoot him, damn it!"

Rascal had no idea, then or later, what he was about to do. He took a few steps forward and told Jeters to stay behind. He raised his arms up in a non-threatening fashion and hollered, "Hey! Hey, bear."

The bear stopped and looked directly at Rascal. "Bear, it's me," and he tried to make the same laughing noise he had the fall before. Jeters thought Rascal was out of his mind.

The bear sat down on its haunches and raised his right front leg and made a similar laughing noise. Jeters' eyes were bugging out of their sockets. "What in hell are you doing, Rascal? He's close enough now to shoot."

"No, Jeters, I don't think we'll have to."

"Bear we mean no harm. When we leave, we'll leave some food for you."

"What do you do, Rascal, talk to animals? I knew I should have questioned more why Elmo wouldn't come along with you. Rascal, I don't want to end up being his dinner."

"Neither do I, Jeters. Let's get off the tracks and ease our way down to the dam. Don't hurry. Just take it easy."

The first dam was about a hundred feet below the tracks. We'll set three traps on this one, Jeters. Just like we did on the other side."

"What's that bear doing now?" Jeters asked.

"Still sitting between the rails."

"I hope he stays there. No, I hope he gets the hell out of here."

"Jeters, look," Jeters stopped what he was doing, thinking Rascal had seen the bear following them.

"See that V in the water? That's a beaver heading upstream. I bet we get one in one of the traps."

The water behind the dam was six or seven feet deep. By the looks of the dam the beaver had been in there for a couple of years. After they had those three traps set they dropped down to another dam they could see. "We aren't too far from Jack Brook, now."

They set three more traps on that second dam. The beaver houses both had fresh cut wood and mud on them, but no sign of any feed beds yet.

They followed the stream down to Jack Brook and there were no more dams. "What now, Rascal?"

"Well I think we'll have one maybe two beaver on the other side of the tracks."

"I hope that bear is gone."

While they were downstream at Jack Brook, beaver had pulled two traps into the water. They walked out on the dam. "See if you can feel any tension on the chain. If it is still fighting, let it be for a few minutes."

"Okay."

Both beaver had drowned and they pulled them up to the dam. They both were super large beaver. They reset those traps, and carried the beaver ashore, up on a flat shelf away from the dam.

"You make us a fire, Jeters, to roast beaver meat, and I'll start skinning these two.

Jeters wasn't long starting a fire. "There's a pot in my pack. Get some water and we'll have some hot tea with beaver."

He wasn't as long skinning the second beaver. Jeters had the meat on sticks roasting over the fire. Suddenly another trap snapped closed and they watched as the beaver swam for deep water. In two minutes all was quiet. Jeters went down to pull it in. "This one is about the same size as the first two."

Rascal carried it up to the shelf while Jeters reset the trap. "How many do you figure are in here, Rascal?"

"Both flowages, maybe a dozen."

Some of the meat was done and they began eating while waiting for the tea water to boil.

"This meat sure is good cooked over an open fire like this," Jeters said.

"It's pretty good canned too. When we're all through here, Em and I will can as much of the meat as we can and you can have some."

"There goes another trap, by-gorry. I'll get this one, Jeters. You roast some more meat."

Rascal pulled another one in about the same size and reset the trap. While Jeters was roasting the meat and keeping the fire hot, Rascal skinned two more beaver.

They ate their fill of beaver and Rascal cut off what meat he could along with the tails and castors and wrapped it up in one of the hides and put everything in his pack and they moved up to the next flowage. Here all three traps had been pulled into deep water and they pulled in three extra-large beaver while Rascal was skinning those and cutting away the meat, tails and castors, Jeters kept watch out for the bear.

Jeters stood to stretch his back. "Hey, Rascal! That damned bear is still on the tracks. I tell you, Rascal, he's waiting for us!"

"Well what do you expect, I promised to get him some beaver to eat."

"You're not funny, Rascal. This isn't funny."

"While I skin these why don't you go back to the other flowage and bring up those carcasses."

Rascal stood up and he too could see the bear. "Boy, I hope you're only waiting for these beaver carcasses. Oh I do."

Two more traps snapped and two beaver disappeared in deep water. Jeters had to make two trips to bring all of the carcasses up. "How many beaver do we have now?"

"Nine. I think there might be more than a dozen. You know, Jeters, I think we'll have to come back tomorrow to finish up."

"You would have to say that. What about that damned bear?"

"Well, he really hasn't bothered us. I don't like him here anymore than you do, Jeters. But so far all he has done is watch us. He has shown no hostility at all. There's no doubt in my mind that he can smell the beaver and maybe that's all he is waiting for." Then in a whisper so Jeters couldn't hear he said, "I hope so."

As they sat there talking about the bear another trap snapped. After five minutes Jeters went over to pull the beaver in. "Another large one. That makes ten."

As Rascal was skinning he said, "That might be the last of the adult beaver, except for what might be across the tracks."

"When are we going to check those?"

"Not until we're ready to leave."

"That suits me."

"While I skin this do you want to go down and check those traps?" Rascal asked.

"Sure."

Jeters pulled in another large beaver and one small one. He reset the traps and walked back up carrying the two beaver. "Here's two, Rascal. What does it mean when we start catching the small ones?"

"Hopefully that the large adult beaver had already been caught.

"Look, it's 3 o'clock now. We might as well leave the traps set and go check across the tracks then go home."

"What about that bear, Rascal, or have you forgotten?"

"No—I haven't forgotten him. Help me put this pack basket on, it's heavy. And I'll help you carry the carcasses up."

There wasn't much left to the twelve carcasses and surprisingly they were able to take them all in one trip. "You go first, Rascal."

Rascal didn't say anything. He wasn't liking this any more than Jeters was.

At the edge of the right of way they stopped and checked to see if the bear was still there. "I don't see him, Jeters, come on."

The bear had been lying down between the rails and when he heard Rascal and Jeters coming he got to his feet. "Bear!" Jeters said. He was almost in tears now.

There was nothing else to do but continue on, so Rascal walked over to the track bed and stepped behind the handcar. The bear stood there watching.

The bear was watching every move. "Come on, Jeters. He hasn't moved."

Slowly and cautiously Jeters worked his way onto the track bed and behind the railcar with Rascal. "Both traps are gone from the coffer dam."

"So, what do we do about this bear?"

"Well, we have to do something. Stay behind me, Jeters, and walk slow."

With their hands full of beaver carcasses they started walking towards the bear. Who hadn't moved for hours. When they were beyond the end of the coffer dam they threw the carcasses as far as they could off the tracks. The bear was still watching. "Now what, Rascal?"

"We remove the beaver from the traps and reset them."

They walked backwards to the handcar. Jeters helped Rascal remove his pack basket and set it on the handcar. And then they left the tracks and walked out on the dam. The third trap Jeters had set in a run at the end was also gone.

They pulled in three more extra large beaver and reset the traps and carried the beaver up to the handcar. "You going to skin them here, Rascal?"

"No, I think we should leave. Leave the two rakes on the other side of the tracks."

"Rascal, how are we going to get past that bear? He hasn't moved all day."

Let's get on the handcar and see what he does."

They climbed on and leaned against the handles. Rascal was standing at the front and Jeters was behind. "He's not moving, Rascal. Oh man, I knew this wasn't a good idea to come up with you, Rascal. If I didn't know better I'd say you were trying to get back at me for a year ago when I got you drunk while we were fishing. But this ain't funny, Rascal."

"No, it isn't. Release the brake, Jeters. Maybe if he sees us rolling towards him, he just might leave the tracks."

"And if he don't?"

"I'll listen if you have a better suggestion."

Jeters didn't and he released the brake. They began to slowly roll. The bear saw this and he stood up on his hind legs and reached out with one front leg. "Oh my gawd, Rascal! We've had it now! Shoot the S.O.B."

Rascal could never explain to anyone, not even his wife, why he did what he did next. "Hey, bear, we are leaving," and he outstretched one arm like the bear had done. Jeters wanted to run. But he knew you should never try to outrun a bear.

Much to their surprise the bear dropped down to all fours and left the tack and walked up to the carcasses and snatched one in its jaws and laid down with it on a small knoll and began eating.

"We'll be back tomorrow, Mr. Bear."

"Can we go now, Rascal?"

Rascal didn't even answer he started pumping the handle. This was the answer Jeters was looking for and he began working the handle also. They had only gone a short distance when Jeters asked, "What's he doing now?"

"I can't see him." Jeters turned around to look.

There wasn't much said between them until they were at mile twelve and Ledge Swamp. They both were thinking about the bear, tired and hungry. "It's downhill from here to the village.

Let's sit down and take it easy."

They both sat on the leading edge hanging their legs over the side. "What is it, Rascal? You talked to that bear as if you seemed to think he would understand you. And you know what the strangest thing is . . . I think he could understand you. Don't ask me how. How long have you been able to talk with Bear? Did you know that you could?" Jeters had many questions which Rascal honestly had no answers.

Rascal sat silent for a long time, trying to find a way to answer. Finally he said, "I don't know, Jeters. It just seemed like the logical thing to do." Then he told him the rest of the story, about the bear burying his traps and following him back to the railroad.

"But what about that sound he made and then you made the same sound? It sounded almost like laughter."

"I only tried to mimic the sound he was making. It really scared me last year when he did it."

"Well you scared me more than that bear when you laughed. I couldn't imagine what you were doing."

"You coming back tomorrow?"

"I'll come back. We lived through this day."

"You have to promise me one thing though, Jeters."

"What's that?"

"Not a word to anyone."

"Who would believe it. The man who talks with Bear."

"I don't hunt or trap around Ledge Swamp anymore. That Bear made his point last year. After freeze-up I'll go after beaver, but nothing else. And then only if I'm sure Bear—he's hibernating."

They could see the village now and Silvio and Anita were sitting in the sunshine on their porch. "What, no bear this time? Hah, hah, hah."

"Nope no bear, Silvio," Jeters hollered back.

"Jeters, you might as well come up for supper."

"Hello, Jeters."

"Hi, Emma."

"I hope you don't mind; I asked Jeters to stay for supper. We've had a long day."

"Certainly, you can wash up in the bathroom."

"I thought you might be later than this. How'd it go?" Emma asked.

"Good, actually; we caught fifteen beaver. But we'll have to go back tomorrow and hopefully finish up."

"I was counting on fresh beaver meat. I was planning on boiled potatoes and cabbage. When I saw you two coming down the tracks I set them on to simmer."

Rascal gave her some beaver meat and took everything else out to the root cellar and put the hide and meat on ice that was covered with sawdust.

* * *

Rascal met Jeters at 6 o'clock at the cafeteria and they went to see Greg for a train line-up. "Regular schedule boys. The morning train from Beech Tree will leave here at 8 o'clock and return from Lac St. Jean at 4 pm. It might be just as easy to have the engineer drop you off at twelve and a half and pick you up in the afternoon."

Both Rascal and Jeters said at the same time, "No! That is, we'd rather have our own transportation. We'll take the handcar up and get it off the rails in time for the train. The handcar isn't that heavy." Rascal looked at Jeters and he nodded his head.

Neither one of them wanted to be up there without a way to leave in a hurry if the need should arise. (The Bear.)

"We may be able to finish up today," Rascal said.

"Good."

As they were working the pump handles, Jeters said, "I wonder if that Bear will be waiting for us?"

"I don't know, but he surely should have a full belly after

yesterday."

Neither Rascal nor Jeters seemed to be as nervous this morning as they had been the day before when they had started up the tracks to twelve and a half.

They stayed on the handcar for a few minutes surveying the area and waiting to see if Bear was going to show. "We'd better get this car off the rails, Rascal."

"Okay, maybe he will leave us alone today." Jeters understood who the 'he' was.

There were two small beaver in the coffer dam traps. "We might as well reset these and work our way downstream. We'll take the rakes along with us. And we might as well leave those two beaver for Bear."

At the next dam just below the tracks they had only one large beaver and the other traps had not been touched. At the next flowage they had two more small beaver. "This makes twenty beaver Rascal, how many more do you think there are?"

"I'm going to say none. But we might as well reset these also and while we wait we can roast some beaver meat."

"I'll get a fire going while you cut off some meat," Jeters said. "You know we just might make it back in time for my shift."

The train was going by and the engineer blew the whistle.

Jeters also put some water on the fire to boil for tea. "You know, Rascal, this is a pretty good way of life."

"Yes it is, unless we get an early winter and the snow is deep. Then at times I wish I had a warm cushy job like tending the boiler fires." They both laughed.

They ate all they wanted of roasted beaver and had drunk enough tea. There was no activity in the flowage and Rascal said, "We might as well pull these traps, Jeters, and pull the dam out."

With the rakes Smitty had made, pulling the dam apart enough so the flowage would drain was an easy and quick job. They waited there until there was very little water left. The beaver house was now high and dry.

They moved up to the next dam and there, too, there was no activity and they began to pull the dam apart. It took this one a little longer to drain as it covered a bigger area.

The coffer dam was next and there was only a little water behind it. "What about these beaver, Rascal?"

"Leave 'em for Bear and let's get back to the village."

They hadn't moved more than a hundred feet down the tracks when Bear came out of the woods and onto the tracks. Jeters was in front facing back and when he saw Bear he screamed, "Bear!"

"Where?"

"Right behind you maybe seventy-five feet and he's running towards us, Rascal!" They began pumping the handle faster and Bear began running faster.

"Oh damn! I knew this wasn't going to be a good day."

"Where is he now, Jeters?"

"Maybe fifty feet and coming fast. Pump, Rascal!

"Rascal, he was so docile yesterday, what in hell is going on? He's only forty feet behind you now, Rascal."

"Pump harder, Jeters!"

"I am, damn it, and he's running faster!"

Bear ran after them for a quarter of a mile and then abruptly stopped and stood up on his hind legs. "He's stopped and is now standing up and I'll be damned—he's reaching out with his front paw again like he's waving goodbye. Listen, Rascal! Do you hear that? That SOB is laughing at us. I swear to God, Rascal, Bear is laughing at us."

Rascal turned around and raised his arm and tried to make the same kind of laughing noise.

"He's sitting between the rails like he did yesterday."

Rascal began laughing then and Jeters did also. Bear stayed on the tracks until they were out of sight. Rascal and Jeters just looked at each other and began pumping the handle.

"How do you figure, Rascal?"

"I don't know, Jeters, unless he was just having some fun

with us."

"You don't suppose he was lonely and only wanted some company, do you?"

"A playmate, perhaps?"

"That would be funny, wouldn't it. I know one thing for sure, I'll never hunt around Ledge Swamp or ever shoot a bear. I'd hate it to be him that I shot. No one would ever believe us would they, Rascal?"

"Probably not. They'd say we're crazy or just telling stories and they'd laugh at us. That's why, Jeters, I never said anything about him last year."

"Okay, do we agree not to say a word?"

"I won't."

"Me neither."

It was early afternoon when they arrived back at the village, the handcar and rakes were put away and then they went to see the station master.

"How many beaver did you remove in all?"

"Twenty."

"And the dams?"

"There were three and we tore them apart and drained all the water."

"Good job, men, and here's your money."

"Thank you, Greg," Rascal said.

"Yes, thank you," Jeters also said.

* * *

When Rascal was home he found a note on the table:

Rascal; If you get back in time, would you finish canning the beaver meat. I have it all in canning jars in the root cellar. You'll have to tend to the canner.

He first started the fire in the cook stove and then went

out for the mason jars and canner. Emma had filled twenty-four pint jars. All he would have to do was to get the water boiling and watch 'em.

While the canner was boiling, he began stretching the hides. He had fifteen hides, but not enough stretchers. The last five he had to nail 'em wrapped around a large pine tree. When he had finished that, Emma was home.

"I'm glad you're home, Em. I'm tired."

"Well, go sit down and I'll fix supper. Are you through at twelve and a half?"

"All cleaned out and water is drained."

Chapter 4

The next morning at the cafeteria with Silvio and Jeters, Silvio asked, "Did you two get the beaver cleaned out?"

"Yes, and the dam's torn apart and water is drained."

"What about that bear?" Silvio asked.

Rascal and Jeters looked at each other and smiled and they both said, "What bear?"

Silvio had noticed the smiles and the exchange of looks between the two and he knew there was something about the bear after all. But why wouldn't they talk about it?

The morning train from Beech Tree arrived and this morning a crew of men stepped onto the platform and began unloading crates from the freight car.

"I wonder what that is all about?" Silvio asked.

"Must be something for the mill," Jeters said.

Rascal got up and went after another pot of coffee and another plate of donuts. "Thanks, Elly. Do you know what's going on out on the platform?"

"Surely do. Them boys are unloading a gasoline driven electrical generator. This hotel is going to have our own electrical power supply. Times are changing, Rascal."

He went back and sat down with the coffee and donuts. "Elly said they are unloading a gasoline generator for the hotel."

"Whiskey Jack seems to be joining the modern times. First, women now have the right to vote, prohibition, so's a man can't have drink in his own home. Then a telephone here, now a machine to produce electricity for the hotel—what's next? A road into Whiskey Jack? I hope I never live to see that," Silvio said.

"The whole world is changing, Silvio," Jeters said.

"I know, but me and Anita aren't changing and it's hard enough to make do on what little income I get from C&R for my injury. With all of these improvements—well, I just can't afford them."

Rascal understood where Silvio was coming from, but all the same, he didn't mind the improvements. He just didn't know what to think if a road was ever put into Whiskey Jack.

Full of coffee and donuts, Rascal went back to his own cabin and started harvesting most of the garden. The potatoes he could leave until cold weather as long as he broke the tops down to stop the potatoes from growing. He'd leave Emma's lettuce for as long as he could. Everything else was picked and put in the root cellar for now.

That morning in the cafeteria, Silvio had said he and Anita had been without any venison all summer. He and Emma only had two pint jars left. So he went out back with a pair of pliers and some wire.

At first he thought about setting the snare where he had the year before, but when he got to the trail it was so well used it was too obvious. And it was the same on the other side of the road. So he walked out to the end looking for another deer trail. Fifty yards to the left was a small heath with only a few alder bushes growing. There he found another deer trail running north of east. And no moose tracks. This was a good sign.

The trail snaked through some of the alders and he found an excellent spot to hang a snare, and there was a two inch cedar growing six feet away. A perfect anchor for the snare.

When he had finished he circled the heath for ideas for fall trapping. He liked what he saw.

Emma was home fixing supper when he returned. "Where have you been?"

"We're low on venison and the Antonys haven't had any red meat besides beaver since June, so I went out back and set a snare."

"Oh good, just yesterday I was wanting some fresh steak. Have you seen the new warden around since he was here with Jarvis?"

"No, I haven't. The garden is all taken care of except for your lettuce and the potatoes. I know you like to keep the vegetables as fresh and as long as you can and that you make stewed tomatoes, so I put everything in the root cellar."

They sat out on the porch after supper. The moon was just coming out. "Looks like a full moon tonight. The animals will be moving around, feeding tonight."

The lightning bugs were making quite a display. Somewhere in the village a screech owl started screeching. Then someone with a shotgun shot it and all was quiet again. Neither one of them said a word. They only laughed. The air was beginning to cool and Rascal wanted to be up long before daylight to check the snare, and Emma was tired.

Rascal was awake by 3 o'clock the next morning and he got out of bed without waking Emma. He dressed and pulled on his boots without lighting a lantern. With a gunny sack in his pack basket and hunting knife he closed the door quietly and started hiking out back to the heath. The moon was below the tree tops, but there was still plenty of light for him to see.

When he came to the end of the twitch road he noticed drag marks in the dirt, but there wasn't enough light to see what they were. He stood still at the edge of the heath surveying the area. He could see about where he had set the snare but there was no deer. But the bushes had all been mauled. He began to wonder if the deer hadn't broke the wire snare and run off.

He started walking closer and the closer he came the more he wasn't liking what he was seeing. There was the head of a small crotch horn deer on the ground and torn hide, blood and innards. Something had come along and killed the deer in the snare and then after eating some had dragged the rest of it off.

His first thought was a bear, then he remembered the

mother and cub mountain lion. This had to be her work. The deer had obviously been caught in the snare the way the bushes had been mauled and there was a definite mark around the neck— what was left of the neck. He pulled the snare and put it in his pack. With that mountain lion still in the area there wasn't any sense in setting it again. He would make a point to trap her when the season began.

He went back to the drag marks and he followed them looking for cat tracks. And in some soft dry dirt he found them. The mother and cub. He had seen enough. Daylight was coming and he headed for home.

Not wanting to be seen this early in the morning with a pack basket by anyone in the village he cut through the woods and came out behind his cabin.

Emma was just fixing breakfast. "Are you hungry?"

"Yes."

"How did it go?"

"I caught a deer alright but that she-lion took it."

"What are you going to do about the lions?"

"Set traps for them when the season opens. I think we'll have to wait for some fresh venison until the fall. I don't dare shoot one so close to the village, just in case the new warden happens to be around."

"Good point. So what are you going to do about some fresh meat?"

"I'll think on it."

* * *

Rascal walked with Emma to work and he went for coffee and donuts.

"You're unusually quiet this morning, Rascal." Silvio said, "What, did that bear get your tongue?"

Again Silvio noticed the exchange between Jeters and Rascal. There was something.

"Oh, I was just thinking about that new warden. Until this guy builds up a routine, it won't be safe to do anything around here."

"Why has he got you so spooked all of a sudden?" Silvio asked.

"Oh nothing really, but I'd like to get some fresh meat, but I don't feel safe doing it now and I surely don't want to get on the wrong side of him."

As he sat there listening to Silvio and Jeters talk an idea began to form in his mind. He would wait until later to think more on it.

"Have the men finished wiring the hotel for electric lighting, Silvio?"

"Yes they worked all weekend and finished up late last night. Now every room has an electric light and won't have to depend on the mills generator. Maybe that'll leave more electricity for the rest of the village to use. Elly was saying yesterday that next summer on hot days they'll have electric fans for each of the rooms plus the cafeteria here, and she and Oleman were thinking about installing an electric water pump, instead of a hand pump. There would be a storage tank upstairs in one of the closets and they would only have to fill it once a day. Maybe twice depending on how busy they were. I believe she mentioned they were going to do that this fall before cold weather."

"Well, Silvio, what do you think of all of those changes? Wouldn't you agree they would be better than naught?" Jeters said. Silvio only grunted.

All that day Rascal kept thinking about his new idea and the more he thought about it the more excited he became.

While he and Emma were having supper he asked, "How would you like a trip to Lac St. Jean Saturday morning and come back Sunday afternoon?"

"I would love a trip up. But why all of a sudden?"

"I have me a plan how we can get some fresh meat."

"How?"

"Bow and arrow. They're deadly and silent."

"Do you know how to shoot a bow?"

"No, but it can't be that hard to learn."

"There are some things I need too."

For the next two days Emma was overwhelmed with excitement about the trip to Lac St. Jean.

"You and Emma heading up to Lac St. Jean for any special reason, Rascal?" Silvio asked.

"We just wanted to get away for a couple of days, that's all. And she wants to do some shopping before cold weather. Anything I can get for you, Silvio?"

"You know there is, by-gorry—a bottle of some nice whiskey."

"I'll see what I can do, Silvio. No promises."

Both Rascal and Emma were up early Saturday morning. Rascal packed their clothes in his pack basket and put on a clean shirt and a clean pair of pants. Emma put on a dress.

When they walked into the cafeteria to wait for the northbound train Silvio looked at Emma and whistled. "My, don't you look grand this morning, Emma. You look good too, Rascal," he added.

Everyone wished them a nice weekend and the train left on schedule. At mile twelve and a half he showed her where he and Jeters had been trapping beaver. "It looks pretty dry," Emma said.

"It is now but the water was up on the track bed before we tore the dams out."

"How much did Greg pay you and Jeters?"

"$40.00 each plus the hides and the meat."

"That was good wages for two days work."

The train only slowed as they passed the custom building at the border. Once in Lac St. Jean they took a taxi to the same hotel and requested the same corner room.

They didn't spend much time in their room; they had

some shopping to take care of. First they found a trading post where Rascal looked at several bows. He had to have help to show him how to string it. "This is a very fine bow, Monsieur; are you going to use it to hunt or target shoot?"

"I'll have to target shoot until I feel comfortable with it. But I intend to hunt with it."

"Then this is the bow you should have. It is a 50 pound pull and will be excellent for hunting or targets. Will you be needing arrows?"

"Yes, target arrows and hunting arrows."

"How many of each?"

"Six of each."

"And may I suggest protection for your fingers. If you do not wear something, when you release the string it could tear the skin off your fingertips, I would recommend this light weight archer's glove."

"Okay, can you wrap everything up?"

"This bow comes with a box and your arrows will fit inside the box also."

It was just a simple cardboard box with no printing on the outside. "This will be good," Rascal said.

"Now, Em, what would you like?"

"I would like a braided rug for the bathroom so we don't have to get out of the warm tub onto a cold floor."

"Okay, anything else?"

"Material for curtains for the big front window and a curtain rod." They had everything wrapped up inside the rug and tied securely.

"We'd better take this back to the hotel. And I told Silvio I would bring back a bottle of whiskey for him."

"Okay," No arguing or scolding, and she even added, "Maybe we could take a couple of bottles of that wine we like."

"We sure can."

"But how will we get that back without anyone knowing?"

"In the pack basket with our clothes."

"You know with all this running around today I'm getting tired; maybe we should go back to our room and lay down for a little before supper."

"Yeah, my leg is beginning to bother me. I guess walking on concrete all day is more stressful for my leg than in the woods."

Back in their room everything was put on the floor for now and they lay down to rest. It wasn't long before they both were asleep. After an hour Rascal woke up. He was still on his back with his arm around Emma and she had her head on his chest. He was enjoying the quiet moment with his wife lying beside him. He began thinking about the miraculous changes he had seen in her this summer. The summer hadn't started off so good with her turning him and his friends in for making brandy, but later when she had spent a night alone in jail for shooting that deer, something marvelous had happened. A terrible burden that she had been carrying was suddenly gone and she was once again the Emma that he had fallen in love with.

She stirred and started breathing heavy and then snoring. His stomach was growling and it must be close to supper. He awoke her and kissed her and said, "Perhaps we should get up and dress for supper."

Emma rolled over and got up and washed her face and put on a clean dress and brushed her hair. Rascal put on clean pants and shirt and washed his face and combed his hair. "Wow, you sure look pretty tonight, Em. You have color back in your cheeks now. You look happy."

"I am, Rascal, and you look pretty swell yourself."

In the dining room Rascal asked to be seated next to one of the bay windows. "We can watch the sunset from here."

"Would you like something to drink while you are deciding, Monsieur?"

Emma spoke up, "Yes, we would like a bottle of white wine. I think it was a chateau."

"You have made a very good choice Madame, at once." He left them with menus and went after a chateau wine.

They both had the seafood platter. "Why does food always taste better when someone else does the cooking?" Emma said. "This fish is so much better than I remember."

"It is good."

"How long will it take you to learn to shoot with your bow?"

"I don't know. But I'll practice every day until I think I'm ready. You understand the bow will have to be kept quiet. I won't even tell Jeters or Silvio about it. If that new warden knew we made a special trip to Lac St. Jean to find one he would know something was up. At least Jarvis would have."

"I won't say a word to anyone."

"I have an idea. Let's take the rest of this wine and go sit outside and watch the sunset."

"Let's go."

The sunset was a fiery orange and red, promising a nice day on the morrow. When the air started to be too cool Emma said, "I'm cold, Rascal. You know, if I'm correct, there is going to be music tonight. Let's ask someone."

"Yes, Madame, the music started a half hour ago in the ballroom."

"Can we have some wine while we listen?"

"Most certainly, Madame. There will be someone to help you."

They found the ballroom and there were already many people there. They were shown to a table and Emma said, "We would like some wine, a chateau."

"Yes, Madame."

Rascal was chuckling to himself. As he was observing the change that had come over Emma. "What are you smiling about?" she asked.

"I just like to see you happy like this."

They danced some and had more wine and finally Emma said, "If you'll help me up to our room, I'll give you something special."

In their room Emma laid down on the bed and she was soon sound asleep. Rascal only smiled and then began laughing.

* * *

After breakfast the next morning they went back to their room and packed. "I'm sorry about last night, Rascal. I'll make it up to you."

"I won't let you forget, Em," and he smiled.

So not to raise any suspicions, they put everything in the baggage car. It was late morning before they arrived back in Whiskey Jack and nobody was around to ask what they were carrying. Rascal had the pack basket on his back and they each carried one end of the carpet bundle.

The wine, whiskey and bow and arrows were taken out to the root cellar out of sight. While Emma finished unpacking Rascal changed his clothes and went outside. He filled a gunny sack with sawdust from the root cellar and tied off the top and found a place in the woods behind the cabin where he could practice and not be seen. He found a clear sight lane about fifty feet long and tied the gunny sack to a tree limb. He went back for the bow and arrows and glove. He strung it like he was shown, nocked an arrow, pulled the string and arrow back and sighted along the arrow shaft to about midway in the sack and released the string. The arrow glanced off a tree on the right and broke. "Um."

He nocked another arrow and this time he remembered to have the odd colored fletching on the outside. He hit the target this time but low. He kept practicing all afternoon until Emma hollered, "Rascal, supper is ready."

He left the target there and returned the bow and arrow to the root cellar."

"How'd it go?"

"Not bad. I only broke two arrows."

Emma almost fell out of her chair laughing.

"But I'm coming along pretty good. Maybe in another two days of practice I might be ready."

She laughed again and said, "If you don't run out of arrows."

He took the ribbing good and said, "If I do I'll take you back to Lac St. Jean for more."

* * *

The new game warden Marcel Cyr boarded the train for Whiskey Jack Saturday morning. He was planning on spending two days in and around the village to get acquainted with the layout and the cutting operations there.

"Mr. Whelling, is there any chance of letting me off maybe a half mile from the village?"

"Certainly, I used to stop the train all the time at mile nine and a half for Jarvis."

Ten minutes later Tom Whelling said, "Nine and a half coming up."

Marcel picked his pack up and waited for the train to slow before jumping off. "Thank you, Tom," Marcel said.

Instead of following Jarvis' trail that skirted the village Marcel crossed Jack stream and followed alongside that until he could see the dam then he faded back into the trees and came out to the twitch road that crossed over the dam that ran up and behind the Ambrose cabin. He wanted to be able to wander around and look at things without the villagers knowing he was about.

There wasn't any activity around Rascal's cabin. He continued on through the trees until he was on top of the knoll and out of sight of both the cabin and the village. He could see where Rascal had been cutting firewood and twitching the tree length wood down the road.

At the end of the road he found the same drag marks Rascal had seen and he followed those until they disappeared.

But backtracking the drag marks into the marsh he found the remains of a deer. And the remains didn't look to be that old. All the meat had been stripped clean and he had no idea how the deer had died. But from the looks of the alder bushes it looked like the deer had put up a terrible struggle.

He made a circle back to the road and found another kill. Perhaps a couple of days older. He checked the ground and there were no drag marks. If Rascal had shot these two, he figured there would at least be drag marks to the road and not like the drag marks he had followed into the woods and then they disappeared.

He eventually left there and came out to a knoll where he had a pretty good view of the lake. There was no one out there fishing.

He sat down and leaned up against a tree overlooking the lake. He decided this would be a good place to sit and listen until supper would be served at the hotel. Then he'd get a room for the night also.

As he sat there he was thinking, *Jarvis probably would have spent the night out under a tree somewhere, but what was the sense of doing that when there would be a comfortable bed at the hotel.*

Marcel was up early the next morning and after eating breakfast he left before anyone was stirring in the mill yard or village. He walked out to the road where Rascal had guided several hunters the fall before.

He walked to the end of the road and he knew the farm wasn't far beyond there, but he didn't feel comfortable striking it through the woods, so he backtracked to the village and circled around it staying in the cover of the trees to the road that he knew would take him to the farm. So far, other than Elly Douglas at the hotel, no one knew he was around.

It was a longer walk to the farm than he had first thought and he went directly to the house to introduce himself to Earl Hitchcock. Earl was just walking across the yard from the barn when he noticed Marcel. He waved his arm for him to come in.

"I heard there was a new warden that had taken Jarvis' place. I'm Earl Hitchcock," and he extended his hand to shake Marcel's.

"Good to meet you Mr. Hitchcock. I'm Marcel Cyr."

"Come on in for some coffee. Have you eaten breakfast yet?"

"I would like a cup of coffee and I ate at the hotel this morning."

"Martha, this is the new game warden, Marcel Cyr. My wife, Martha."

"How do you do, ma'am."

"Any coffee left, Martha?"

"I just put on a fresh pot."

"What brings you out here on a Sunday morning?"

"Oh, nothing really. I'm just out meeting people and getting acquainted with the land."

"I don't have my usual crews yet. Just a few men to lay out lines and swamp new twitch trails and tend to the animals and crops. We're almost self-sustaining in here. Not quite completely, but we do a good job of it."

After a couple of hours of talking with Earl and Martha and several cups of coffee, "I should be on my way. Do you have any problem if I look around your operations here?"

"Certainly not. Help yourself. Why don't you figure on having supper later with the wife and me. If you do we can put you up just as easy here as at the hotel and it won't cost you either. We'd enjoy the company."

"That sounds good. I'll plan to be back here in time then. Thank you."

As Marcel crossed the mowed hay field to the lower corner there were several deer feeding on the clover that was now growing. With deer in the open like this and not the least bit nervous he decided there wasn't any illegal hunting happening here. And he doubted very much if Earl Hitchcock would condone anything illegal occurring on the farm if he was aware of it.

He made an afternoon of walking through the old choppings. He saw many deer and although they would run off it was never in alarm of his presence. There were bear tracks in the soft dirt and mud, coming and going from the clover rich field. And an occasional cow moose with calf tracks. No big bull tracks. They were probably lying down in the shade.

He found a cool spring the men had dug out and a dipper hanging on a tree limb. He looked around him, "Yes sir, this is nice country and the crews have left a lot of nice trees that'll get big enough to harvest again in another ten or fifteen years."

There were twitch trails and roads all through the choppings and this made him feel a little more secure. He was beginning to question his competency with the big woods. He had to admit the big woods made him nervous and uncomfortable. He hoped he might grow out of that in time.

He returned to the farm just in time for supper. Martha had anticipated his return and had set a place for him at the table.

Afterwards he and Earl sat outside enjoying the last rays of the sun. Martha joined them after she had the kitchen picked up and the dishes were washed and dried.

* * *

Marcel left the next morning soon after eating breakfast. "I must catch the morning train back to Beech Tree. I want to thank you for your hospitality, food and letting me spend the night."

"Anytime, young man," Martha said.

He was back in Whiskey Jack in plenty of time and he joined Silvio, Jeters and Rascal for coffee and donuts.

"What are you doing here so early?" Silvio asked.

"Actually I came 2 days ago and I have been familiarizing myself with the woods and lumbering operations here."

The fact that he was on his way back to Beech Tree and not just arriving in Whiskey Jack had the men more than a little concerned.

"I found the remains of two dead deer, Rascal, beyond your house."

"Two you say?"

"Yes, two."

"Hum, that SOB; There should only be one."

That statement caught the men off guard. More especially Marcel. This wasn't going like he had planned.

"Damn, if they don't clear out of here there won't be a deer left around Whiskey Jack," Rascal said. He hoped he was being convincing.

"What are you talking about, Rascal? Who's they?"

"About a week ago a mother and two cub mountain lions killed a deer and then an old male, I guess, probably tried to take it away from her. They got to fighting and woke up the whole village. Me and Em thought they were right outside our cabin. Em was scared and I don't mind telling you I didn't sleep much the rest of that night.

"In daylight I went looking and across the twitch road I found the remains—or rather where a deer had been dragged off. And where the two cats had been fighting. I found a patch of hide as big as my outstretched hand that the mother lion had torn off the other one. I followed the blood trail only a little distance and found blood on some bushes when the cat would rub against them. Then I found his paw print in some soft dirt and it was huge. I decided not to follow a wounded mountain lion any farther, so I followed the drag marks and found the mother's tracks and much smaller cub tracks.

"I tell ya if that lion comes into the village I intend to shoot it before it hunts or kills someone," Rascal said.

"Was that one of the remains you found?" he asked Marcel.

"No, the two I found were at the end of the road. And

there I too found drag marks."

"So that makes three deer those SOBs have killed. I wonder just how many more they have killed." Rascal said.

Silvio didn't know whether to believe Rascal or not. Jeters—he wasn't quite sure what to believe. But apparently young Marcel Cyr believed every word.

"If you see that cat heading for the village you have my permission to shoot it."

"When I came up on the train two days ago I noticed there was a beaver problem at mile nine. Jarvis said you usually take care of those problems, Rascal?"

"Yeah, I'll talk with the station master this morning."

Everyone at the table heard Marcel when he said he arrived in Whiskey Jack two days ago. But no one had seen him arrive. Maybe this new warden was someone to be aware of.

The southbound was boarding and Marcel excused himself and left. No one said a word until Marcel had left the cafeteria. "Maybe we have underestimated this new warden," Silvio said. "He said he has been here for two days, and not until this morning did anyone know he was around."

They talked for a while longer before splitting up. Rascal went to see Greg. "Yes, Rascal, what can I do for you?"

"Warden Cyr tells me there is a beaver problem at mile nine again."

"Okay thanks, I'll have Elmo meet you in the cafeteria tomorrow morning and the two of you can work out a time to take care of it. He's with the track crew today."

Rascal went home and with Marcel now gone, he figured this would be a good time to try out killing a deer with his bow. He changed clothes, put a gunny sack in his pack basket and with his bow and hunting arrows he left through the woods to his trap line where there was a natural salt lick.

The water near the lick was muddy. A deer had been there and had probably heard him coming through the woods. He found an ideal spot, about forty feet away and behind a large spruce tree. He hadn't gone close to the salt lick so there would not be any of his scent there.

No sooner had he got settled in and a doe and lamb stepped into view. He wouldn't shoot a doe with lamb. He enjoyed watching them and they being there meant they were not alarmed by his presence.

After only a few minutes they wandered off. As he waited for another deer he was thinking that his arrow would have to be well placed so the deer wouldn't run off. An hour later he could hear something coming towards the salt lick. He waited patiently, hardly even breathing. It was a crotch horn and he was smelling the doe's earlier tracks. He was coming in straight on towards Rascal. The deer walked up to the salt lick and stopped and looked around with its head held high. When it was satisfied it began licking the salt. Rascal stepped out from behind the tree and pulled the bow up and pulled the string back. He was waiting for a good shot and he didn't know how long he could hold the string back. He whistled and immediately the deer lifted its head high in the air and Rascal took his shot at the base of the neck.

The deer was hit and hit good, but it managed to run off. Rascal didn't believe it would go too far. At least the deer was running deeper into the woods and away from his trap line trail. The deer had collapsed about twenty-five yards away.

He removed the arrow and wiped all the blood off. Then he began deboning the meat and putting it in his gunny sack. It wasn't a huge deer and he figured he might have forty or fifty pounds of meat, plus the heart. The arrow had actually severed the large artery on top of the heart.

He clived the meat away from the bones as close as he could. As much as he hated to, he would have to leave the ribs and he only took a small piece of liver. He put everything in his pack basket and looked around to make sure he wasn't leaving anything. He had left no tracks at the salt lick and here the ground was hard and covered with leaves.

He shouldered his pack and started for home through the woods. The day wasn't that warm but he was sweating. Before going directly to his cabin he stopped and made sure there was no blood or hair on him. He broke off a spruce bough to use to brush his clothes. There was plenty of deer hair on his pants. Satisfied he walked in behind his cabin out of sight from across the lake, and into the root cellar.

He cut off about twenty pounds and wrapped it in some paper and set it on the cool sawdust. He took the heart and the piece of liver inside and washed them and left them on the sideboard. Emma would be home soon.

Just in case there might be some deer hair still on his clothes he changed. The meat would stay fresh for several days in the root cellar, but he knew they would have to can some of it. So he cut off the best steaks and took the rest inside to can.

By the time Emma was home he had the heart and liver sliced, frying with onions, with boiled potatoes and corn on the cob—and the deer meat cut into small pieces and packed in canning jars.

The minute Emma opened the door she knew Rascal had somehow managed to get them a deer. "You have been busy."

"Everything is ready."

While they ate Emma said, "Something is going on at the mill, or rather in Rudy's office."

"How do you mean?"

"Two men arrived on the morning train to see Rudy. They talked in his office for most of the day—until the afternoon train left—behind closed doors. He never closes his door even if they are talking business. I have no idea what is going on."

"Maybe more customers."

"Maybe, but he never before closed his door to talk business."

"I don't know what to tell you. Has business been good?"

"Yes, we're 20% higher than a year ago."

Before going to sleep, Rascal said, "I'll be getting up

before daylight as I want to take some fresh meat down for the Antonys before anyone is around."

* * *

Before sunrise the next morning, Silvio and Anita woke up to a loud knock on the door. Silvio was already thinking about getting up so he went to the door and found a box of wrapped deer meat. He looked around and he knew there wouldn't be anyone. "Hey, Anita, we have some fresh deer meat left at our door. I'd like eggs with some deer steak this morning." The air was cool and Silvio made a fire in the cook stove.

Later that morning while Rascal, Jeters and Silvio were having coffee and donuts, Elmo joined them. "Greg said you had some beaver problems that you needed help with. Where is it, back at twelve and a half?"

"No, mile nine," Rascal said.

"Count me out. That's where we got chased by that bear, or have you forgotten?"

"What's the matter, Elmo?" Jeters said. "Maybe all that bear wanted was someone to play with," and he looked at Rascal and he was smiling. Silvio saw the exchange between the two men and knew there was something there. Something about that bear that they didn't want anyone else to know. *But what?*

"I'll go down with you, Rascal. As long as you clear it with Greg."

"Okay, I'll go see him and if there isn't any problem meet me at sunrise tomorrow."

Greg had no problem hiring Jeters to help, but he couldn't understand why Elmo wouldn't want the overtime.

* * *

The sun was just peaking over the treetops the next morning, and Rascal and Jeters started down the tracks to mile nine. "Give me an honest answer, Rascal, do you expect to find Bear at mile nine?"

"I don't know, Jeters. I hope not."

They rode the rest of the way in silence. At mile nine they lifted the handcar off the rails and set it aside out of the way. Jeters put his ear on the rail. "Train is coming, although it is a long ways away."

This year the dam was fifty feet below the tracks and not plugging the inlet to the huge culvert. But the house and the beginning of a feed bed was above the tracks. "You know what to do, Jeters."

They dug out four troughs and set traps. Before they had finished, the morning northbound went through. "How many beaver would you expect to find in the flowage?"

"I'll guess maybe only a pair of two-year-olds."

There was another large dam upstream and no beaver house or feed bed. "We'll set three here. Then hike upstream a ways and see what else there is."

They followed the little inlet upstream for a half mile and didn't see any more beaver workings. When they returned to the first dam they had one two-year-old. "If you'll build a fire, Jeters, I'll skin this and cut off some meat to roast."

Jeters also set a kettle of water on to boil for tea. All while Rascal was busy skinning, Jeters kept close by, watching for Bear.

"Are you nervous, Jeters?"

"Some. I don't want to be Bear's play thing."

Jeters set some meat to roasting while Rascal finished skinning. He watched as Rascal cut off the meat, the tail and castors.

They sipped hot tea while they waited for the meat to cook. The train whistle blew in the distance and it had a lonesome tone. Nothing had come to the traps while they ate lunch, so they crossed the tracks to the lower dam. There they had two large beaver. Jeters reset while Rascal took care of the beaver.

"I'm guessing there'll be one more beaver in here, Jeters. And it is probably inside the house. Maybe if we jumped up and down on it the beaver will leave and my guess would be that it would head for Jack Brook."

They made their way to the top of the house and started jumping up and down and driving stakes down through the top. "There!" Jeters said, "He just left and you were right, it's heading downstream." They could hear the trap snap closed and the beaver splashing back into the water.

"I'll get this one, Jeters, if you want to pick up the other traps."

"Sure."

Rascal pulled in another large beaver and he figured they now had them all. He pulled those four traps and began taking care of the beaver. Jeters was back and started pulling the dam apart with a rake. When Rascal finished the beaver, he helped Jeters.

Then they went up to the second dam and took that one apart and watched as the water drained. Both flowages were drained now and everything was at the handcar as they waited for the Lac St. Jean southbound. "Jeters, see if you can hear the train coming."

He put his ear to the rail again and he said, "I don't hear anything. Maybe we have time to get back before it comes through."

They put the handcar back on the rails and loaded everything and started for home. "No Bear this time," Jeters said.

At mile nine and a half Jeters could see the southbound train coming. "Train!" he hollered. "Rascal we need to get off the tracks." They stopped and by the time they had the handcar safely off the train was only a hundred yards out.

"That was close," Rascal said, "I thought you said you couldn't hear it coming."

"I couldn't. It must have been stopped in Whiskey Jack."

They put the handcar back on the tracks and returned without further incident.

Jeters went to bed, before his night shift started, and Rascal went home and took the dried beaver hides off the drying boards and put the new hides on. Even though the beaver hides did not have their winter fur, these hides looked very good.

Chapter 5

Silvio never let on that someone had left he and Anita some fresh deer meat. But he knew without any doubt it had to have been Rascal. He was the only one who would have the time to get a deer in closed season and clever or sneaky enough, however you wanted to look at it, to do it without raising the interest or hackles of the game warden. He would have liked to say thank you, but he knew it would not be necessary. And it would have taken the excitement out of the ordeal for Rascal to be discovered.

The mountain lions had not made an appearance again, nor were they heard. Rascal wanted to hike out and see if the cats had found the remains of the deer he had killed. But he was paranoid that Marcel Cyr would be out there watching.

So when trapping season began he was more than anxious to lay traps. And his first line was out back. All day he would check each mud flat or soft soil for cat tracks. By the end of the day he figured the cats had probably moved on.

The next day he went up to the head of the lake and up along Jack Brook for a mile and then he crossed the brook and worked his way back laying traps.

The following day he checked traps behind his house and much to his surprise he had the female lion in a cubby set with a #4 trap. She had fought the trap and had tangled the chain around the cedar tree and bushes and was not able to stand. He dispatched it and removed the trap. He knew it would take a long time to properly skin the cat and didn't want to do it here. So he picked the cat up and threw it over his shoulder and returned home and hung it up in the woodshed. And then he went back to his trap line. He figured the cat weighed about ninety pounds. He had not seen any cub tracks. Maybe the male had returned after his wounds had healed and killed the cubs.

He only picked up one pine martin on that trap line and he began to wonder if the presence of the mountain lions might not have something to do with that. Now with the female removed from the area he hoped the other fur animals would return.

The next day up along Jack Brook he had set eight traps going up the brook and four coming down the other side. He picked up fur in each of the twelve traps: two otter, one fisher, two mink, one raccoon and six martins. Maybe the presence of the mountain lions had driven the animals over and along the brook. He would see.

Two weeks had passed before he started picking up more than one piece of fur on each tend behind his house. It was as if the fur animals had all migrated back to this area.

When he was done for the season he had caught along Jack Brook, two more fisher, two more mink, four more raccoons and a red wolf. And the male mountain lion with a piece of hide missing from his right shoulder. He was heavier than the female.

Behind his house he caught four more pine martin, a fox and a bobcat. He would have liked to have continued trapping but he did not want to overtrap the area. Besides it was two weeks into the deer season and there were more hunters than last year. Some of the sport hunters were having some success while the others, not knowing anything about the woods or hunting, were spending much of their time in the cafeteria.

Marcel Cyr was around a lot during those first two weeks, keeping an eye on Rascal Ambrose to see if he would be trying to sell deer again this year. And taking advantage of an unseasoned game warden. But Rascal was hardly ever seen. Running two trap lines was keeping him busy.

Sunday morning, the beginning of the third week, Rascal, Elmo, Jeters and Silvio were sitting at their usual table drinking coffee and eating donuts. "Are you still trapping?" Silvio asked.

"I pulled everything yesterday."

"You're done early this year, aren't you?"

"A little, but I thought I might pick up a sport or two to guide."

"How was the season?" Silvio asked.

"I don't think I have quite as many pieces as last year. But this was a good year. I caught the two mountain lions that were fighting. The cubs I think high-tailed it out of here. I haven't seen their track since I started trapping."

"Or the adult male could have killed them," Silvio said.

"That could be so."

Marcel walked into the cafeteria and joined the men for coffee and donuts.

"You coming or going?" Silvio asked.

"I just come in on the morning train. Looks like the hotel will be full of hunters this week. Are you going to guide, Rascal?"

"If I can pick up a sport or two. Do you remember me telling you about the mountain lions?" Rascal asked.

"Yes."

"Well, I caught the two adults, and I haven't seen any tracks of the cubs."

"Where do you sell your fur?"

"Jarvis is new at the business, I'll give him a chance if his prices are good."

Two sports came over to the men's table. "Excuse me, Mr. Ambrose?"

"I'm Rascal Ambrose."

"My friend and I are new to this hunting and we really don't know much about it or this country. It is much grander than either of us thought it would be, and the woman at the front desk said we should talk with you about guiding for us."

"Well I do guide, but you haven't even introduced yourselves yet."

"I'm sorry, my name is Oliver Pierce and this is John Fox. And we're from Trenton, New Jersey."

Rascal stood up and shook hands with each man. "Rascal Ambrose and it will be $50.00 a week per man and paid up front. Oh, and you'll have to shoot your own deer." Everyone laughed even Marcel.

"Let me introduce you to our new game warden, Marcel Cyr."

"Gentlemen," Marcel said.

"And this is Silvio Antony, Jeters Asbou, and Elmo Leaf."

"Now you eat a good breakfast tomorrow morning. We'll be out all day. I'll bring fixings for lunch. Do each of you have a compass, knife and matches? If not you'd better go to the general store next door and get 'em.

"What do each of you have for a rifle?" Rascal asked.

John Fox answered, "We both have .30-30s."

"Those are good rifles."

"Thank you, Mr. Ambrose. We'll see you at breakfast."

Pierce and Fox went to the general store for compasses. "You'll have your work cut out for you, Rascal, with those two," Silvio said.

"Oh, it won't be so bad. I doubt if either one of them will want to do much walking."

The men broke up and Marcel remained; he still had to wait for the morning southbound to come through from Lac St. Jean. He was exhausted and he folded his arms on the table and lay his head down to rest. He was sound asleep and snoring in minutes.

Back at the cabin, Emma was cooking and trying to wash clothes. "Rascal, will you hang these out for me."

"Sure. I have a party of two to guide this week."

"Well, there's plenty of venison stew in the root cellar and I have already made a double batch of biscuits. You'd better tell your hunters it's beef stew and not venison. Word might get back to Marcel."

"He had coffee and donuts with us this morning. He was looking pretty haggard. He was waiting for the southbound. I have no idea how long he has been here."

"I think I'll bake some bread also. Those biscuits won't last you long."

"Have you heard about what went on in Rudy's office?"

"Not a word. Earl is coming in from the farm tomorrow. I don't know if that has anything to do with those two other men or not," Emma said.

Rascal put together what he would be taking in the morning and he even cleaned his rifle. Then he pulled all the fur pieces off the stretchers and put them in the root cellar. "Next week if I don't have any hunters to guide, I just may trap."

"We haven't had any ice on the lake yet and that's unusual," Emma said. "Don't get me wrong, I like this warm weather right now."

Before leaving the next morning, Rascal started a fire in the cook stove and put a pot of coffee on for Emma. Then he packed his pack basket and with rifle in hand he hiked down to the cafeteria to meet up with John and Oliver for breakfast. The two men were already there and Rascal joined them at their table. It wasn't quite daylight yet.

"Rascal, why are we going to start hunting so early?" John asked. "I mean the sun isn't even up yet."

"The best time to hunt is between sunrise and eight o'clock. Usually the deer are still feeding then. Later they'll start looking for a place to spend the day and where they might eat a little. Then between 3 pm and sunset deer are coming out to feed again."

Before leaving, Rascal bought a half dozen donuts. He looked at Oliver and John and said, "Mid-morning tea break."

They crossed the mill yard and the mill workers had not even started yet. But just as they were entering the woods on the road, Jeters let blast the 6:30 am steam whistle. Both John and Oliver jumped. "What was all that about?" John asked.

"6:30,am wake up call for the crew. There'll be another blast at 7 o'clock when the work day starts."

Rascal took them out to the same area where he usually took all of his hunters. In a low voice he said, "One can sit here and the other one comes with me. In the afternoon we'll swap off."

John said, "I just as soon sit here. Where?"

Rascal showed him a slight bank on the left side of the road and then he showed them the well-used deer trail that ran the length of the valley and crossed the road. "I'll take Oliver up to the further end and we'll hunt our way back. Keep a sharp eye out, John. If we jump anything it'll probably run down the trail and cross the road."

"Okay," John said.

"Follow me, Oliver."

John sat on top of the bank where he could clearly see the road. He had never been in the deep woods before and now he was alone. As long as Oliver was with Rascal, he was feeling very comfortable in the woods, but he'd hate to be on his own out here.

Rascal followed the hardwood trees for a mile up through the valley and then he cut across it to the game trail that ran down the middle of it and across the road John was on. "Okay, Oliver, I want you to stay on this game trail all the way to the road. Hunt slowly don't simply walk along. I'll be just off to your left at all times. If I think you are going too fast, I'll whistle twice. There is no wind so the deer won't be as spooky."

"Okay, Rascal."

Rascal tried to keep within sight of Oliver, but there were times when he couldn't and Oliver would stop until he could see him again.

About half way to the road Rascal heard a deer blow and he stopped, he could see Oliver had stopped also. The deer blew five more times as it ran down the valley. Oliver had never heard a deer blow. At least he thought it was a deer. Hell, he didn't even know deer made any noise at all. And he was glad it had run off. Rascal thought it was probably only a doe signaling its fawn.

A pine martin ran across the deer trail in front of Oliver and chased a red squirrel up a cedar tree. The squirrel jumped to another tree and when the martin saw Oliver it started screaming at him. A high pitched eerie scream.

Rascal knew it was a martin and he wanted to laugh, but he didn't. When the martin stopped screaming, it moved on in search of the red squirrel. Oliver wiped the sweat from his face and continued. There were no more surprises all the way to the road.

Rascal made a fire and put water on to boil for tea. "Was that a deer making that blowing noise?"

"Yes, it was probably a doe warning its fawn."

"And there was a big ass red squirrel chasing another and making that awful screaming noise."

"That big red squirrel was actually a pine martin and he was after the red squirrel to eat it."

"John, did you see anything?" Oliver asked.

"No, but I heard that screaming and thought it was a little kid."

When the tea was ready, Rascal poured three cups and opened the package of donuts. While they ate donuts and sipped tea Rascal explained to them how to use a compass. This was all foreign to them both.

"What now, Rascal?" John asked.

"Well, I'd like you to remain here and I'll take Oliver with me and we'll go back on this road some and make a sweep back to the valley. I'll try to plan to be back here at noon."

Rascal dumped the tea water on the fire to put it out before leaving.

They went back about two hundred yards and started to make a wide arc back to the valley. Rascal had Oliver lead off and he would follow correcting his course occasionally. After about five minutes Rascal tapped him on the shoulder and pointed to a partridge on the right. There were beech trees here and Rascal could see where the deer and bear had been after them. This area was looking really good. Maybe a first hunt tomorrow morning.

They came across an old rotten stump that a bear had torn apart after the honey. There was honeycomb still on the ground.

They were an hour making the arc back to the edge of the valley. Rascal liked what he saw there for deer sign. They stopped and Rascal motioned towards a slight high spot and they sat down to watch the valley. Rascal looked at his watch and figured after an hour here they would have to leave.

They met up with John at noon and Rascal started a fire and put the venison stew on to warm up and the biscuits on the fire pit rocks to warm up. "John will you get some more water for tea?"

As they were eating, Rascal said, "Well, we know there are deer here. They have been eating beechnuts where we went through those hardwoods, and Oliver and I jumped two deer this morning. There were bear eating beechnuts also."

"I'd like to shoot me a bear, too," Oliver said.

"No. No bear," Rascal said.

That caught them both off guard and John asked, "Why not?"

"The carcass would rot before you were home. And it is much harder dragging a bear back than a deer." And which he didn't say, he didn't want Bear shot.

"What are we going to do this afternoon, Rascal?"

"Well I figured it would be best if we stayed right here until about 1:30, then John and I'll hunt south of the road and work our way back here about sunset. Deer will be laying down now and there's no sense of us spooking them out of their beds and run off. Later they'll be feeding again and moving around more. If this was the middle of November when the bucks would be in full rut then we'd go back to hunting and not taking it easy.

This might also be a good time to take a nap if you were so inclined."

John and Oliver didn't have to be told again. They both lay back and were soon asleep. As Rascal sat there thinking, a whiskey jack—gorby—flew down and landed on the toe of his boot, and perched there looking at him and wanting him to toss him a morsel of food. There was only one biscuit left and he reached into his pack, half expecting the whiskey jack to fly away. But he waited until Rascal broke off a small piece of biscuit and tossed it into the air. The whiskey jack flew up and caught it and flew away.

In a few minutes the whiskey jack flew back and landed on his boot. He threw up another small piece and the whiskey jack caught it and flew off. The whiskey jack kept repeating this until there was no more biscuit. Sensing this, he flew off in search of more food.

At 1:30, Rascal woke John and Oliver and said, "We'd better get to it. If you shoot a deer, Oliver, and it runs off, wait for us. I don't want you chasing after it on your own. We won't be long."

Rascal stopped and checked the direction of the slight breeze. It was blowing south. That meant the deer would be moving north into the wind. He and John hunted south of the road following the hardwood tree line. Not much had changed from a year ago. They followed the tree line down about a mile. "I want you to remember this big rock here, John, for tomorrow." Then they cut across the valley to the deer trail. John was to hunt along this trail, Rascal off to his right. John seemed to be more relaxed than Oliver. John was doing a good job. He stopped often and looked around, and he wasn't simply watching the trail and where he was going.

About 3 o'clock Rascal heard two bucks fighting just out of sight straight ahead from them. He whistled softly and John stopped and Rascal walked over. "Did you hear that clash?" and there it was again.

"What is it?"

"Two bucks are fighting just out of sight. They won't be paying too much attention to anything else, so let's get closer," he motioned for John to go ahead.

One footstep at a time. After fifty yards they could see movement. "When you see the one you want John wait for a good shot. Right behind his front shoulders," he whispered very low.

John nodded his head. The two bucks were making a lot of noise now. A little closer and they could see the two bucks. Their antlers were locked together and they both were on their knees. They never saw the two men and John raised his rifle and did just as Rascal had said and sighted in on the one on the left and he pulled the trigger. Both deer went down. "What ta hell," Rascal said. One deer was dead and the other one was trying to free its antlers. He was now up, thrashing and swinging the dead deer by its antlers.

"I wish Oliver was here to shoot the other one."

The standing buck was still fighting trying to loosen his antlers from the dead deer. "What do we do now?"

Rascal leaned his rifle up against a tree and said, "Maybe if we grab the dead deer we can twist his antlers enough to free them. Set your rifle down."

John did and the two of them grabbed ahold of the dead deer. The live buck was dragging all three of them backwards. Rascal grabbed the dead deer's antlers and twisted with all he had. The live deer was able to twist his antlers enough and freed himself from the dead deer. He walked off, not running, with his tongue hanging out.

John looked at Rascal and the two started laughing. "You know, John, if we hadn't have come along both deer probably would have remained locked together and died."

"Boy, do I have a story for Oliver and to take home. Rascal, you're one hell-o-va guide."

They started dragging back to the road and they hadn't

gone very far when they saw the same buck standing in the trail looking back at them. Only momentarily and then he disappeared towards the road. "Oliver should be able to shoot that one, no faster than he's traveling."

"He's probably asleep," John said. "I have to admit I fell asleep when I was sitting."

Rascal didn't say anything.

By the time they reached the road there was still an hour before sunset. They pulled the deer upon the road and looked at Oliver. His head was resting on his chest. "Ye-up, he's asleep," John said.

They dragged the deer right up to the fire pit and John had to kick Oliver's foot to awaken him. Slowly Oliver opened his eyes. "I guess I fell asleep." He looked at John's deer and exclaimed, "Holy cow, John! Did you shoot that?"

"I surely did and we chased another across this road for you."

"I'm sorry, I fell asleep—couldn't help it. I didn't even hear you shoot."

"That was an hour and a half ago, Oliver."

While dragging it back to the hotel, John said, "You must think Oliver and I are a couple of wusses. I mean we each fell asleep on stand and neither of us feel comfortable in these big woods."

Rascal was some time before he replied and then he said, "I was overseas in the war and saw some pretty big cities here also, and you know something, I felt as uncomfortable in the cities as you two probably do out here in the woods. It all depends what you're used to, I suppose."

John's eight point buck weighed out at 185 pounds. "That's a nice deer, John. Now we need to take out the heart and liver before they spoil. Oliver, would you go into the kitchen and ask Elly for a pan."

When he was back, Rascal removed the liver and the heart and put 'em in the pan. "We'll hang it up now at the north end of this building. There's an overhang there and the deer will stay out of the sunshine in the day."

"How long before the meat spoils, Rascal?" John asked. "I mean will we be able to get them back to Trenton, New Jersey, before it does spoil?"

"If the nights and days stay cold enough there won't be any problem. But two days in a row of warm temperatures and they probably will spoil."

"Maybe if Oliver was to get his deer right off we could leave early," John said.

"Do you want the heart and liver, Rascal?"

"I would, but I think Silvio and his wife, Anita, would appreciate it more and it would be a good gesture if you two would take it to them. The last cabin up the tracks is theirs."

* * *

At supper that night Rascal told Emma all about the two fighting bucks. ". . . and then we had to pull 'em apart. That buck actually pulled both John and I and the dead deer backwards. His strength was unbelievable.

"Neither of the two are much in the woods, but they know this and admit it and they don't argue when I want them to do something.

"If I can get Oliver a deer tomorrow, I'll have the rest of the week to trap, and I intend to trap next week also."

After a good breakfast the next morning Rascal took Oliver back out in the same place. "You go sit where you did yesterday. I'm going to circle up where we saw the beechnuts yesterday and then down to the deer trail in the valley. The wind is from the south this morning so the deer will travel into it. I'm guessing there are deer feeding on the beechnuts now. So you go get settled and stay alert."

Rascal waited a couple of minutes for Oliver to get settled, then he started up towards the beechnut grove. He got there just in time to see three flags disappear towards the valley. He looked around some and found a huge bear dropping, and he instantly began to wonder if this was Bear.

He continued on slowly. He didn't want to spook the deer into running. He knew that once they reached the marshy valley they'd turn into the wind and head south towards Oliver. All he had to do was corral them without spooking 'em. He hoped one of them was a buck.

Watching the ground and their tracks he tried to stay on the uphill side of them. Then he knew they would have to turn towards the road. When he reached the edge of the tree line sure enough all three deer had turned south into the wind. Still staying high he worked his way to the deer trail and waited momentarily before continuing on. When he found their tracks again, all three deer were now following the trail in a relaxed stride, not hurrying. This was good. He only hoped Oliver was awake. Rascal knew he was close to the road and he was sure the deer were still between him and the road. He stopped to listen and just before he was about to start walking, Oliver fired one shot. Rascal waited where he was. When he was satisfied there was only the one shot he walked out to the road.

Oliver was standing over his deer with a happy smile. Rascal looked the deer over, a nice six point and not the one that had been fighting with John's deer. He rolled it over to look for the entry wound; in front of the left forward shoulder. "Nice shooting, Oliver."

While Rascal dressed it Oliver never stopped talking. Rascal smiled—this is what hunting was all about. "There were three deer together. First the doe came out and stood on the road followed by a fawn and then the buck and they all three just stood in the road with their heads up, I guess sniffing the wind."

"You know, Oliver, you and John have turned into two capable hunters. And this is a well-placed shot."

They dragged the deer back to the hotel and it weighed 175 pounds. It was hung up with John's deer and it was still too early for lunch.

"Maybe we should take the afternoon train out, Rascal," John said.

"Oliver's deer is still too warm. It would be better to let it cool overnight and board the morning train south."

"Okay, that sounds like a good idea."

The heart and liver was given to the Antonys again and they were certainly happy to have it.

At supper that night Rascal told Emma all about that day's hunt and about the two young men. "You're impressed with them, aren't you?"

"Yes, I suppose I am. They were two green boys when they stepped off the train Sunday morning and I have to admit I thought I'd have my work cut out for me. Like those two boozers last year. But these two were interested and they listened to me."

"So, are you going to trap now?" Emma asked.

"Yes, after I see them off tomorrow and all next week also. On a good day I can make more trapping than all week guiding."

* * *

The next morning when Rascal joined Jeters and Silvio, Silvio asked, "Are you all done guiding this week?"

"Yes, I'm going to trap the rest of this week and next week."

"Sure didn't take you long to get those two fellas a deer," Silvio said.

"They shot them theirselves too. They turned out to be pretty good hunters."

Just then Oliver and John walked into the cafeteria for breakfast. "Hey you two," Silvio said, "you might as well join us this morning."

While the others had coffee and donuts the two hunters had a big breakfast.

The train rolled in and John and Oliver were just finishing breakfast. "It was cold enough last night so maybe the two deer froze. You shouldn't have any problems."

Jeters and Rascal helped the two carry the deer to the freight car. "I gotta go, it's time for me to sleep," Jeters said.

"Thank you for your help."

"You two were good hunters. Maybe you'll think about coming back sometime."

"We just might." They each gave Rascal a $25 tip. "You were worth every penny of it, Mr. Ambrose," John said.

"Most certainly," Oliver added.

"You have a good trip back."

After the two had boarded, Rascal went home. He had his pack basket and trapping gear all set to go.

He headed for Jack Brook. He usually had great success around water. He set two otter and mink sets and a few covey sets and a few leaning tree sets for martin and fisher. Then he crossed the brook and crossed the tracks just below nine and a half. He had planned to circle back to his deer hunting road. He hadn't gone very far when he came across a well-used trail heading in the same direction. There were no scarf marks on any of the trees and the trail had not been cleared, only used quite often.

Then he thought about Jarvis and how he seemed to appear in the village from nowhere when no one had seen him get off the train. "Well I'll be damned, you ole fox. I never gave you enough credit." He laughed to himself and began setting traps along Jarvis' trail. And that's what he would call it from now on.

This trail was taking him away from the water but he wanted to know where it would lead. And he did find a few nice sets.

The trail eventually came out to his hunting road and crossed that and circled down towards the railroad and out onto the farm road. "No wonder he could sneak around so much without being seen. And this must be how Marcel came into the village a few weeks ago."

He had had a late start for the day and returned home at sunset. Emma arrived home a few minutes later.

"Something is still going on with the company, and I haven't a clue what," Emma said.

"What makes you think anything is going on?"

"Well, in all the time I have worked for Rudy, he hardly ever closed his office door when he was talking with someone until lately."

"I don't know what to say. I haven't heard anything."

* * *

The next day Rascal tended his trap line and was pleasantly surprised with his catch of 1 otter, 2 mink, 2 raccoons, 3 martin and a red fox. That wasn't bad for a first tend on a short trap line. This day he was home early enough to have supper ready when Emma came home from work.

"You know, I miss the long daylight days, this time of year," Emma said.

"Me, too."

The nights were cold but the lake had not frozen over yet. Once in a while on her walk to work in the morning she would see thin films of ice in shallow mud puddles. Then the day would warm into the 40s or low 50s.

As he followed the Jarvis trail to the road, Rascal kept chuckling to himself thinking about Jarvis and how good he was at his job. And no one in the village ever knew about this trail. Some day he decided he would talk with Jarvis about it.

That Sunday morning four more hunters arrived and Rascal had earlier told Elly he wouldn't be available to guide that week. The weather turned off cold and in the middle of the week; eight inches of snow fell during the night. This is what Rascal had been looking for. Now he could see where fur animals were traveling and he even relocated a few traps. And if a nice buck should happen to cross his path he would take it. The days were cool enough now so the meat wouldn't soon spoil.

That Thursday afternoon he already had a pack basket full of fur and a hundred yards from the road he saw a huge buck standing broadside all alone with his nose into the wind. The snow had made it quieter in the woods and the buck had no idea he was not alone. Rascal took a fine bead on the deer's neck and squeezed the trigger. The buck never knew what happened. He fell in his own tracks.

Before leaving Rascal made a covey with the innards and set a #3 trap. He was sure come morning he would have something. If not for the snow he would have had to go to the village for help to drag the deer. The antlers had fourteen long points and a thick heavy beam. He guessed the deer would go well over 200 pounds.

Marcel had been waiting for the afternoon southbound and saw Rascal come into the open mill yard with a deer. He went out to meet him. "Want some help, Rascal."

"Sure, I'm all sweaty."

"That must have been your shot I heard a while ago."

"Yes," he didn't want to let on he knew about the Jarvis Trail.

They dragged the deer to the scales and it weighed 230 pounds. "I thought he was heavy."

"You guiding this week?"

"No, trapping it's more profitable."

"I think the train is about to leave."

"Thank you, Marcel."

Jeters was still asleep and everyone else except Silvio was at work, and he knew Silvio would help if he asked, but Anita would have a fit. So he borrowed a horse from the stables and dragged his deer across the mill yard to the cabin and then returned the horse.

While the deer was still warm he pulled the hide off and

cut the neck off. There was just enough room to hang it up in the root cellar. He put the heart and liver in the sink in the cabin and stretched his fur. He had done so well trapping this week he decided to pull his traps the next day.

Emma was soon home. "How was your trapping today?"

"Not quite as good as yesterday, but I did get a deer. Heart and liver are in the sink. I'll be in as soon as I have finished with these hides."

The next day in the covey he had made and baited with deer innards he caught a fisher. And he picked up two more pine martins. It was time to call it a season.

He had coffee and donuts with his friends that Friday morning. "How was your trapping this week?" Silvio asked.

"It was good but not what I was hoping for. I was in a new area and I thought, or hoped, I'd have done a little better. Maybe I would have if I ran 'em another week"

* * *

Friday, late afternoon, one of the hunters from New York came back to the hotel all in a tether. He stopped and talked with Elly. "Mrs. Douglas my friend Alex is lost. Is there anyone who can help?"

"There is only one person in the village that might be available to help. Rascal Ambrose. His wife works in the Hitchcock company's office. You might ask her where Rascal is. I'll place a call to Beech Tree to see if the warden will come out here."

"Mrs. Ambrose?"

"Yes, how may I help you?"

"I'm looking for your husband. I need his help."

"He should be home taking care of his fur pelts. What's the problem?"

"My friend is lost."

"If he isn't home, I don't know where else he might be."

"Thank you, ma'am."

Stanley Brown hurried to the cabin and Rascal was splitting cedar kindling.

"Hello, Rascal?"

"Yes, what can I do for you?"

"My friend Alex and I were hunting this morning and after lunch we were supposed to meet up again but he never showed."

"Have you heard him do any shooting?"

"No, and that's what bothers me. I need your help, Mr. Ambrose, to find my friend. I don't know these woods at all."

"Have you sent word out to the warden?"

"Yes, Mrs. Douglas said she would make a phone call."

"Okay, I'll put my pack together and I'll meet you in the cafeteria."

Stanley left. Rascal left a note for Emma and put on his rubber boots, he shouldered his pack and put an outdoor kerosene lantern in his pack and strapped on his .45 instead of carrying his rifle.

Rascal found Stanley Brown outside watching the mill yard. "Come on, Stanley, we'd better have supper before we go out."

"How can you think about eating when my friend is lost?" Stanley said.

"I've been on these before, Mr. Brown, and we could be out there all night. And it ain't no good to start looking on an empty stomach. Besides it is almost dark. If he is lost, he won't be moving much."

They went inside and had beef stew with biscuits and plenty of coffee. Just as they were finishing the late afternoon northbound for Lac St. Jean arrived and Marcel Cyr walked into the cafeteria. "Have you eaten, Marcel?" Rascal asked.

"No."

"Then you'd better have a bowl of beef stew and biscuits. This might take all night."

As Marcel ate, Rascal asked Stanley a few questions. "Where were you hunting?"

"We were hunting through to the field at the farm, and then swung down into the alder cuttings; we found places to sit and watch, and at noon we got together, had lunch and split up. We were to meet up again at the edge of the field at 3 o'clock. When he didn't show up I talked with Mr. Hitchcock at the farm and no one had seen or heard anything from him."

"When you split up which way was he going?"

"Alex was going to follow the contour of the land and drop down below, before where the crews are cutting. I went straight down and found a spot to sit."

"Well we're going to need a horse and wagon to get us out to the farm. I'll go see Owen Haskel at the stables," and he left.

As they rode out to the farm they could see quite well because of the snow cover. If and when the moon came out they would be able to walk through the woods without much difficulty. They pulled up at the farmhouse and the three of them went to the front door. Earl answered the door. "Mr. Hitchcock, we are looking for this man's hunting partner, Alex Bowman. By chance has he come here?" Marcel asked.

"No, and no one has heard any shooting either."

"Thank you. Okay, we'd better start where you two split up."

They rode down to the edge of the field and walked down through the old cuttings. "This is where we ate lunch. These are my tracks going downhill and those are Alex's going off in that direction."

"Rascal—eh— I have never had to look for a lost hunter before; I'm afraid you're going to have to help me out here."

"Okay, Stanley, you go back to the wagon and build a fire. Not a small cooking fire and not a huge bonfire but a large one. Don't go wandering off."

"Marcel, you and I will take his track." Before leaving

Rascal took his .45 and fired up into the air. They waited and waited. Alex did not fire back."

"He's too far away to hear that, isn't he?" Marcel asked.

"That, or maybe he can't."

They started following Alex's track. The snow was still providing enough light so they were able to follow his tracks. But not fast. It was obvious by his tracks that he was heading more downhill than following the contour of the land. "He is heading for the valley where I guide my hunters."

Two hours after leaving Stanley the moon came out. It wasn't full but it turned the darkened woods into daylight. Almost. But they were able to quicken their pace. After a while dark clouds covered the moon and it was now darker than before. Rascal took the lantern out of his pack and lit it. "Hold on a minute," and Marcel brought a brass tube from inside his jacket. "I was saving this until we needed it," and he turned on his flashlight.

"Yeah, we had something like that in the war, but the battery wouldn't last long."

"They're using a different kind of battery. But I don't know how long it'll last. So we'll have to use it sparingly."

Rascal kept his lantern lit. They came to a draw and there were boot tracks going back and forth in both directions. "Looks like he was trying to get warm. I think I'll fire another shot. Even if he can't fire back, he'll know we're close and maybe he 'll start hollering."

Rascal fired into the air and they waited. And then there was a faint cry straight down the hill and not in either direction where he had been walking back and forth. Rascal cupped his hands around his mouth and hollered back. No answer this time.

"Now what?" Marcel asked.

"I took a compass heading from his hollering and we follow that."

"But his tracks are going to either side."

Rascal took off, "You coming?" Rascal knew where they were now. At the lower end of the little valley below the road.

Marcel hollered again and this time Alex immediately hollered back. He was maybe a hundred or two hundred yards straight ahead.

When they found him his feet and clothes were soaking wet and he was cold. Rascal built a fire so Alex could warm himself before they started out.

When Marcel looked at Alex's rifle it was clear he had been running at some point and had fallen down ramming the barrel into the ground. The barrel was full of dirt. He unloaded it.

"Do you know where you are, Rascal?" Marcel asked.

"Yeah, that little valley we crossed is where I guide my hunters. We are maybe a mile or a little more from the road."

Rascal sat down on a log and pulled his pants down and put a hand full of snow on his right hip. "Does your leg hurt? I noticed you were limping more than usual."

"Yeah, it's pretty tired."

"What happened?"

"I was shot in the war."

While Alex got warm, Rascal cooled the inflammation in his hip. The clouds had blown out and everything seemed brighter than before. "We have the moon again. We should leave."

"Which way?" Marcel asked. "Back to the field or out to the road that goes to the mill yard?"

"Well, we can't leave his buddy in the cold. And I ain't about to hike from the village out to the farm. No we go back to the field from here." Rascal took out his compass and checked the heading and said, "Let's go," and he started off.

Marcel marveled at Rascal's competence and knowledge of the woods and even more how comfortable he was way out here in no man's land.

At first Alex was having difficulty keeping up and Rascal would have to stop often and let him rest. "You're the one with the bad leg and I can't even keep up with you," Alex said.

"Well, as soon as your blood begins to circulate better you'll stop feeling so cold."

Half way through his muscles finally loosened up and he was more able to keep up.

Marcel didn't know what to think of Rascal. He was out here helping with a bad leg when he didn't have to be. *And without him I'd be lost out here,* he thought.

Two hours after leaving they came out to the field and only a hundred feet from Stanley and his fire. "How did you do that, Rascal? You only looked at your compass once," Marcel said.

"I don't know. I feel as natural out in the woods as city folks do in the city."

"I mean it took us two hours to get out here and only a hundred feet from the wagon. Unbelievable, just unfreaking believable."

They stood around the fire for a while talking. Alex and Stanley were both happy Alex had been found safe, but they were not as impressed with Rascal's woods-wise ability as Marcel. He hoped he would never have to chase him.

It was 4 am when they were back at the hotel. "Marcel, you're welcome to come up to the cabin and sleep for a while. I only have to take the horse and wagon back."

"I'd appreciate it. How's your leg, Rascal?"

"Sore, but a little sleep and it'll be fine."

They took care of the horse and wagon without waking Owen. Marcel talked all the way up to the cabin until they reached the door. "Ssh, I don't want to wake up Em. She'll be getting up in an hour or so. When we get up, I'll make us a good breakfast."

He eased the door closed quietly. "I'm awake, Rascal. I haven't been able to sleep much worrying about you." She slipped out of bed and stepped into the kitchen. There was still plenty of moonlight to see she wasn't wearing anything and when she saw Marcel there, she let out a little scream and rushed back into the bedroom and pulled on a bathrobe.

When she came back out no one, not even Emma, wasacting as if anything had just happened. "What time is it?"

"Fifteen to five," Rascal said.

"Well, I might as well stay up. I'd have to get up soon anyhow." Rascal turned on the lights.

"You guys must be tired and hungry. I'll fix breakfast for us and then you can get some sleep. Marcel, you can wash up in the bathroom."

She fixed scrambled eggs, ham and biscuits. The coffee would wait until they had slept. "This is the last of our ham, Rascal, do you want me to order some from Douglas and we could use some bacon too."

"Yeah, go ahead."

As they were eating, Emma said, "Marcel, next week the whole village gets together on Thursday for Thanksgiving, why don't you and your wife come up if you don't have any other plans."

"I'd like that. I'd like her to meet the people in Whiskey Jack."

"Okay, it is settled. I'll see you next week. Now I must get to work. Leave the dishes for later, Rascal."

She went to work and Rascal showed Marcel the spare bedroom. Then he lay down without taking his clothes off and was instantly asleep.

Marcel lay awake for a few minutes thinking about Jarvis's and Rascal's abilities in the woods. Everything in the wild seemed to come so naturally for them both. Abilities he hoped to learn.

Chapter 6

Before leaving Whiskey Jack, Alex Bowman and Stanley Brown met Rascal in the cafeteria and thanked him profusely, and Alex gave him $50 for coming after him and possibly saving his life.

When Marcel arrived home he told his wife, Arlene, all about the people of Whiskey Jack and in particular about Rascal and Emma Ambrose. And that Emma had invited them for Thanksgiving in the village.

"After hearing you talk so much about these people, I'm intrigued and I want to meet them."

Two hunters from Lac St. Jean stepped off the southbound train out of Lac St. Jean Sunday morning, with plans of returning on the northbound train Wednesday afternoon. These two, as they walked into the cafeteria, carried themselves like seasoned hunters, and they each were carrying a Marlin .32. A good rifle. And neither one of them were interested in hiring a guide.

With no one to guide this week Rascal was almost inclined to set out a few traps. But he decided he had taken as much fur as the area could stand and still leave fur for next year. So he busied himself around home after coffee and donuts. He cut fir boughs and banked the cabin and shoveled what little snow there was on to the boughs to keep the cold out from under the cabin.

He cut off meat from the deer that would be canned. He filled four quart jars and there would be more as they ate the steaks. Cold weather usually followed close behind Thanksgiving week so he wasn't worried the rest of the deer meat might spoil. The lake had finally frozen over, but not strong enough to walk on. Sometimes the wind would blow the light snow down the length of the lake making it appear like the dead of winter.

As the fur pelts dried he took them off the stretchers and combed and primed the hair, pulling out all the hair knots. When he was finished with each piece they were looking very good. Even the greasy raccoon hides he had looking exceptional.

On Wednesday, the day before Thanksgiving, Rascal stayed home and baked biscuits all day; the evening before, Emma had made a large batch of biscuit dough and she showed Rascal how to bake them. When she returned home from work she was surprised how well he had done.

"I ordered the ham and bacon on Monday and Mr. Douglas said they should be in Friday."

"The first thing I want to do Saturday morning is go hunting. I want to shoot my deer," Emma said.

"That sounds like a good idea."

* * *

Thursday morning Marcel and Arlene boarded the train for Whiskey Jack. "I don't understand, Marcel, why there are no roads to the village."

"Well, it's a lumbering town that grew up around the Hitchcock saw mill. They own most of the land around there," Marcel said.

"And the only way in is by train?"

"Yes. It's too far for most people to hike in."

"It's just difficult to understand why people would choose to live there."

"I don't think the village will always be there. Someday the company will run out of lumber to saw and the mill will close, and in all likelihood move. Then the people will have to move."

The train pulled to stop at the platform in Whiskey Jack, and Arlene said, "This isn't at all what I expected. I hope you never expect me to live in a place like this."

Everyone was happy to meet the new game warden's wife, Arlene, and they all feasted and ate and talked until they couldn't eat any more. And this year instead of the men going off by themselves to have a drink of hard cider they all had coffee and were just as merry. Emma had brought three dozen biscuits and not one was left.

Any food left, and there was plenty, was divided up between the families. Even Elmo and Jeters got to take back some leftovers this year.

When the afternoon southbound from Lac St. Jean arrived, Marcel and Arlene said goodbye and boarded. "I can see why you talk so much about Whiskey Jack and the people. You like them. I do also, Marcel, but I still would not want to live here."

Many people stayed to help clean up. Elly Douglas said, "I want to thank all of you for helping out and the food you brought."

* * *

Friday morning Rudy Hitchcock and his wife, Althea, boarded the northbound train for Lac St. Jean. Everyone, including Emma and Rascal, knew that they were taking a mini vacation. But Rudy had other plans. He had an appointment with Jacques Colong of Colong Lumber and try to make a deal to sell spruce and pine logs to the Colong Lumber Company. Some of the details had previously been worked out over the new telephone system and now they simply had to sign contracts.

The Colongs took Rudy and Althea out for dinner that evening and they didn't return to Whiskey Jack until Sunday.

Saturday morning Marcel boarded the train for Whiskey Jack and had plans of getting off at the border and searching out any deer and moose hunting stands and burning them now that the ground was covered with snow.

Rascal and Emma, dressed in hunting attire, had a big breakfast at the hotel and then headed out along his favorite hunting road to the valley. Emma carried Rascal's .38-55 and Rascal his .45 handgun. Emma was determined to shoot her own deer.

They left the cafeteria later than Rascal would have liked. As they walked across the mill yard the muddy ruts had frozen solid overnight. When they reached the road, Rascal said, "You go ahead of me, Em. The snow is quiet so you can walk right along without worrying about making too much noise."

Once they were well away from the village they began to see many deer tracks in the snow. When they reached the cut off to the beech grove, Rascal stopped Emma and said in a low voice, "I'm going up through here to a beech grove and circle back to the valley. You follow this road until you see a rocked up fire pit. There is a rock to sit on beside the road. And there is a deer crossing about fifty yards further up the road. If I jump a deer, and I think I probably will, it will go down the valley and follow a nice deer trail to the road. I'll be thirty or forty-five minutes before you see me."

"Okay," Emma whispered and she walked on. Rascal headed up towards the beech grove. There were more deer tracks here heading for the same beech grove than there were in the road.

Emma found the fire pit with no problem and the rock. She sat down and immediately she could see movement about where Rascal had said the deer cross. She kept watching. Then she saw movement again as a deer's nose poked through the bushes smelling the ground. All she could see was the nose. She waited and she had to pee really bad, but the deer was more important. Now she could see the nose and part of the antlers. She waited some more, gritting her teeth. The deer moved forward a little with its nose still to the ground. Now Emma could see the entire head and antlers. She couldn't wait any longer. She sighted in on the deer's head just below the ear and fired. The deer dropped with its head laying on the edge of the road.

"There." She leaned the rifle up against a tree and peed. Then she walked down to look at it.

When Emma fired, Rascal had turned towards the valley at the beech tree where all the deer workings were. He waited to see if there would be another shot. When there wasn't he continued on at a little faster pace.

Marcel had just stepped off the platform at the train station when he heard one shot. He asked Elly if she had any guests today. "No, the only hunters are Rascal and Emma."

There were two sets of tracks crossing the mill yard and those had to be Rascal's and Emma's. Rascal had already shot one deer and he naturally suspected he had just shot one for his wife. He started following their tracks along the old road.

Rascal didn't waste much time. Steam was still rising into the air from the bullet wound when he arrived. Emma was standing on the road shaking with nervous excitement. When Rascal saw the bullet wound just below the ear he said, "Holy cow, that was a good shot," And then laughing he said, "You know, Em, you could have picked a smaller spot to shoot at. But that's one hell of ah nice shot."

The deer was lying in a perfect position to dress it. Emma watched in fascination as he carefully slit the hide from the butt end all the way up to the brisket and around the anus and the pecker without any urine leaking into the cavity.

Marcel saw the two tracks separate, it was obvious Rascal had circled to the right. He kept following Emma's track. Before rounding the curve in the road he could hear them talking and it was obvious they had a deer down. He kept walking towards them and he spoke before nearing them so not to unexpectedly surprise them, "That's a nice deer."

They both looked up at Marcel. Rascal was just beginning to pull all the innards out, without puncturing the stomach, "It sure is a nice buck," Emma said excitedly, "it's a ten point." Then she added for Marcel's benefit, "The first legal buck I ever shot."

He didn't reply but he was thinking. He was also looking around. Rascal's tracks were not on the road anywhere and Emma was holding the rifle and it was also obvious that the buck dropped where it was standing when shot.

"Where did you hit it Emma? I mean he dropped where he was standing," Marcel asked.

Emma rolled the head just enough to show him the entry wound. "Wow, where were you?"

"I was sitting on that rock behind you next to the fire pit."

There was no way Emma didn't shoot it herself and he'd be damned if he'd embarrass himself by asking. Instead he asked, "Anything I can do to help you, Rascal?"

"Yeah, pick the head up some so the blood will all drain out."

Marcel helped Rascal drag the deer back. "I'm surprised to see you up here today, Marcel. There are no hunters at the hotel."

"Actually I was on my way to the border when I heard a rifle shot, I thought I'd come and have a looksee. This is really a nice buck, Emma. You should have the head mounted."

That began her thinking.

The buck weighed 235 pounds. Five pounds heavier than Rascal's. "You're welcome to come up for lunch, Marcel. I'm going to fry the liver and heart with onions and biscuits."

As Rascal and Marcel were in the living room, "Those sure do smell good, Emma."

"You know, Rascal, at first I thought you shot that buck. But when I started to put all of my observations together I knew there was no way you could have."

"I must admit the idea did cross my mind when Em said she wanted to go hunting. But she also said she wanted to shoot it herself."

Between the three of them they ate the heart and half of the liver with onions and biscuits. "Do you want some help hanging that up, Rascal?"

"Sure." But Rascal had decided to hang it in a tree to skin it and not the root cellar. He just didn't want Marcel in there. After it was hung Marcel said, "I might as well take the southbound home I couldn't get up to the border until tomorrow now. I'll have to wait for next week some time."

"Thank you for your help Marcel."

* * *

After Rascal had the deer skun he used a meat saw and cut the deer down the middle of the backbone. He hung one half in the root cellar and then he went inside to see Emma.

"Em, what would you think about giving half of your deer to the Antonys?"

"It's okay with me. Two deer I think might be more than we could use."

Rascal shouldered one half and hiked down to the Antonys. Silvio was getting some firewood when he saw Rascal. "Em thought it a good idea to give half of her deer to you and Anita, Silvio. We don't need two deer."

"Was that her shot we heard this morning?"

"Yes."

"We'd appreciate it. We'll hang it up in the shed for now." Rascal helped him.

December came in cold and at night the wind would blow all night and then it suddenly stopped and began to snow. The frozen lake was now thick enough to walk on. The snow was dry and fluffy and one night of wind and the lake was swept clean again.

Marcel did manage to get to the border and burn the one hunting stand and then he looked around for more without finding any. He was back at the custom building in time to catch the southbound.

"Are you going to trap beaver?"

"I thought about going up to the swamp and check it out and then I found another flowage on Jack Brook."

"What about Bear?"

"Well, he should be hibernated by now. If I see any tracks I'll turn around."

"Remember last month I said something was going on."

"Yeah."

"Well I think I know. The company now has a contract to ship—daily—one railcar of four-foot softwood pulp and one railcar or more each day of spruce and pine logs to Colong Lumber in Lac St. Jean.

"Also when Rudy and Althea went to Lac St. Jean, he hired four men to be responsible for loading the two railcars daily. And Earl has hired six more men, also from Canada, for two more three-men crews. Plans are for another four men to handle the extra teams needed to haul the pulp and logs to the mill and two men to process the pulp at the farm. And the mill is going to operate an extra hour each day and all day on Saturdays.

"The company is moving so much more lumber now, and that makes me wonder what is going on," Emma said.

The next day the first two railcars left Whiskey Jack; one loaded with pulp and one with spruce and pine logs. The company was boarding the four men doing the loading at the mill at the hotel. The farm now had thirty men. Emma wasn't sure if the company's business had picked up that much or if there was something else happening.

With the temperatures so cold each night, Rascal and Emma would lay in their bed at night and listen to the lake making ice. There were times when the snaps were as loud as a rifle shot and echoing back and forth in the mountains. The cold hung on for two weeks before subsiding some.

Rascal hiked up to Ledge Swamp, figuring Bear was probably safely hibernating. He found a huge house and feed bed at the upper end of the flowage. There was snow over the ice and there was only four inches of ice. He set two bait sets in what he assumed was the beaver run between the house and the feed bed and he set up two ideal runs in clear channels through the bushes. He was satisfied with this flowage and he packed up and went down to, and then upstream on Jack Brook about a quarter of a mile to the other flowage he knew of. He set up this flowage about the same as Ledge Swamp.

By the time he was back home, he was tired and he saw Emma walking across the ice for home and he hurried to join her.

"Busy day?" she asked.

"Tiring, it's a long hike to Ledge Swamp and then up Jack Brook and home."

"Don't overdo it, Rascal. Are you going back up tomorrow to check your traps?"

"No, I'll wait maybe two days and take what I have and pull the traps. When those hides are dry we'll take a trip to Beech Tree."

The next day the temperature warmed up slightly and stayed like that for the rest of the week. "Hope we don't get any rain," Silvio said.

"Does anyone know why Hitchcock is doing so much more business now?" Silvio asked.

"I don't know, maybe they saw the tops of the fir and spruce trees could be turned into money, instead of left to rot on the ground."

"Well, for whatever the reason the village sure is busy," Jeters said.

And the village was busy. Every day a carload of four foot pulp went south and every second day the men were able to send two cars out.

Rascal went back to Ledge Swamp and pulled all of his traps. Of the four sets he had three large beaver. He built a fire and then began skinning. And he set some meat to roasting. The meat was cooked before he had finished all three and he ate that and set more to roasting, finished the three beaver, cut the meat and castors off and put everything in his pack basket. He knew there were more beaver here but the trip up and back again was too much for his bad leg.

On Jack Brook he only had two large beaver. That would have to be enough. After he skun the beaver and cut off the meat and castors, his pack basket was full. His traps he hung on the back of his neck and shoulders and started for home. He figured he had over a $100.00 worth of fur and castors, and enough fresh meat to last he and Emma for a while. The pack was heavy and he had to cut off a walking stick with his axe. He didn't want to take a chance of falling on the ice.

He waited until the next day to stretch 'em and nail 'em to his drying boards. With the cold temperatures now, the fleshy sides would turn white. He left the hides in the root cellar for two days and then moved them to the wood shed for three days. The hides were then cured and white.

"Do you suppose Rudy will give you tomorrow afternoon off, so we can catch the train to Beech Tree?"

"I'll ask when I see him this morning."

* * *

Emma came home that evening all excited. "Mr. Hitchcock said I could have it off and this time I won't have to come in on Sunday to make up for it. We'll have the whole weekend."

She took a bath that evening and made sure Rascal did also and then she packed a few clothes and wrapped one bottle of wine in a sweater and put it in the pack. "Rascal, I'd like to buy a grip while we are in Beech Tree. I'm tired of walking into hotels and have people staring at us carrying a pack basket."

"Okay," Rascal had never thought twice about using his pack basket. But he guessed he could understand how Emma might feel.

At coffee the next morning "Silvio, I have some more beaver meat. Do you and Anita need any more?"

"I don't think so. We still have some."

"How about you, Jeters?"

"I'd take some. That was surely good what we had. I'd never eaten beaver before. It is so sweet and none of it was chewy or tough."

"You'll probably be asleep, but I'll bring some down before noon."

"Just leave it by the door, if you would. If that door opens I'll wake up."

"Sure no problem."

Silvio wasn't as talkative this morning and he wondered why. He was looking pale too. But then again in the winter he seldom got outdoors except to come for coffee. He forgot about it.

"These French fellas from Quebec surely are hard workers. After supper each night they load pulp on the freight car usually until 10 or 11 pm."

"Hey, Silvio, are you sure you're okay? You're almost asleep," Rascal said.

"Yeah, I'm okay. I just ain't been sleeping too well."

They split up after a while and Rascal watched Silvio as he walked home. He was acting like an old man now. He was worried about him. Rascal went home and shoveled more snow up against the cabin and filled the wood boxes inside. Emma was home shortly after noon and Rascal had made lunch for the two of them.

"After we finish eating I'll carry your deer head and cape down to the terminal platform."

"What about your deer, Rascal?"

"I've thought about it too. I've kept it frozen so it is still good. I'll bring back another box for that one."

Before leaving, Rascal stoked both fires and filled them with round beechnut wood. Rascal had earlier bundled his pelts and now he put them on his back and they hiked down to the station. They were early and so too was the train as it was just coming around the bend above Antony's cabin. They still had a few minutes to wait as the train had to couple on the car loaded with pulpwood. They left the station on time.

In Beech Tree they had to hire a driver to take them to the Beech Tree Hotel. "Oh, Rascal, will you hire an automobile to take us. I don't want to sit in the cold."

"Sure," There was an auto taxi parked outside waiting. They went first to Page's Furrier. Would you wait here, please. I want to drop these off."

They had to make two trips. "Hello, Jarvis. Is it alright if we drop these off and come back in the morning? The crated boxes each contain a buck's head and cape that we would like mounted."

"Sure thing, no problem. We'll put them in the back room. It is always kept cold."

"We must leave, Jarvis; a taxi is waiting for us outside."

"See you in the morning. Why don't the two of you come for breakfast. Say about 7 am?"

"That would be fine."

Jarvis knew they were in a hurry because of the taxi waiting for them, so he didn't want to delay them. "See you in the morning."

The taxi took them straight to the hotel. "You know, Em, why does traveling tire one out so much?"

She laughed and said, "You know, I don't know. Maybe because traveling breaks up the routine."

"Anyway, I'm hungry."

They unpacked and went downstairs to the dining room. "I wish they had the same fish platter that we get in St. Jean."

"How about a roast pork dinner?" Rascal asked.

"You know we seldom have pork; that sounds good."

The waitress took their order and as she was about to leave Emma asked, "And how about a bottle of chateau wine?

White, please." She knew what the answer would be.

"Sorry, ma'am haven't you heard of Prohibition? Where do you live, in the woods?"

Rascal just sat there watching and listening to his wife, "As a matter of fact, Miss, we do. In Whiskey Jack."

"Well, I'm sorry, no alcoholic beverages, ma'am."

"Then a glass of water and two coffees," Emma said. She looked at Rascal and smiled and said, "I had to try. You know I really enjoy a glass of wine."

While they waited for the roast pork the waitress gave them a plate of hor d'ourves to sample while they waited.

The roast pork was worth waiting for, "Oh my, have you ever tasted anything so good?" Emma exclaimed.

"You know, Em, with this cold weather we could take back a couple of pork roasts with us. It would stay good for a long time in the root cellar, especially if we froze them first."

When they had finished eating Emma said, "Before we go upstairs let's go for a walk and let this pork settle. I think we both need to walk it off."

It was cold outside and the wind was blowing a little, just enough to make them feel the cold. They didn't stay out for long.

Up in their room, Emma said, "You take a bath, Rascal. I had one before we left."

He didn't argue. In fact he kinda enjoyed lying back in the tub with hot water. While he was bathing, Emma took out the bottle of wine and poured two glasses and then she took her clothes off, except for her panties and bra and brushed out her hair and applied just a hint of perfume. Then she waited on the bed for Rascal.

The hot water was feeling so good, Rascal was staying in the tub for a long time. Finally Emma said, "Did you go to sleep or something?"

"I'll be out in a minute."

"When you do, I want you to shave."

After he had dried off, combed his hair and shaved, he

stepped into the bedroom and saw Emma lying in a seductive pose on the bed and he stood there enjoying what he was seeing and wearing only a big grin.

"Don't just stand there grinning, come here," and she gave him a glass of wine. They clinked glasses for a toast and Emma, "To the French."

Rascal grinned again and said, "I'll drink to that."

They sipped wine and talked long into the night. When the wine was gone they talked some more. And then—and then they made wild passionate love.

* * *

They were up early the next morning so they would not be late for breakfast with Jarvis and his wife, Rita. The hotel concierge telephoned for a taxi for them. "These modern conveniences are going to spoil me, Rascal."

The taxi driver came into the hotel after his fares. It was a short ride to the Pages and they were out of the cold.

Emma offered to help Rita, and Jarvis and Rascal sat at the table talking. "I notice there are two buck heads. Do you want both mounted?"

"Yes. Em shot one the last day. She hit it just below the ear."

"Good shooting, Emma. But you've had practice," Jarvis said good naturedly.

"What did Marcel have to say?"

"At first I think he suspected I had shot it, but all the evidence was there in the snow."

"What do you think of him, Rascal?"

"I think he feels awful uneasy alone in the woods. His own words. We were out all night with a lost hunter and he didn't feel comfortable at all and I don't think he had any natural woods-wise ability. He may learn to feel more comfortable, but I'm not certain."

Oh, I found how you seemed to appear in Whiskey Jack when no one knew how you got there. I found your trail. I trapped from it this fall."

Rita and Emma were serving up breakfast and all four kept talking even while they ate. Both Rita and Emma were glad for company.

"Do you know someone who will mount the deer heads for us?"

"Yes, there is an excellent taxidermist right here in Beech Tree. Leave the heads with me and I'll talk with David Rubert."

"Well, let's go take a look at your fur pelts," Jarvis said.

Rascal untied the bundle of pelts and separated each species. Jarvis was very interested with the two mountain lion hides and the story behind them. "These summer beaver pelts look almost as good as these five. These five I can offer you $30 each and the summer pelts $22 each. How many castors are there?"

"Three pounds."

"I can offer you $5 for the three pounds." He looked over each pelt very closely. "I am impressed how well you take care of them. These are all prime pieces. For everything, including the castors I can offer an even $2000.00."

"I tell you what, Jarvis, $2000.00 plus a coat for Em, one of those in your shop with a fur collar."

"Okay."

"The coat I want to be a surprise for Em for Christmas, so if you would send it to me, I'll pay the charges. And do you want a deposit for the heads?"

"Oh, how's $20 each head."

"Okay. When the mounts are done, can you ship them to us also and if you'll do that I might as well pay you now for the mounting."

"Okay, how's $60 sound for both mounts?"

"That'll be fine. Take it out of the fur."

"Okay, here's $1940.00."

"Thank you, Jarvis."

They had another cup of coffee and then Rascal and Emma had to leave. They still had some shopping to do. "Thank you for breakfast, Rita. You and Jarvis must come see us some time," Emma said.

"Thanks, Jarvis."

Even though the temperature was still cold they decided to walk to town. It wasn't that far. Emma found her two grips. They next went to find a meat store that had pork.

The meat or butcher shop was surprisingly close to the train station. "Hello, may I help you with something?"

"Yes, do you sell pork loin?"

"We certainly do."

"Would it by any chance be frozen?"

"Yes, during the cold months of winter I can keep meat frozen. How much would you like?"

"A full loin and could you cut it in half and wrap each half separately? Double wrap if you would. We'll have to carry it in our luggage."

"Certainly."

"We won't be able to leave now until tomorrow morning. Is there any chance we could leave that here and pick it up in the morning before the northbound train leaves?"

"The train leaves at 7:15 am so if we were here by 6:30 am . . ."

"I'll be here at 6:30, then. And I would appreciate it if you would pay for it now."

"Do you want anything else, Em? I mean while we are here?"

"We have our ham and bacon, maybe a bushel basket of apples."

"Oh boy, yes."

Rascal paid for the pork and apples and it was now time for lunch.

"How much did you get for your fur?"

"$2000.00 and after I paid to have the two heads mounted $1940.00, minus hotel and food. We'll have just over $1900.00 to bank."

"You know Rascal that'll give us somewhere between $5000.00 and $6000.00."

* * *

After breakfast they took a taxi to the meat shop and put the loins in the pack basket and left that out on the platform where it was cold, until it was time to board. The apples they took inside with them.

Rascal and Emma were the only ones going to Whiskey Jack, the other six passengers were going on to Lac St. Jean. It was cold inside the passenger car and Rascal and Emma huddled together.

At Whiskey Jack the train had to couple on two flat cars with logs this morning for Colong Lumber. The inside of their cabin was cool but not cold and Rascal knew none of the water pipes would have frozen.

* * *

After the deer season things had pretty much fallen back in to routine at Whiskey Jack. And Warden Cyr was not seen at all during the month of December. The train had hit a couple of deer on the tracks near Ledge Swamp and the track crews divided up the meat. It had been a while now since the train had hit a moose.

At the Christmas gathering the day before Christmas this year, Elly and two other women cooked up a boiled dinner, with plenty of ham. Emma baked her usual biscuits and this year she also made two apple pies which everyone enjoyed. Silvio and Anita were enjoying themselves, although Rascal thought Silvio was being unusually quiet. Later in the afternoon there was pie and coffee and hot chocolate for the kids.

It had been a warm day and going up the slight incline from the dam Emma and Rascal kept slipping. So they had to set over in the unpacked snow. The crews this year were cutting straight back from where the road ended, and not off to the left where Rascal had his trap line. They would have that side of the lake, what they were going to cut, all harvested by the middle of February. And then they would help the crews with the four foot pulp.

On Christmas morning Rascal slipped quietly out of bed and stoked the fires and put the coffee pot on. Emma awoke to a warm cabin and the smell of fresh coffee making. Before she had a chance to get out of bed and dress Rascal gave her a large box.

"What's this?"

"Open it."

"Oh my word, Rascal! It is so beautiful. When did you find the time to buy this? And how did you ever get it home without me knowing about it?"

"I saw it at Jarvis' and asked him to send it to me."

She climbed out of bed with nothing on and tried the new coat on. "It fits perfectly. How did you ever know the right size to get?"

"Oh, there was this beautiful woman in the shop that tried it on so I could see."

"You're kidding right?" all serious like.

"Of course; I guessed."

"It feels so soft next to my body. And I love this fur collar."

"Your gift isn't ready yet. It took me a long time to decide to do it, so tonight after supper I'll give it to you."

"You'll have me wondering all day."

Emma was so happy with her new coat she kept it on until she began to sweat. Then she got dressed. Rascal was busy making breakfast. Scrambled eggs and thick slices of ham with coffee. "You know, Em, after breakfast I think we should walk down and check on the Antonys. I don't think Silvio has been feeling good."

"I'll make a hot batch of biscuits to take with us."

While Emma was baking biscuits Rascal filled both wood boxes and packed down a snowshoe trail beside the twitch road by the cabin and another down to the lake in front of the cabin and across to the village.

When he had finished Emma had just taken the biscuits out of the oven. "You ready?" he asked.

She pulled on her new coat and said, "I'll carry the biscuits if you hold onto me and keep me from slipping."

It was still cold outside, but the wind had stopped blowing. No one was about outside in the village.

As they approached the Antony's cabin, Silvio was just emptying a bucket of ashes on the walkway, so people would not slip and fall on the ice.

"Merry Christmas folks and come on in out of this damned cold." He held the door open for them. "Don't worry about your feet. Sit down and how about a cup of hot coffee?"

"That would be good and Anita, here's a batch of biscuits I baked this morning."

"Hum, these are so good, Emma. You always bake the best biscuits in the village. Someday you'll have to tell me your secret."

"How about a Christmas cheer, folks?"

Rascal knew what Silvio meant and he wasn't too sure how Emma would react. "Anita, get four glasses down would ya? We'll all have a drink to Christmas and good friends."

Silvio poured two fingers in each glass and then they each raised them in a toast and all said at once, "To good friends."

Emma had never tasted whiskey before. She sipped it and liked the taste but she could feel it burn all the way down. But she wasn't going to say anything and spoil the happy mood for anyone.

Silvio's was gone in two swallows. Rascal's lasted a bit

longer and Anita and Emma nursed theirs.

A few minutes after the drink Silvio seemed to act more like his old self, not so worn out. He even began telling stories about his days on the railroad before he injured his ankle, and shooting moose for his family. Emma saw the difference also and she began wondering if the whiskey didn't have a lot to do with the change. *Maybe that's all he needed to get his blood flowing again*, she was thinking. *Maybe alcohol in moderation was actually good for the heart.*

After two hours Rascal and Emma decided it was time to leave. "Thank you so much for the biscuits, Emma," Anita said.

The sun was out bright and this made you think it was warmer than it really was. "You better hang on to me, Rascal."

Emma was planning a venison steak supper with baked potato and beet greens, so for lunch she fixed sandwiches and more coffee.

After lunch Rascal read the day-before newspaper and then went outside looking for something to do, to take his mind off what surprise Emma had for him. Emma cleaned the inside of the cabin. When she was finished she opened two windows to fill the inside with fresh air and blow the old air out. The air was cold and she decided it didn't take long at all to fill the inside with fresh clean air. She inhaled deeply and was satisfied.

Rascal strapped on his snowshoes and followed the twitch road out back to see what the crews had been doing. Much to his surprise there were deer everywhere feeding on the slash left behind. The bucks had all lost their antlers and it was difficult now to tell the difference between them and the does. But they all looked fat and healthy. He saw ravens fly up and he went over to see. There were the remains of a dead deer. He looked it all over and circled it looking for other animal tracks and there were none. The body of the deer was there, head and neck also, but the four legs were missing. One of the cutting crews had killed it. As much as he wanted to, he could not begrudge them. As he had done the same many times.

Dark clouds had moved in. There was no wind and the air was not as cold. Everything was silent. Not even the whiskey jacks were flying around looking for food.

Rascal returned home and said, "I think we are in for a storm."

"You have plenty of wood in the boxes, don't you?" she asked.

"Yes, but I think I'll bring a little more and some kindling."

He piled the wood up on the floor beside the wood boxes. "There that should be enough for tomorrow too."

"I'm glad I won't have to work tomorrow," Emma said.

"I'm going to get some potatoes. You take a bath. I took one while you were out."

"Oh, Em, I just had one not more'n two days ago."

"Do you want your Christmas gift or not?"

"Okay."

"And shave."

"Yes, Em."

She put two lighted candles on the table, lit one of the larger kerosene lanterns and put that on the mantle in the living room and brought in the last bottle of wine from the root cellar and opened it and filled two glasses. Then she took her clothes off and slipped on her bathrobe and took Rascal's to him in the bathroom. "Here, put this on when you're done. And holler when you start to shave and I'll put the steak on."

She combed out her hair and let it float on her shoulders. "Ok, Em, I'm shaving."

She put the steak in the already hot fry pan, and put the beet greens on to warm up. The potatoes she knew would be ready as soon as the steak was done. She was careful not to overcook the steaks. She wanted the centers to still be a little raw. This way there was more flavor and she had also noticed that after eating wild meat, especially beaver, if it wasn't overcooked, gave her an adrenaline rush and aroused her sexual appetite.

Just as Rascal was leaving the bathroom Emma was putting everything on the table. Rascal just stood there astonished and grinning. "This is great, Em."

She gave him a glass of wine and she held hers and they took a sip. "Wow, this all smells so good and I am hungry." They sat down and he looked at his wife again and grinned and said, "You are really beautiful, Em."

"The night has only begun."

They talked all through supper and when they had finished eating Emma refilled their glasses, "Let's go sit in the living room. The kitchen can wait for morning." With only the lantern and the two candles the semi-darkness was romantic. They talked and laughed and when their glasses were empty Emma filled them again. She could really feel the wild meat doing its work.

When that glass of wine was gone Emma refilled their glasses again, "That's the last of that," she said.

Emma was happy and having fun giving herself as a gift for Rascal. And oh, wow, was that wild meat ever working now. She emptied her glass and slid off Rascal's lap and went into the bedroom and came out with a thick quilt that she spread on the floor in front of the stove. She opened the stove door to let the fire illuminate the room and she blew out the lantern, and left the two candles burning on the table. "There," she said, "That's much more romancier," and she laughed at the use of that word.

She untied her bathrobe and the front she brushed aside exposing her nude body. Rascal's eyes were glazed in place watching her. She bent down and kissed him and when he started to pull her down to him, she pushed his arms down and said, "Not yet."

She stepped back onto the quilt and in the romantic glow of the fire and the candles she let the bathrobe fall to the floor. Then she began to slowly dance in place moving her hips side to side and humming a tune. *Boy was the wine and wild meat working,* she thought. Rascal was smiling and watching and enjoying every move. She reached down and took his hands in hers and pulled him to his feet and slid his bathrobe over his shoulders and let it fall to the floor.

They danced there on the quilt in the soft glow of the fire and then she went down on her knees and pulled him down with her and when she lay back, Rascal was on top of her.

At first it was passionate love making, but Emma could really feel the wild meat working inside her. She wanted more and more of Rascal. She needed to fulfill her debauchery needs and hunger and Rascal was getting just as much enjoyment.

They had been at it for hours now trying to fulfill their own needs while trying to please the other. It was well after midnight when they finally had to stop from exhaustion. The candles had burned out and the only light now was from the fire and Rascal closed the door to the stove, pulled the edge of the quilt over them and they slept on the living room floor.

Before either of them had drifted off to sleep Rascal said, "Thank you for my Christmas gift."

She rolled over to look at him and grinned and said, "It was my pleasure."

* * *

When they woke up the next morning the fire in the stove had gone out and the cabin was cold. Emma started to move and she said, "Ooh, the inside of my legs hurt."

Rascal got up and started the fire in both stoves. Then they both dressed.

"Em, look out the window. It must have snowed two feet last night."

While Emma was fixing breakfast, Rascal went outside to shovel out the paths.

The snow was deep but it was dry and fluffy. Rascal could walk through it without any trouble. After breakfast he put on his snowshoes and broke out the path to the twitch road and then he went to check on Silvio and Anita. Silvio had not even been outside yet. So Rascal cleared his paths to the outhouse and wood shed. Then he went inside to visit.

"Thank you, Rascal. I was just having difficulty getting started this morning. How much did we get?"

"Two feet, but it's a dry fluffy snow. The wind will blow it off into the woods." Rascal stayed and had coffee and then he went home.

The crew loading the flat cars with pulpwood had cleared the snow and were now back to loading four foot pulp. They didn't work yesterday, and now they wanted to make up for it.

Everyone was busy on Sunday shoveling out from the snow. On Monday the village was back to its regular routine. On New Year's Eve, Friday night, everybody got together in the cafeteria for some friendly talk and Rudy Hitchcock had produced a gallon of hard cider. Emma had a glass and she didn't like it as well as the wine.

* * *

More lumber was being sawn now in the mill than anyone had thought possible and the company was now regularly shipping two carloads of pulpwood south and two carloads of spruce and pine logs to Colong Lumber in Lac St. Jean. A lot of money was passing through the company and Whiskey Jack village. "At the rate the lumber, and pulp and logs are being shipped out of here I find it difficult to see how much longer they can operate like this. There has to be an end to the wood some time," Silvio said.

The annual January thaw arrived right on schedule, January 15th. The snow was settling and the villagers were happy for a reprieve from the cold temperatures and snow.

One morning during the thaw when Rascal arrived at the cafeteria for the usual coffee and donuts, Jeters was sitting alone with a long drawn face. "What is the matter, Jeters? Where's Silvio?"

"Silvio ain't coming, Rascal. He died in his sleep last night."

"Where is Anita now?"

"She's with Elly in the kitchen."

Rascal went to see Anita and offered her any help she might need. Anita had a sister in Beech Tree that she would go and live with. But not until a funeral could be held in Whiskey Jack. This is the only home Silvio had and the people there were all like family. The body would be buried in Beech Tree.

Everyone was affected by his passing. Some even cried when they heard the news. For Jeters, Silvio was like a father and he would really miss him.

Death of the human body was only part of life, but for those left behind, Silvio would be missed. Rascal accompanied Anita and Silvio's body to Beech Tree and he made sure she was settled at her sister's home before he returned to Whiskey Jack.

"Rascal, I can't thank you enough for all of your help. Would you close up the cabin for me? Maybe this summer I'll come back for a while."

"I will look after it, Anita."

Before leaving Beech Tree, Rascal stopped to see Jarvis. "It was a shock to us all. He hadn't been feeling good, though, for a month. He said he was just tired. I worry about Anita, though."

"I'll check in on her, Rascal. She'll be just fine."

"Thank you, Jarvis."

Chapter 7

Rascal and Jeters missed their friend the most. He was, after all, one of the coffee and donut crew.

When Rascal had returned from Beech Tree after accompanying Anita and Silvio's body, he had made sure that their cabin was secure for the winter. He emptied all containers of water and he took all food stores to the cafeteria to be given to other families, or the food would have spoiled. He found a few items he was sure Anita would want, along with their clothes.

He packed everything and left them in the bedroom for now. Later he would see that they were taken to Beech Tree.

By mid-February the crews had finished cutting out behind the Ambrose cabin and now those two crews were helping the teamsters to bring the four foot pulp and logs to the mill to be shipped out.

"You know, Em, I think Silvio was right when he said the Hitchcock Company is up to something."

"I know, and I agree with you, but so far Mr. Hitchcock hasn't said anything to me about it. But strange businessmen are still coming here and talking with Rudy."

The snow had settled much during the January thaw and then refroze and hardened again making it ideal for lumbering. With solid frozen ice roads the teams were not getting as tired hauling wood from the farm to the mill. That winter was proving to be ideal for lumbering and both Rudy and Earl were satisfied with the pace of operations.

In early March one afternoon as Emma was closing the office, Rudy stepped in to talk with her. "Emma, does Rascal have plans for tomorrow?"

"Not that I know of, Mr. Hitchcock."

"Good, after his morning coffee, I would like both of you to come to my office. There is something I would like to talk to you both about."

"I'll make sure he is here, sir."

That evening as they were eating supper Emma said, "Mr. Hitchcock would like to talk to us tomorrow morning in his office after you have had your coffee."

"Do you know why?"

"He didn't say."

"I wonder if it has anything to do with the fast pace of harvesting lumber this winter."

At coffee the next morning with Jeters, he didn't say anything about Rudy Hitchcock wanting to talk with him.

"I miss Silvio," Jeters said.

"Yeah, me too. He was like a grandfather to you and me," Rascal said.

"I feel bad for Anita"

Rascal excused himself and said, "I need to drop by and see my wife," and he left the cafeteria. Jeters went back to his room to sleep.

Rascal walked into her office.

"He's waiting for us."

Rudy's office was at the end of the hall, "Come in, please and close the door—sit down, please; we may be here for a while."

Rascal was really curious now. He had no idea what to expect.

"I'll get right to the point. As of the end of February all harvesting will be terminated, and as many loads of logs that we can, will be sent to Colong Lumber, as well as any four foot pulp left. When the inventory of logs in the mill yard are gone the entire company will begin moving to relocate and people will have to leave the village. We will take as many worker families with us that want to stay with Hitchcock Lumber."

"We have a crew now that is assembling a new saw mill with more modern equipment. The big saw here will be left here for now, as most of the equipment in that part of the mill. Everything is old. We are installing a new band saw instead of the rotary saw blade that we use here. The farm will be closed up and all water drained. The C&A station master and crews will be leaving and all the other buildings—except the mill, lumber shed and the hotel-general store will remain—will be burned.

"I'm assuming you'll want to stay on. I think I have heard you say that once or twice."

"Yes," they both answered.

"Now here's the proposition I want to make. The company is going to need someone to look after what is left here at the village and the farm. That's where you two come in. The company owns all the buildings in the village except your home and ten acres, so as I said earlier everything will be burned and covered over. I am prepared to give you two the hotel/general store building. The hotel would make you a marvelous sporting lodge. I will also need you to look after the farm and what is left behind here, as I said before. And I am prepared to give you $500.00 a year for looking after them. If you'll accept my offer of the hotel and general store, the buildings will belong to you."

"What about the Douglas's?" Emma asked.

"They have already said without the railroad and mill there is no point in the keeping the hotel."

"When do you expect to have everything moved, burned and covered up?" Rascal asked.

"By mid-summer we plan to be out of here. That's July 1st."

"The C&A crews will be out of here by May 1st and the Douglas's do not see any point in their staying beyond May 1st either. So as of May 2nd it could be yours, if you want it."

"Where are you moving the company?"

"The west branch of the C&A out of Beech Tree, a half township bordering the Canadian border."

"Do you expect to ever come back here?"

"Yes, we have left a good healthy forest and when we come back what we have left this time will be ready to harvest then. Also I have been talking with Senator David Lowe and he tells me that the United States Army Aircorp is looking to the possibilities of building thousands of airplanes and the manufacturers will need high grade hardwood which we have a lot of. So when building these airplanes becomes a reality we'll be back for the hardwood and the mature softwood.

"I know you have a lot to think about and I don't need your answer right now. Tonight, talk it over and give me your answer in the morning.

"And do me one favor, don't say anything about any of this until I have a chance to tell everyone."

* * *

Emma went back to work and Rascal went home and boiled a pot of coffee and sat at the table digesting everything Rudy had said, and his offer. Emma could hardly keep her mind on her work.

After he had finished all the coffee in the pot he put his coat and hat on and walked out back where the crews had been. There was still many deer living in the choppings and no sign of any predators. All the while thinking about Rudy's offer. It was too good to pass up, but even without Emma's income they could survive quite well.

The wind was beginning to blow and although it wasn't all that cold he decided to walk down to the mill and walk back with Emma. Besides, there was so much caffeine in him now, he couldn't sit and relax for long.

"I'm glad you came down to walk me home, Rascal. Have you been thinking about Rudy's offer?"

"That's all I have been thinking about."

"Yeah, me too. I couldn't keep my mind on my work today."

All through supper they talked about it. "It's a wonderful opportunity, Rascal,"

"I know and we would be stupid to pass on it."

"I'm hearing a . . . but . . . there somewhere."

"Well, what I make trapping and what I get for disability amounts to over $3000.00 a year. That's more than most people make. And I'm doing something I like."

"I can still hear the . . . but."

"Okay, let's say we don't accept, what are you going to do but get bored. There won't be anyone here to socialize or talk with. I think you would soon become bored and fat. We would argue all the time. It would be a lot of work, you know."

"But we wouldn't have time to get fat or argue."

"You see what I've been thinking about all day. There are pros and cons on both sides."

"Okay, I agree with you there, Rascal. Let's not think or talk about it anymore today. Let's sleep on it and in the morning we'll know what to do. Okay?"

"Okay," Rascal agreed.

They went to bed listening to the wind blow overhead and measuring the pros and cons of Rudy's offer.

The soft music of the wind eventually let Emma fall asleep. Rascal stayed awake on his back long into the night.

For a brief while the wind blew harder and Rascal was beginning to enjoy listening to it. He laughed at himself and thinking he had a decision to make that would affect his life as much as the night he had lain awake thinking about asking Emma to marry him. He continued laughing silently and then he thought to himself, *My life turned out alright with Emma. So why not take Rudy up on his offer.* With that last thought echoing back and forth in his head he fell asleep.

In the morning when they awoke they were facing each other. Their eyes open and began to focus. Emma smiled and brushed the hair back on his forehead. "Tell me, Rascal, yes or no before you have a chance to think on it."

"Yes. And you?"

"Yes."

"Well I'm glad that is settled. I have lain awake worrying if it was the right thing to do or not, for a long time," he said.

"When did you ever lay awake worrying?"

"The night I made up my mind to ask you to marry me."

"You worried about whether you should marry me or not?"

Right then Rascal was regretting saying anything about it. Emma saw the hurt look on his face and she began to laugh. "Come on, you, it's time to get up."

* * *

At work that morning Emma told Mr. Hitchcock, "We have both been doing a lot of thinking about your offer Mr. Hitchcock and we both accept."

"Good. Sunday I'll call a town meeting and tell the folks about the changes."

Rudy had made up some posters to put up throughout the village announcing a special town meeting Sunday morning and requesting everyone be there. He put one in the cafeteria, the general store, the train terminal and several within the mill. He wanted everyone there.

* * *

At 10 o'clock Sunday everyone in the village was in the cafeteria. "First I want to thank everyone for coming. And I want to thank everyone for your work this season. The pulpwood market this winter has yielded more money than we had budgeted.

"Now to get down to more important things. At the end of this winter's harvest period the company will be terminating business here in Whiskey Jack. The company will be moving to the Kidney Township, only accessible by the C&A west branch line out of Beech Tree. The company has been working on preparations for our move since last September. Instead of log cabins, everything will be frame construction. There will be a new band saw, which will be quieter, safer and faster. The company purchased half of Kidney Township and it lies next to the Quebec border.

"I will leave a roster here on the table for those will move with us to Kidney Pond."

There was murmuring among the villagers. This announcement had surprised everyone. Rudy continued and explained the Ambroses would be taking possession of the hotel-general store on May 2nd.

"Any questions?"

"Yes, when will this move start?"

"All harvesting stopped yesterday and the remaining crews will help load the pulpwood and logs on to the railcars. Then the farm will be closed up. When the logs have all been shipped from here we start removing things. The C&A crews will no longer work from Whiskey Jack. Instead they will come out of Beech Tree. Once everyone has left, the buildings will be burned and buried."

"Will the Hitchcock Company ever come back to Whiskey Jack?"

"Yes, but probably not for fifteen years."

"Oh, there is one important fact that I forgot to mention earlier. Every single worker will be receiving a $1000.00 bonus. Now if there are no more questions, I must return to my office."

After Rudy left, everyone was trying to talk all at once. All but two people signed the roster to go to Kidney Pond. Rascal and Emma went home.

"That went better than I had supposed," Rascal said.

"How do you mean?"

"I would have thought there might have been some grumbling about having to pick up and move."

"Maybe what these people need is a little change."

Chapter 8

With all of the pulpwood and logs now hauled down from the farm, Earl began closing up things there. The livestock were all butchered and given to the people in the village. There wasn't that much. The tools and wagons were stored in the barn, the horses and harness were taken to the village and loaded into boxcars and taken to Kidney Pond. Earl and Martha's personal items and some furniture were all shipped to Kidney Pond.

The water was all drained and the outhouses cleaned out and the doors nailed shut. The barn and shed doors were also nailed shut. Old two-man crosscut saw blades were nailed across the lower windows to keep the bear out.

Finally the day came when Earl and Martha turned and walked away. "It's sad, Earl. We had so many good years here and the friends we made."

"Some of those friends, Martha, are going to Kidney Pond with us. We'll be back here in fifteen years or so."

They were at the station in time to board the afternoon southbound. There was only a skeleton crew left in the village now to see to the last preparations. The mill had stopped sawing two weeks ago and all of the sawn lumbar had been shipped. Jeters was one of the last to remain and he was staying with Rascal and Emma, as his living quarters were torn down and ready to be burned. The track crews were gone, but the station master, Greg Oliver, would be there until everything had been shipped out.

The Douglas's offered Rascal and Emma a deal they couldn't turn down. "There is too much stuff here for us to pack and ship to our new home. We'll leave everything for you two for $150.00."

Rascal and Emma didn't hesitate, they accepted the offer.

Now all that remained besides Rascal and Emma, was the station master and Rudy Hitchcock; his wife, Althea, had already gone on to Kidney Pond.

Rudy Hitchcock was the bank for the entire village and when he gave Rascal and Emma their account in full they were surprised. $7143.50.

"That's more than I figured we had on account."

The next day the train delivered a new Allis Chalmers bulldozer that was offloaded onto the log ramp. "The first rainy day, Jeters will set fire to all of the cabins. I understand you'd like to keep the Antony cabin."

"Yes, and maybe a couple of the sheds."

"I'll leave the shed that is full of sawn lumber and the one next to it. You'll probably want the slab pile for stove wood."

"Yes."

"I'll be leaving tomorrow morning. Jeters will stay on until everything is buried. When the bulldozer is loaded back on the train, Jeters will leave then. Later a crew from Beech Tree will come up and pull up the tracks in the mill yard.

"I would advise you, Rascal, to get yourself a small bulldozer. One with a bucket on the front. Here is the $500.00 for this year and every year on May 1st I'll send you $500.00 for taking care of things. If you need to get in touch with me you can reach me by telephone at Kidney Pond. The lines have already been installed."

The next morning Rudy and Greg left, and that left Jeters, and he was busy learning to operate the big bulldozer. Rascal and Emma were there to say goodbye to Greg and Rudy. "We don't know what to say, Mr. Hitchcock. You have been so good to us."

They had coffee and donuts while they waited for the morning train. The northbound to Lac St. Jean had already gone through and C&A were sending another special train with crews to pull up the rails and they would be spending at least one night at the new Whiskey Jack Lodge, but not until Jeters had burned the buildings and buried the remains and finished his work with the bulldozer. He had to have the ramp so the train could back up a flat car to it so the bulldozer could be loaded.

"Jeters, how many days do you think you'll be here? I need to get to Beech Tree and buy a small crawler and I'll need a ramp to unload it."

"That'll depend on the weather. I can't burn unless there is rain. To finish everything I'm looking at close to a week."

"Okay, I'll take the southbound this afternoon and I'll be back as soon as I can."

Emma wanted to go to, so Rascal asked Jeters if he'd be okay there alone. "Sure, I'm used to my own cooking."

"Em, we'd better take our money and put it in the bank after we pay for the crawler. We'll keep the $500.00 that Rudy gave us to live on and ready money."

"How much will you have to pay for a crawler?"

"I have no idea. Hope it won't break us before we even get started."

Emma packed one of their new travel grips and put the money in her purse.

Whenever the train was supposed to stop at Whiskey Jack, Greg Oliver had told Rascal to flip the red metal flag up on the signal post on the platform, whether a passenger wanted to board or there was mail going out.

The red flag was up and they waited for the southbound. And right on schedule it pulled to a stop. There were only a few other passengers. It was a nervous ride for them both. They had no idea how much a crawler would cost them. And they hoped they were doing the right thing.

The Beech Tree equipment warehouse was only a block from the terminal. "We might as well get it done now."

"Let's go."

Mr. Walter met them at the front showroom and after Rascal described what he wanted a crawler for Mr. Walter said, "I think I have just what you are looking for. The boys finished putting it all together this morning.

"It weighs three tons and is powered by a four cylinder gasoline engine." Walter showed him how to start it using the key ignition. "And if your battery is low, leave the battery connected and use this hand crank, just like the model As and model Ts." He showed him how to hand crank it. He showed him everything that he would need to know. The bucket when turned right could also be used as a blade.

"I'll need a steel drum with a hand crank pump for gasoline and grease."

"We have all that. This machine is guaranteed for five years. If you have any problems let us know and we'll send out a mechanic to help you."

"I'm going to need this loaded on the northbound train for Whiskey Jack."

"I'll take care of that before night, and tomorrow morning it'll be loaded on a flat car."

"Okay, the big question. How much?"

"The steel drum and pump and grease I'll throw in. If you want it filled with gasoline I'll have to charge you for that. We can fill the drum here and load it in the bucket and strap it down secure."

"How much?"

"$920.00. That includes the gasoline."

Rascal looked at Emma and they stepped away from Walter and Emma gave him $1000.00. Rascal counted out $920.00 and gave it to Walter.

"We'd better go to the bank, Rascal, before it closes."

They deposited $6300.00 in both their names. "Now I'm tired after all this running around. I was going to suggest we go to the hotel but what if we stopped by Page's Furrier to see if our deer heads are done yet?" Emma said.

"I guess that would be okay. Then we can go to the hotel."

"I talked with Fred yesterday and he said he would have both of them finished soon. So what's left in Whiskey Jack?" Jarvis asked.

"Just us now, and the first rainy day the remaining buildings will be burned and buried. We have the hotel and store and we're going to make it a hunting and fishing lodge."

"I think you'll do okay. The newspapers every day are exclaiming how fast the economy is growing. The New York papers are calling the 1920s *the Roaring 20s*. Because the pace of life is speeding up and everyone has money to spend.

"The price of fur pelts has already gone up."

"That sounds good."

"Maybe some weekend you and Rita can come for a visit," Emma said.

"We'll try to do just that—before fall."

* * *

The next morning the northbound stopped at Whiskey Jack and Rascal's bulldozer was unloaded. He was unsure about driving it off so he asked Jeters. "Sure, no problem."

Once he had it off the ramp, Jeters stopped and said, "Here, you take it now."

Rascal climbed on and he was surprised how easy it was to operate. Now all he had to do was get used to using the bucket and blade. For now he parked it in the empty shed and Jeters helped him roll off the fuel drum and stand it up. "This will come in handy hauling out a moose," Jeters said.

"You know, dragging a moose back was the only reason I was never interested in shooting one."

At supper that evening, Jeters said, "Are you two going to be okay out here all by yourselves?"

"I'll admit, it'll take some getting used to, but I think

we'll be alright," Emma said.

They sat up and talked while watching the sunset. Dark clouds were blowing in from the south. "Looks like rain tomorrow."

Around 3 am it began to rain—softly at first. Then by sunup it began a heavy rain. Jeters went out before eating and one by one he began to torch the buildings. Once they were all burning he came back inside for breakfast.

The day before, Jeters and Rascal had gone through each cabin, shed and building salvaging anything that could be used. They found a few tools, some telegraph wire, rope, some canned food and they took out all the windows and doors. Rascal found a nice new axe under one of the beds. Everything was put in the mill shed.

"It'll probably take all day to burn and then another day to bury it all."

It rained steady all day and by darkness the flames had burned out but there was still smoke rising from the ashes. It rained all night and by morning the smoke was gone. Jeters was all day burying the ashes and what didn't burn.

When he had finished the old mill yard looked like a field ready for planting.

"Is there anything you want me to do, Rascal?"

"Yes, over by the crawler shed would you level a place for a large garden?"

"Sure, it won't take long." Jeters had become quite proficient with the big bulldozer.

When he had finished he said, "I need to telephone the train station in Beech Tree and have them send up a flatbed tomorrow to haul this out."

When he made the call he was told the morning northbound would drop off a car and in the afternoon the southbound would couple it.

There was still five hours before sunset and the three of them put the canoe in and paddled up to the inlet to catch supper and breakfast. Rascal let Emma and Jeters fish while he paddled them around.

"It seemed to me, Rascal, the last time I came up here fishing with you, we got drunk and you were trying to fly cast with a streamer and you kept hooking me in the head." They began to laugh, even Emma, and she knew what they were talking about.

"But, Jeters, you hooked yourself once too," they laughed some more.

They caught eight large brook trout. Plenty for two meals for three people. Then in a more serious tone to his voice, Jeters said, "I'll certainly miss those times. Hell, I'm already missing Whiskey Jack. It's gone."

That was a sober note for them all. They were quiet all the way back.

The northbound train dropped off the flatbed car, pushed up and secured to the ramp. Jeters drove the big bulldozer on and Rascal helped him secure it in place with chains.

"What are you going to do with the Antony cabin?"

"I don't know. I didn't have the heart to burn that one. Too many memories and maybe Anita might want to come back for a visit."

"We had some good times here didn't we," Jeters said as he looked first at Rascal and then Emma, over his cup of coffee.

There was nothing else to do but wait for the southbound. So Emma made another pot of coffee and the three of them sat out on the platform. It was a beautiful day with enough wind to keep the blackflies at bay. At noon Emma made sandwiches.

Between eating their sandwiches and drinking coffee they retold stories of their life there at the village. The second pot of coffee was almost gone, and Jeters said, "I can hear the southbound it's about a half mile out."

Rascal put up the red flag. The train went by slowly and then stopped while the switch was turned and then the engineer backed the train up and coupled the loaded flatcar. It came forward so the passenger car was at the platform. "Well, ole buddy," Jeters said, "if you get lonely that Bear is always at the swamp and needs a playmate."

"Thanks, Jeters."

Emma hugged him and kissed his cheek.

"All aboard."

Jeters boarded and looked back, smiling.

They stood there watching the train until it was out of sight. "Everyone is gone now, Rascal," Emma said with a croak in her voice. "It's only you and me now. I wasn't expecting to feel like this when we would be here alone."

Chapter 9

Two days later the A.M. northbound stopped and dropped off the two buck mounts. They took 'em inside and unpacked them. "Rascal, these are beautiful. I know just where to put 'em. On either side of the stone fireplace."

When they had finished hanging the mounts up they stood back by the kitchen door and looked at them. "They go good there," Rascal said.

"Are you going to plant a garden?"

"Yes, I think I'll take the crawler out to the farm and bring the harrow back."

"While you're doing that I'm going to take inventory of what there is in the cold storage room in the cellar."

Rascal started the crawler and headed out the farm road. He was having fun learning to operate it. He knew there was a harrow behind the barn, or maybe it had been put inside the barn. It seemed strange to be there and no one around. The harrow was in the barn and he had to move two wagons first.

There was a drawbar on the crawler and with a clevis pin he hitched the harrow to it and pulled it out of the barn and closed the doors.

He didn't want to damage any of the disks on the way back so he went slower. "Boy, this is so much easier than a work horse."

He was back in two hours and he began harrowing the garden. The soil was dark and rich and not many rocks or roots. When he had finished he unhooked the harrow behind the garden plot and put the crawler back in the shed.

Emma was sitting at the table with pencil and paper making a list of the food stores she had found in the cellar. "You looked good on the crawler, Rascal. Did you have any problems?"

"Not at all, and the harrowing is done. What did you find?"

There's enough food in the cold storage room to feed the village for a year. All kinds of canned vegetables and beef. There is so much ham and bacon it looked like a butcher shop. It is so cold in there the meat was almost frozen. You'll have to look at it when you have time.

"I'm going to start supper now."

"While you're doing that I'm going to walk up to the cabin and get the vegetable seeds and tools. I'll be right back."

He found the seeds and the hoe and rake and walked back. What he didn't have for seeds he found in the general store. Emma hollered, "Supper is ready!"

* * *

The next day the C&A track crew arrived to pull up the tracks. The wooden ties were piled up close to the tracks and the iron rails were laid beside it. It was a lot of work and they had to stay over one night. Emma didn't charge them for the rooms but she did for the meals. Fifty cents a meal.

While the tracks were being pulled up, Rascal finished planting the garden.

The next morning the train slowed as they went through and threw off a mail pouch, with one letter inside and the day's newspaper.

Rascal took everything inside and gave the letter to Emma. Rascal, do you remember Alfred and Beverly Cummings from Pennsylvania?"

"Yes."

"This letter is from them and they would like to come up

fishing. There is a number here so we can telephone them."

"You call, Em."

"Alright." It took about five minutes to get through all of the operators.

"Here, Rascal, it's Alfred; you speak to him."

"The spring fishing is best right now."

"Al and his wife Beverly are coming up fishing. They read in the newspaper the village was dismantled and that we had turned the hotel into a lodge. They're leaving on the train tomorrow morning. They might be here in two days."

"Oh my word, that didn't take long. We never talked about how much to charge."

"Didn't the Douglas's charge $100.00 per guest for six days?"

"Yes."

"Then we do also."

"Okay. Rascal, you have got to help me clean upstairs and down. The sheets in the three rooms the crews were using have to be changed and washed. Everything in the rooms has to be cleaned and the entire floor swept. You can help me with the beds first."

"With all these preparations, I think you have forgotten to be lonely."

For two days Rascal helped Emma scrub, wash and sweep both floors. "I never knew owning a lodge would require so much work," Rascal said. Emma only smiled.

"You clean the tables, the windows and sweep the floor, Rascal. I'm going to do some baking. Do we still have jars of frog legs or beaver meat?"

"Yes, two jars of frog legs and six beaver."

"We never had time this spring to pick any fiddleheads."

"Could you pickle fiddleheads?" Rascal asked.

"I don't know why not; you can pickle anything."

"Next year."

For two days Emma kept going up and down the stairs

making sure everything was clean. She even made out a menu for meals during their stay.

On the morning of the third day the northbound pulled to a stop at the platform and the Cummings stepped off. Rascal rushed to carry their luggage.

They shook hands and hugged, and Al said, "My, have things changed here."

"Doesn't it get lonely out here, just the two of you?" Beverly asked.

"At first we were, but we soon got so busy we didn't have time to be lonely."

Rascal showed them up to their room and asked, "Would you like some coffee. I think Em has a pot brewing?"

"Yes, we'll be down shortly."

"Those two head mounts look nice. Did you shoot them, Rascal?" Al asked.

"One of them. Em shot the biggest one. She hit it right under the left ear."

"Wow, I'm impressed, young lady."

"Right where you shot yours, Al."

"They look so decorative there with the fireplace," Beverly said.

They talked and drank coffee until lunch time and then Al asked, "When is the best time to go fishing?"

"Right at sunrise or after 6 pm."

"I'd like to have a go at it later this afternoon. How about you, Beverly?"

"Not today. I'm worn out after two days of traveling. Maybe tomorrow morning if the weather is good."

They both went up to their room for a nap. "Be sure to wake me in an hour."

After eating an early supper of venison stew with fresh biscuits and sour pickles, Rascal and Al canoed up to the head of the lake. "We must sit still for five minutes, Al, and be quiet.

155

We scared the trout off when we came in; now we must wait for them to come back."

Finally Rascal whispered, "Okay."

Al whipped his line and fly out there like an expert and he waited for the ripples to disappear before he began inching the fly back. And then almost instantly a big brookie came up for the fly and cleared the water by two feet. "Holy cow!" Al exclaimed. "Did you see that?" Then the trout dove for the bottom. Al wasn't impatient. He stripped the line back a little at a time, always keeping a taut line and not hurrying.

"That's a beauty, Al."

Al was having fun playing the trout as he brought it in alongside the canoe. Rascal slowly dipped his net in and scooped the trout up. "Two pounds I'd say, Al."

"What's the limit?"

"Twenty-five fish. We're not able to freeze the fish, Al. Close, but not frozen."

"I think I understand what you're saying. What if I keep enough for breakfast tomorrow?"

"That'll work."

Rascal didn't have to tell Al to wait a bit before casting the fly out again. But he didn't wait any five minutes either. He put the fly down exactly where he had before and no sooner had the fly hit the surface and another two pounder came flying out of the water with the fly.

"Maybe one more. That should feed the four of us in the morning. Then we can leave and on the way back I'd like to try trolling for a really big one."

Rascal netted the second brookie and after things quieted Al cast way up to the mouth of Jack Brook. He stripped the line back about six feet and another took it and immediately dove for the bottom. "This one is much bigger, Rascal. And he sure is a fighter."

He brought him in a ways and the fish took off again. "Wow! Did you see that? I have never had a trout fight like that."

"I don't think it is a brook trout Al. I think it just might be a togue."

"A what?"

"A togue."

"I don't know what that is."

"I guess you'd call it a lake trout. Here in Maine we call it a togue. They don't jump out of the water like a brookie. They usually will immediately dive for the bottom."

Al played that fish for a half hour before he could bring it close enough to the canoe to see it. When it rolled Rascal said, "Yup, that's a togue. And a big one, maybe eight pounds or more."

The touge was tiring and so was Al. Finally Rascal was able to net it. "Holy cow! Look at that!" Al exclaimed. He was grinning from ear to ear.

"Are these any good to eat?"

"Certainly. They make a terrific chowder and they're pretty good baked too."

"Well, I guess we can go home now."

Rascal swung the canoe around. "That togue must have been following a school of smelts. Smelts spawn in Jack Brook about this time of spring. We'll know for sure when we clean it."

It was almost dark when they were back inside the lodge, and just like Rascal had figured, the togue was full of almost transparent small smelts.

"What would you like, Al, use the togue for a chowder or bake it?" Emma asked.

"What would you do?"

"I was planning on having frog legs and beaver for supper; how about a nice trout chowder for lunch with biscuits?"

"That sounds good to me. How about you, Bev?"

"Certainly. I kind of enjoyed those frog legs and beaver meat," Beverly said.

* * *

In the morning they had scrambled eggs with brook trout and biscuits. "For the life of me I don't understand how you two stay so slim eating like this every day."

"Well, life out here requires a lot of work just to survive."

"Today, Bev and I would like to do some hiking around here and tomorrow morning get up and fish. The two of us."

"That'll be fine. Just let us know where you plan to go."

"I'd like to take Bev out and show her where I shot my deer. And then maybe if we feel up to it hike out to the farm."

After the Cummings left, Emma said, "What are you going to do today?"

"I want to look things over around here."

"Okay, I'm going to start the chowder."

The first thing Rascal wanted to do was look at the basement and the cold storage room. Rudy had told him that when they dug the hole for the basement there were not enough rocks to rock up the cellar walls, nor could they find enough close enough, so they used peeled hemlock logs with a dirt floor. The logs all looked to be in good shape. No rot and the logs that were above ground were well chinked with cement. The well for the lodge was right in the middle of the cellar floor. This way the piping would not freeze in the winter.

The cold storage walls were a foot thick, boarded in on both sides and filled with sawdust to insulate it. On the outside wall there was a vent that could be opened in the winter to allow cold air in. He used to help Mr. Douglas in the winter cutting out blocks of ice from the lake to keep the room cold in the warmer months. If he was correct, they would haul in a ton of ice and bury it with sawdust to insulate it from the warmer air. As the ice gradually melted the water would just soak into the dirt floor.

Everything in the cellar looked in good shape. He then walked around the outside. Some of the cement in the fireplace was loosening and would need to be pointed. But not an emergency. The chinking between the cellar logs was weathering but everything was intact.

The general store had not been built over the cellar but adjacent and attached to it. Sometime, two of the support pads for the support columns would need to be leveled, but the building itself was in good shape like everything else. The game pole on the north side of the building and partially shaded by the building would need the dirt cleaned out from under it. He would have to do this before fall.

There was a woodshed which made up part of the support for the overhang of the store and it was only half full of wood. He would have to fill it before trapping and hunting season.

He looked the shed over and the pile of slabs. And he wandered throughout the mill. He had never seen the inside. He found some chains hung on one wall, clevis pins, a box of assorted nuts and bolts and a wooden keg of 8d nails and another of 16d spikes. "These will come in handy."

He walked back to the lodge. "How did your inspection go?" Emma asked.

"I am surprised, really. Everything is in good shape. I found a few things that'll need some attention, but nothing immediate."

"That's good."

"That chowder smells good."

"You know, I've been doing some thinking this morning."

"What about?"

"Wouldn't it be nice to have milk, eggs and our own butter? Instead of a cow we could get some goats and maybe twelve laying hens and a rooster."

"I've always liked goats milk and goat cheese. We could get enough hay from the farm in the summer to see the goats through the winter."

"Couldn't we use the Antony cabin for both the goats and chickens?" Emma asked.

"You know before we get too busy, maybe we should make out a list of things we need and take a trip into town."

"I'll do the food stores and what we need for the lodge

and you make a list of what you need."

The Cummings walked in then and sat down in the cafeteria. All they wanted for the moment was a glass of water.

"I still find it difficult to believe the company just picked up and moved. This used to be such a nice little village," Al said.

"We feel the same way. Mr. Hitchcock did say they would be back maybe in fifteen years."

Al saw a newspaper on the table and picked it up and was truly surprised that it was that day's issue. "How do you get today's newspaper out here?"

"I made a deal with the station master before he left to have the train engineer throw off each day's paper."

"How convenient."

* * *

"This chowder is so good, Emma," Beverly said. "But how do you keep fresh milk way out here?"

"It's canned milk mixed with water."

"It's delicious."

After they had eaten Al said, "Maybe we forgo the hike to the farm for another day. And I think we should have a nap before going fishing."

"Why don't you and Rascal go, Al. I promise I'll go with you in the morning."

They had an early supper of baked togue, potatoes, fried onions and carrots. "Don't eat the dark meat. It is very strong."

"It has been a long time, Em, since we have had baked togue. I had forgotten how good it is," Rascal said.

"The Cummings both agreed.

When they had finished eating, Al and Rascal paddled to the head of the lake and Al said, "Today, Rascal, instead of fishing here, I would like to try trolling."

"Okay. I would tie on a warden's worry streamer and I'll turn the canoe."

"That's a good idea."

"Let enough line out so the streamer will be about six feet under the surface.

He started paddling along the north shore. That would be where the coldest and deepest water was. About two hundred feet out in front of the other no-name brook inlet, something hit the streamer, but Al was slow in setting the hook. "Don't worry I'll make a wide circle and make another pass over the same area."

This time a huge brook trout took the streamer and it cleared the water and then dove for the bottom. "Did you see that, Rascal! Holy cow! I have never seen such a large brookie."

It weighed just over six pounds and measured twenty-five and a quarter inches. Al was adamant, "We're not going to eat that one. I want it mounted."

"Can Jarvis help you with that, Rascal?" Emma asked.

"Yes, he said if anyone wanted a fish mounted that the same taxidermist that did our deer heads also did fish. But we would have to get it to him as soon as possible.

"I could take it on the southbound tomorrow afternoon and I could be back here the next morning."

"Would you be willing to do that, Rascal?" Al asked.

"Surely."

The sun had set and tomorrow was promising to be a long day, so they all went to sleep early.

The next morning, "Do you have room for me, too, in the canoe, Rascal? I'd like to go. I could tend the fire and cook the fish while they fish."

"I think we can make room."

Emma packed a kettle and some tea. "I'm already."

Rascal gave Al another paddle. "It'll go easier with four people if you help."

"Certainly."

It was early and there was a little chill still in the air. The surface of the lake was as smooth as glass. "It is so beautiful out here," Beverly said.

Rascal pulled into shore so Emma could step out. Then she pushed the canoe back out. No one had spoken a word. She went to work and started a fire and found four green sticks she could use as spits to roast the fish on.

Al pointed up to the mouth of the inlet and Beverly laid a fly at the mouth. "Aah, I got one!" she screamed.

"So much for being quiet," everyone laughed. As soon as they had four Rascal pulled the canoe along shore and Emma took the trout and cleaned them and put them on to roast. Al and Beverly went back to fishing. Because of the noise they were not coming as fast.

"These four are almost done."

"Okay, we only need one more." Al brought that in and they all went ashore.

"The tea is all made and the fish are done."

Each took a stick. Beverly waited and watched the others . . . how they were going to eat it.

"Just like corn on the cob, Bev," and he started eating. "Why does food always taste better when it is cooked outdoors over an open fire?"

Rascal put the other four back over the fire to cook while they finished eating.

Beverly had been raised as a young girl in a prime atmosphere, and even after having a family she had always tried to conduct herself with grace. Now she was eating food cooked on a stick over an open fire and eating it while holding the food in her hands. This was a completely new experience for her. And she was loving it.

They returned to the lodge in plenty of time for Rascal to take the afternoon southbound to Beech Tree.

"Hello, Rascal, what can I do for you?" Jarvis asked.

"I'd like this brook trout mounted. Do you remember Al Cummings from Pennsylvania? He shot a nice buck last year. He caught this yesterday."

"Well let me see it. And I do remember him. If I'm correct he used a .38-55 octagon barrel."

"That's him."

Rascal unwrapped it. "Holy cow! This came out of Whiskey Jack Lake?"

"Yes, he was trolling a warden's worry streamer. I'll pay the cost now and could you have it shipped to this address when it is finished?" Rascal handed Jarvis a slip of paper with Al's address.

"That'll be $30.00 for the mount and probably another $10.00 for shipping. Do you need a receipt?"

"Yes."

"How much did it weigh?"

"Six pounds and twenty-five and a quarter inches. It took him almost an hour to bring it close enough to the canoe so I could net it. The day before that he caught an eight pound togue that Em baked. We've been eating fish all week. To tell you the truth I'd like to sink my teeth into a juicy beef steak."

"I tell you what, Rita is off visiting our daughter and won't be back for two days. Why don't we go to Beech Tree Restaurant and have a beef steak? I'll close up here."

* * *

Rascal boarded the train the next morning and he couldn't wait to return home. He noticed a pair of beaver were back at mile nine. They weren't a problem yet, but soon would be. He'd wait and let the station master in Beech Tree contact him.

When the train pulled to a stop at the platform, Emma was there waiting for him. "I was afraid you might forget milk and eggs."

"Almost did. Where are Al and Beverly?"

"They hiked out to the farm—said they'd be back for lunch."

Rascal carried the milk can down to the cold storage

163

room and Emma the eggs.

Al and Beverly were having the time of their lives. The fishing was only an excuse to come and get away from their tiring life on the farm. They enjoyed the fishing immensely and they enjoyed the hikes and the peace and quiet and more than all this, they were enjoying visiting with Rascal and Emma.

For supper that night Emma had roasted one of the pork loins with whipped potato—"What are these? Little apples?" Beverly asked.

"Yes, spiced crabapples."

She watched the others as they picked them up in their fingers and ate around the core, and then she did also. "These are delicious. I have eaten so many strange and different foods here. This is all so marvelous, Emma."

"Yes," Rascal said, "The pork is outstanding."

"When you go fishing afterwards, I'd like you to bring back four two pound trout. I have something different planned for supper tomorrow."

"We'll try," Rascal said.

"Where did this cold milk come from?" Al asked.

"I brought a milk can on the train this morning. Oh, here is the receipt for the mounting. When it is finished it'll be shipped directly to you." Al gave Rascal $40.00 for the receipt.

"You are a marvelous cook, Emma," Beverly said.

"Maybe you two should think about advertising your lodge in—let's say Pennsylvania and New York," Al said.

"How would we do that?" Emma asked.

"If you could write a brief description of Whiskey Jack Lodge and what you have to offer and the price per person per week I know some people in the advertising business that would take care of that. You write something up and I'll take it with me."

"Okay, while you're fishing this evening I'll put something together," Emma said.

Rascal and Al left in the canoe. The air was a little cooler and the blackflies seemed to come at them in swarms. But Al didn't complain. As they were approaching the inlet, Rascal said, "You heard what Em wants for brookies."

"Yes, four nice trout. No small ones."

As Al fished Rascal sat there watching and he suddenly felt a shiver go through his entire body and he felt extremely happy. *Perhaps this isn't going to be such a bad way of life. Em is happy too.*

The sun was behind some clouds and there was a small hatch of mayflies on the water. Al wasn't long catching the four two pound trout.

"Are the frogs out yet?" Al asked.

"It's a little early for frogs."

"Okay, I guess I'm done here, but I would like to troll going back. Do you think the streamer should be down six feet with a hatch of mayflies?"

"I would try closer to the surface. You just might hook into another big one."

Just as Rascal was turning the canoe in towards the wharf another large brookie took the wardens worry streamer and went four feet in the air above the water. "Holy cow! Rascal, did you see that!" Al exclaimed. He was so loud Emma and Beverly could hear him inside the lodge and came out onto the platform to watch.

"This has to be bigger than the other one." The trout jumped and cleared the water twice more trying to shake loose of the hook. And then the trout started coming straight at the canoe, much faster than Al could strip the line in and it just broke the surface of the water enough so its head was clear. Without any tension on the line, he shook himself free of the streamer.

Al sat there laughing and laughing as if it had been a great joke. "My word, Rascal, that was some brook trout. I'm glad though that he got himself free. Let's go in. I'm cold."

"We have fresh milk, Al. How would you like a cup of hot chocolate instead of coffee?"

"That sounds like a great idea. Beverly, how about you?"

"Yes, I would like a cup also."

Emma gave what she had written up to Al to look over while she made hot chocolate for all of them.

"Ah, I see you included your address and telephone number. That is good. And I like it. I won't change a word."

While they were waiting for the hot chocolate, Al said, "Our son is getting married the last of August and we have promised them a week's honeymoon at Whiskey Jack Lodge. In fact I'll pay you now in advance so I don't forget."

Emma handed him a piece of paper and pen and asked, "Would you write down his name and address?"

"Certainly. Mr. and Mrs. Richard Cummings, 14 Sweetwater Rd., Buffalo, NY. My son is a doctor. Our youngest son is the one taking over the farm."

"When will they be arriving so I can schedule them?" Emma asked.

"They are shooting to arrive here the morning of September 2nd."

"If they're newlyweds, Rascal, we could fix up our cabin so they'll be alone."

"That'll be a good idea.

"Al, how many fish would you like to take back with you?" Rascal asked.

Al looked at Beverly and they talked it over for a bit and then Al said, "We don't need to take any back. We have eaten a lot of fish. I have a trophy to take back and we have had a marvelous time. In fact you can book us for next year the third week of May. I have had more enjoyment on this trip than I did hunting.

"And here is the $400.00 for Richard and his wife and our stay."

"You two are just like family to Rascal and me. I hate to charge you."

"Nonsense. This is your livelihood. Here . . . here is the money."

"Thank you. I think the hot chocolate is done now."

They sat in the living room sipping hot chocolate and talking until all four heads began to nod. "I think it is time we all went to bed," Beverly said.

The next morning, they were up before breakfast and canoed this time to the other small inlet. And again the surface of the lake was like glass. Loons were out in front of the inlet. "That is a good sign," Rascal said.

"What is it?"

"The loons. They're feeding. Maybe only on smelts. But if smelts are running, trout and togue will still be feeding on them."

Rascal stopped the canoe and held it in place with his paddle about one hundred feet from the mouth of the inlet. Al whipped out as much line as he could and started working the fly back and almost instantly he had one on. "A two pounder, just what your wife ordered."

With each of his next three casts he caught brookies close to two pounds or a little more.

"Okay Rascal, that's enough for now. I'd like to canoe around the shore of the lake. I'll help paddle."

They stayed about one hundred feet from shore around the lake. Rascal knew Al was really enjoying himself. As a dairy farmer, he probably had not had the time to do much relaxing.

As they pulled into the wharf at the lodge there was a slight breeze now and they could smell fresh coffee. "That's a welcoming smell," Al said.

They had ham and eggs for breakfast and Rascal cleaned the fish and put them in the cold storage room for now. He had no idea how Emma was going to cook them. When they had eaten and had all the coffee that they wanted, Al said, "Bev do you feel up to another walk to the farm?"

"That would be a good way to work off breakfast."

"How about you two joining us?" Beverly asked.

"You go, Rascal. I have work to do," Emma said.

Halfway to the farm a huge bull moose stepped into the road and stood momentarily looking at them and then it continued on to the other side and disappeared in the trees.

"That was a big moose, but why were the antlers so small?" Beverly asked.

"Moose shed their antlers in late fall or early winter and then grow them back again. Those antlers were as we say, 'in velvet.' By September he will have a trophy set of antlers."

They continued on and Al said, "The air is so fresh out here," and then he added, "Whoever built these buildings did a marvelous job. Look how square and plumb they all are."

Down at the lower end of the field a bear must have winded them, as he now stood up. "Look, there's a bear," Al said. "We used to see them in the farm fields at home also. Then some of the local hunters with dogs overhunted them, and you seldom even see a bear now."

"This is a bear's breeding season and that's probably a lone male looking for a female. Sometimes when they're mating the males can be very aggressive. I think we should leave now and head back for the lodge."

"Is there any danger?" Beverly was concerned.

"I doubt it. He probably stood up to get a better scent of the air. Bear can't see very good but their sense of smell is very sharp. He probably scented us when he stood up," Rascal said while hoping that wasn't 'Bear.'

Back at the lodge Al and Beverly sat in the sun on the platform and Rascal walked up to the cabin. He needed to cut the grass and bushes around the buildings. The inside of the cabin was fine and no evidence of mice. Sometime he knew he and Emma would have to move all of their personal things and food down to the lodge. That was their home now. He did fill his pack basket with canned goods and took that down with him. He was going to take his axe, but there was a nice one there in the woodshed.

For now he left the pack basket in the cold storage room

and joined the Cummings on the platform. Emma wouldn't let him in the kitchen.

Close to noon Emma came out and said, "Lunch is ready."

They all sat down. There was a steamed trout on each of the plates, hot biscuits and a side dish of coleslaw and a coffee cup with hot melted butter. "Just peel the skin off and dunk the pieces of meat in the butter like you would steamed clams."

Rascal had never had fish like this. Everyone was silent while they tried the first bite. "Wow, is this good, Em. Where did you ever come up with this idea?"

"Oh, I just wanted to try something new."

"Well it is delicious, Emma," Beverly said.

"Yes, it certainly is," Al confirmed.

Everyone was busy eating and no one was doing much talking.

* * *

At breakfast Saturday morning everyone was unusually quiet. Al and Beverly would be leaving on the southbound shortly. Rascal put out the red signal for the train to stop. "Emma, Rascal, we can't remember when we have had a more enjoyable six days. Thank you," Al said.

"We really hate to be leaving, but we must."

"We'll look forward to you both coming next year. Maybe we'll have some moose meat."

Al handed Rascal a sealed envelope and said, "Addresses and the names of two widely distributed hunting and fishing magazines. I'll get your information, Emma, to the editors of both and you should be hearing from them probably in about three weeks."

The train was a half mile out and the engineer blew the whistle. Emma and Rascal helped them with their luggage. As they were boarding the passenger car, Al said, "You can expect

Richard and his wife September 2nd, even if you do not hear from him before. And goodbye and thank you."

The train disappeared and Rascal and Emma were left alone once again. "Now, I want you to work on a list of things you can think of that we need. I have a short list," Rascal said.

"I have mine. If no one arrives tomorrow we should take the Monday southbound. The first thing we need to do is set up a checking account for the lodge and that'll take both of our signatures," Emma said.

They were sitting back at the dining table with coffee and Rascal gave the envelope Al had given him to Emma. When she opened it she let out a little scream, "Aaahh, Rascal he put $100.00 in here and a note."

"What does it say?"

"Just a TIP, in capital letters."

"Well, I'll be. I never expected that."

"Me neither."

Sunday was fairly cool and Rascal said, "I think I'll go out my hunting road and start working up some firewood."

"Be careful."

He put the saw, axe and wedge and chain in the crawler bucket and went out to a nice stand of beech and ash. The beauty of the crawler and bucket, when he had a tree that wouldn't fall right he could push it with the crawler. He'd top them off and hauled them out to the road where he would buck them into two foot lengths for the fireplace and the ram-down stove on the second floor.

By lunchtime he had worked up five trees and piled the wood beside the road. He would have to get one of the wagons at the farm to haul the wood back.

As they were eating lunch, Rascal asked, "Do you want to take a walk out to the farm? I want to see if there is a wagon there I can hitch behind the crawler for a trailer."

"I'd like to go. Let me clear up the kitchen first."

Ten minutes later, "Okay I'm ready."

They were in no particular hurry and they talked all the way. "I'd like to go inside the house, Rascal. I have never been inside."

"Maybe we can find a hammer in the barn or one of the sheds." As they walked towards the barn Rascal scanned down across the field. No bear and no deer. "Here's the wagon I'd like to use. It's rugged and in good shape with side boards and a clevis hitch. Now to find a hammer."

"Over here, Rascal, on this front wall." She picked it up and they went back to the house and took the 2x4 off that was nailed across the door.

"It isn't anything fancy is it? It looks as if they have left almost everything, like they might come back soon. I'm going upstairs, Rascal."

"Okay, I'm going to look at the cellar." Here, like the lodge, a root cellar had been made in the cool cellar. And the well was in the middle of the dirt floor. Not a bad idea when you think on it.

He went back upstairs and Emma was there. "You ready?" she asked.

"Let's go."

They went outside and Rascal nailed the 2x4 back across the door and hung the hammer on the nail head.

They started walking out the drive to the road and Emma looked to the right. "Bear!"

Rascal turned to look. Yep, a lone bear. There was no doubt in his mid that this was Bear. It was only about a hundred feet away. Emma was clutching Rascal's arm. But Rascal wasn't moving.

"Do something, Rascal!"

Bear started walking slowly towards them. Rascal did the only thing he could think of doing. He raised his right arm and made that same laughing noise that he had done before.

"What are you doing?"

Bear stopped and stood up on his hind legs and raised his

paw and made a similar laughing noise. "Rascal—what is going on?"

"Bear, I want you to meet my wife, Em."

He stood up again and raised his paw and made a noise like *arrahy*.

"Did he just say hi, Rascal? You have a talking bear! Jesus, he's big."

"Let's start walking slowly down the road. Walk backwards."

For every step backwards they took Bear took a step forward. "He's following us, Rascal."

"Just keep walking backwards."

They had gone about a hundred feet by now and Bear was keeping pace. He was not showing any threatening behavior. "Are we going to have to walk backwards all the way to the lodge?"

"I don't know."

"I don't blame Elmo now, for not wanting to go with you beaver trapping. Shouldn't we be running or something."

"We may have to, only I can't run very fast because of my leg."

"I'm not liking this, Rascal."

"You think I am? This is the fifth time I've come up against him."

"Five times! Is there something you're not telling me, Rascal?"

"Later."

They kept walking backwards and Bear was still keeping pace.

"Em, turn around slowly and keep walking."

"Now what?"

"He hasn't closed the distance—that's a good sign. I'm going to turn around also."

Rascal turned around and they kept walking, and so too did Bear. "He hasn't come any closer. Let's try running."

"That's fine with me."

"Okay, let's go."

They ran about fifty yards and Emma looked behind them, "Rascal!" She was almost panicking. "Now he's running! And coming closer! Right now I wish we were back at our own cabin."

"Me too," Rascal said.

Bear kept closing the distance and they kept running. They both were breathing hard now and working up a sweat. Bear wasn't even panting. "He's still coming closer, Rascal!"

"I guess don't stop running. Maybe he'll get tired and stop."

"He chased you and Elmo two and a half miles and you think he'll get tired?"

Bear was following directly behind Rascal, but he wasn't showing any sign of aggression. Only running after them—little by little he kept coming closer. Emma didn't dare look back anymore. Bear was only a couple of feet behind Rascal now and he closed that to within inches and suddenly reached out with his paw and tripped Rascal. He went sprawling to the ground. Emma stopped and helped him up. "Are you okay?"

Bear did a couple of circles behind them and Rascal and Emma started running again. And Bear followed. They had gone running maybe fifty feet or so and Bear tripped him again and then ran in circles behind them waiting for Rascal to get up.

"Are you hurt, Rascal?"

"No, let's go." And Bear followed and this time, Bear bunted Rascal in the butt sending him sprawling again. This time Bear jumped up on the bank next to the road and—"SOB is laughing, Rascal. I swear to God that Bear is laughing."

Rascal started laughing and soon Emma did too.

"He was just playing with you, wasn't he? How long has this been going on, Rascal? You're his playmate!" and she started laughing again.

While they were standing up, Rascal said, "I guess I'd

better tell you the whole story."

Bear was only twenty feet away and Rascal raised his arm and made that same noise and Bear lifted one paw and ran back towards the farm.

"Bear made me pee in my pants."

As they walked back to the lodge Rascal told her the whole story about Bear. "Jeters came up with the idea that he was lonely and was only looking to play. We swore on oath never to say anything to anyone, including you, Em."

"Why not me? I'm your wife."

"Because you would have thought me crazy."

"Probably, and we still can't say anything. No one would ever believe us."

Chapter 10

Sunday came and went and no one had showed up. So Monday afternoon Rascal and Emma took the southbound to Beech Tree. They only had time that day to set up a checking account at the bank and pickup stamps and stationery supplies. "This might take two days."

Rascal went to see about the canoes first.

"Yes Rascal we have some."

"I need three, and six paddles. And now I would like these taken to the train depot and have them sent to Whiskey Jack Lodge. Can you do that?"

"For three canoes and paddles, we sure can."

"Would you have any fly rods?"

"That we do."

"Okay, two rods and an assortment of flies. Have everything sent to the lodge please."

"Yes sir, anything else?"

"No, that's fine."

He went next to the feed and grain store. "Yes, we still have chicks."

"I'll need a dozen and one rooster. Can you crate these and have them taken to the train depot and send them to the Whiskey Jack Lodge. Ah, send them in two days."

He went to the equipment store where he had purchased the crawler and had a case of oil and six filters to be sent to Whiskey Jack Lodge.

He was done his shopping and he went to see if he could find Emma.

All Emma was able to do was purchase a braided rug and chairs for the living room. "That's all I had time for today. We aren't going to be able to leave in the morning are we?"

"No."

"You know if you want to go back in the morning, then I can stay and finish shopping. Most of what I need now is office supplies."

"If you don't mind. I don't like being away with no one there."

They went to the hotel and acquired a room. "I'll be staying two nights," Emma said. Then they had supper.

"Rascal, when we finish eating let's visit Anita Anthony."

Anita's sister's house was within walking distance of the hotel. When Anita first saw them she almost cried with joy. They visited until the sun was beginning to set. "If you ever need any help at the lodge, Emma, call me."

"I will and thank you."

* * *

Rascal was happy to be going home but a little apprehensive about Emma being alone. But she had been alone for two years while he was in Europe.

Once back at home he decided to work on firewood some more. But he was not going to stay bent over all the time sawing the trees into two foot lengths. Before heading for the woods he made a series of sawhorses from wood left at the mill, so he could lay a long piece on the horses. He found this worked much better.

He had five trees down and twitched them to the road to buck 'em up. Halfway through he stopped to wipe the sweat from his head and he sat down to rest, thinking, *Someday someone will come up with something that'll make cutting trees easier.*

By the time he quit for the day he had almost another cord piled up.

After eating supper he sat out on the platform in the cool breeze. The dark clouds coming in from the west were looking like a thunderstorm was coming. The leaves on the trees were turned backwards. "Yep, it'll rain before sunset."

And it did, just before sunset. There were only two flashes of lightning directly overhead. The others were way off. He stayed out on the platform under the eaves. The rain was making the air cooler. And there were no bugs.

The next morning when Emma arrived the canoes and stuff were on the freight car, as was the furniture Emma had purchased. The chicks and rooster and many of the smaller items would be sent the next day according to the shipping manifest.

Emma wanted the braided rug laid down first and then the new furniture set around it. "There, that's much better," she said with a smile.

"I think I'm going to have to build more canoe racks. We now have six. What's in that wooden crate?"

"A safe. You know there might be times when we can't get to the bank to deposit some money and I would feel better if it was locked up."

"Good point."

The next morning everything else arrived, "I guess I'd better get busy and make the cabin over into a hen house." There was a roll of chicken wire in the store and Rascal used that to make an outside enclosure with a gate. He built laying boxes in the kitchen and filled them with clean sawdust. He put sawdust on the floor also, knowing the wooden flooring would probably rot out within two years, but he'd deal with that in two years. He had to make a separate pen for the rooster when it matured. For now it could stay with the other chicks.

There was running water inside and he had to find something he could use to put water in for the chicks. He wanted the top of an old milk can but there was nothing around, so he hiked out to the new dump and looked through things there until he had found one. "Excellent."

He cleaned it up and put it on the floor with water and he put some hen mash in a wooden trough he had made. He'd have to wait until the chicks were bigger before he could let them out in the outdoor pen. For now he was done.

Three weeks after the Cummings had left they received two letters, one from a magazine editor of sporting news in Pennsylvania and another from the editor of a New York trophy hunting magazine. They each had made some minor changes, but would include the advertisement in the next issue with payment.

Emma wrote out two checks and accompanied them with a brief letter for each magazine. And another letter went to Al and Beverly telling them of the new advertisements and thanking them.

The mill yard that Jeters had leveled off now had a green tint to the ground as new grass began to grow. Rascal spent a few hours each day working up firewood until he figured he had about ten cord piled up by the roadside.

One evening after supper Rascal said, "I'm going to drive the crawler out to the farm and bring back a wagon. Do you want to go?"

"Noooo, you go play with Bear." They had four guests and they were looking strangely at Emma. She didn't offer to explain.

Rascal felt pretty safe on the noisy crawler. If Bear was around he could just stay on the machine. But when he arrived Bear was nowhere to be seen. "Maybe you went back to Ledge Swamp. I hope."

He hooked onto the wagon and brought it down to the lodge. He'd wait until tomorrow to start hauling the wood in.

Marcel Cyr arrived in the morning. "I didn't want anything in particular, I was just interested in how you were doing."

"We've had a few guests, but we're just getting started."

"It certainly looks different around here now. Will you stay the winter? In here all alone?"

"We have never thought otherwise. Are the beaver causing any problems between here and Beech Tree?"

"There's a flowage at mile nine, but I don't think it is of any consequence yet."

Marcel talked with the guests before they left to go fishing on the lake. They seemed happy to talk with him.

"You'll have to excuse me, Marcel, I need to haul in firewood to the lodge."

"Could you use some help? I'm here until the southbound comes through."

"Yes, and that reminds me, I'd better put out the red flag or the train won't stop."

It was a hot and muggy day, but Rascal needed to get the wood in before September. Then he could work on other winter projects.

They had hauled in two wagonloads and piled it up in the woodshed by lunch.

* * *

Rascal finished his woodpile and had two more cords for 'just in case,' by the middle of August, and six different couples from New York came to stay a week. Everyone had caught fish and were happy. Two had one mounted at Rupert's taxidermy.

Now that the firewood was done, Rascal concentrated on catching frogs, and canning the legs. These they would keep for themselves and an occasional special guest. While he was busy frogging, Emma was preparing the log cabin for the arrival of Mr. and Mrs. Richard Cummings.

The windows, floors, and kerosene lantern mantles were washed and new clean sheets and pillow casings. Rascal in the evenings trimmed the grass, weeds and bushes around the cabin.

"There," Emma said, "I think the cabin is ready if they want to use it."

There was no electricity to the cabin since the Hitchcock

Company left, but lantern light was softer and more romantic than a light bulb, especially for newlyweds.

On the morning of September 2nd, Emma put on a new dress and made Rascal put on casual pants and shirt. "These are special people coming in this morning, Rascal, and I want to look appropriate. Now go on and change."

They were not expecting any more guests that week. It was a nice day, a little cool, but nice. So they sat on the platform to wait. The engineer blew the steam whistle a half mile out. Emma stood and said as she turned around, "Do I look okay, Rascal?"

"Yes, Em, you look fine. Quite attractive actually."

They could see the train now as it began to slow. As the engine rolled passed the lodge the engineer threw out the day's Sunday paper. "Thank you," Rascal said as he waved.

The conductor stepped off onto the platform first with two travel bags and then a dark-haired, good looking man, looking much like his father Alfred, carrying two more stepped off. Rascal went over to help with the travel luggage. Then a beautiful, well-proportioned woman stepped off and stopped when she saw Rascal. For a brief moment she and Rascal looked at each other. Emma saw the two looking at each other.

Finally Rascal said, with Emma by his side now, "Lieutenant Belle. Or should I say, Mrs. Cummings?"

Emma interrupted then, "Hello, Belle, I'm Emma," and they shook hands.

Belle then introduced her husband. "This is my husband, Richard." They all shook hands.

"I would have known you, Emma, anywhere from Rascal's description of you and how much he used to talk about you." Emma's cheeks were turning red.

"I want to thank you, Belle, for taking care of Rascal."

"I'm glad to see you are getting around better than when we said goodbye."

"You can have your choice where you want to stay. Here

at the lodge or you can have our cabin across the lake," and she pointed.

"Oh, we wouldn't want to put you out of your own cabin," Belle said.

"You won't. We stay at the lodge now. We didn't know but what you may prefer the privacy. You'll take your meals here, of course."

Belle looked at Richard and he said, "That would be fine. Mom and Dad have told us so much about Whiskey Jack Lake. We would enjoy experiencing living in the cabin. We had enough luggage to bring, so I didn't bring any fishing equipment. Dad said you would outfit us."

"Yes certainly. We'll show you to the cabin now," and Rascal carried two pieces of luggage, Emma one, Richard one and Belle picked up a small case.

"Dad said the village was gone. That's too bad. You must get lonely here when you haven't any guests," Richard said.

"Not at all. There is always plenty to do to keep busy. We wouldn't wish to live anywhere else. We had a chance to follow the company to Kidney Pond, but decided to stay."

Rascal had done a very good job cutting back the grass and weeds. "This cabin is just how my folks described it."

They went inside and put all the luggage in the bedroom.

"I wish we could offer you a bottle of wine," Emma said. "We'll let you alone now. Lunch is at twelve."

Rascal and Emma left and walked back down to the lodge.

"So that's Lieutenant Belle," Emma said. "She is beautiful."

"She is dressed up like this, I have never seen her without her fatigues. Emma, you are just as attractive.

Rascal put on his work clothes, clean, and went down to check on the chickens. They were big enough now to let out in the pen. Instinctively they knew what to do, and started scratching the ground looking for bits of food.

The four of them talked almost continuously during lunch. "How do you get fresh milk out here?" Richard asked.

"We buy it direct from a farmer in Beech Tree in milk cans and he ships it up here via the train. We keep it on ice in the cellar."

"Mom told us they had fresh milk while they were here but I couldn't imagine how."

"We love your log cabin, Emma. It is so homey feeling.

"But why do you stay here?"

"Well we have to cook and cater to our guests and it's just easier if we live here."

"I would like to do some fishing this afternoon," Richard said.

"This evening would be the best time."

"I'll plan on an early supper since the sun sets sooner now," Emma said. "About 4 o'clock?" No one objected.

"Now, Belle and I would like to go for a walk. Which road from here would take us out to the farm?"

"The road to the right."

After they had left, Emma asked, "Do you think you should have said something about Bear?"

"I don't think so. I haven't seen him again since the time you were with me. Besides if we said anything at all, we'd have to tell them the whole story and who would believe us. Except maybe Jeters?"

"I just hope they don't encounter him."

Rascal pulled a canoe down to the wharf and loaded it with what they would need.

"How are the chickens doing? I haven't been down to see them for a couple of days."

"I can see them grow from day to day. But it'll still be February or March before they start laying."

* * *

Emma decided not to go with them fishing. And Belle said, "Why don't you two go. I'll stay here and visit with Emma.

I'll go in the morning." She walked with them down to the wharf and watched as they paddled up the lake. Then she went back inside to talk with Emma.

There was a bull moose with huge antlers in the water feeding on aquatic plants near the little no name inlet. Somewhere on the ridge behind the bull, a cow in heat started calling and immediately the bull turned and rushed off, grunting with each step he took.

Rascal explained what had just happened. Five minutes later the cow stopped bellowing. When they stopped at the Jack Brook Cove, Richard was going to start casting. "Wait Richard," he said in a low voice. "Wait for our disturbance to settle and the trout to come back."

After five minutes Rascal nodded his head and Richard lay his line and fly with expert skill. Like his father.

"Let me help you clean up, Emma. I'd feel more relaxed if I'm doing something."

Emma didn't say she couldn't. The two talked almost constantly after the initial barrier was broken.

"Belle, I'd like to ask you a personal question."

"Okay."

"Do you ever talk about the war with your husband? I ask that because Rascal doesn't. Not even with his friends."

Belle thought about it before answering. "I think I can understand why. I have never talked much about what I saw and experienced. And I think it is probably more difficult for someone who was in the trenches to want to talk about seeing your friends and comrades killed right beside you or seeing their heads or limbs blown off. I work in the ER in the Buffalo General Hospital and every time a bad accident comes in, I'm taken back to France watching our boys come in."

"I never considered that. I do understand, though."

"Now, can I ask you a personal question?"

"Okay."

"Where are your two children? Rascal talked so much about you and his son and daughter."

This hit Emma in her stomach and she had all she could do not to start crying. Belle saw the sudden sadness on her face. "I'm sorry, maybe I shouldn't have asked."

"No that's okay. It's something I don't like to talk about. They both died while Rascal was in the war. I didn't tell him until he came home. I was afraid his grief might have gotten him killed. When he did come home, I think I was taking my anger out on him."

"How did you get over it? I mean you two seem fine now."

Emma started laughing and then she said, "I had to spend a night in jail. I didn't sleep much that night because there was so much to think about."

"Why were you in jail?"

Again Emma laughed, "I shot a deer in closed season that was eating my lettuce. The game warden, Jarvis Page, was standing on the dam with Rascal when I shot." They both started laughing then.

This was good medicine for Emma, having another woman to talk with.

The sun was setting and Rascal and Richard were almost back to the lodge. The two women could hear them talking and they walked down to the wharf to meet them.

Richard had caught over a dozen brookies and had only kept four for breakfast.

* * *

Early the next morning after a breakfast of coffee, trout and donuts, they all boarded the 18 foot canoe and went directly to the upper end. Emma had brought the pack basket with tea and a kettle to boil water. Emma went ashore and built a fire and cut four roasting sticks. When Belle started talking, Richard shushed her and whispered, "We must be quiet to let the fish come back."

After five minutes they started fly casting. Belle was good, but she couldn't get her line out as far. But she caught the first trout. When they had four Rascal paddled back to shore and gave the trout to Emma who cleaned them and put them on to cook.

They each caught and released for a while and then Belle said, "Let's go in; my arm is getting tired."

"The tea is ready," and Emma poured four cups. While she had been waiting for the water to boil she found some short dry cedar logs to sit on.

"Those fish sure do smell good," Richard said, "I hope a bear doesn't smell it too."

"We never have had any bear trouble here. The railroad tracks are only a short distance through the woods. When the northbound goes by you'll hear it," Rascal said and looked at Emma, who looked away.

Richard and Belle weren't sure how they were going to eat the fish when Emma handed them each a stick with a fish on it. They waited to see what Rascal and Emma were going to do. Rascal noticed their hesitation and said, "You eat it like corn on the cob," and he took a bite.

"Oh, Em, this is done to perfection."

When they went back to fishing, Emma wanted to take back enough for a good fish chowder for supper.

While Emma was making the chowder, Richard and Belle went back on the lake with the canoe just paddling around and exploring.

Rascal decided to build a smoker. He and Emma liked smoked fish and this way the guests could take some home without worrying if the meat would spoil. He started building near one of the sheds. He would work on it off and on when he had time and it was complete a week later.

Richard and Belle had been catching many one-to-two

pound brook trout, but Richard wanted a large one to have mounted like his father's.

"Well, we'll go out at day break tomorrow. You be here at the wharf tomorrow morning at 5:30 and we'll give it a try," Rascal said.

Back at the log cabin, Richard and Belle sat on the porch in the evening air watching the sunset. "Do you think, Belle, that these people ever sleep in late? I mean growing up on the farm we always had to get up early, but nothing like here. I bet when there aren't any guests they're still up at sunrise."

"It may come from the existence of living in the wilderness like this. I think when the village and mill were here and operating they had to work hard. I have enjoyed these few days here, but I couldn't live here year round," Belle said.

"They are remarkable people though. I wish the village was still here so we would have a better understanding," Richard said.

At 5:30 the next morning Rascal was on the wharf when he could see Richard and Belle walking across the dam. Belle went inside with Emma.

"Before we leave, tie on a smelt streamer. It'll be easier now, than out on the water." When Richard was ready Rascal pushed the canoe out and said, "Let about a hundred feet of line out." And then he began paddling up the center of the lake. To the upper end and circled back in front of the no name brook inlet. There he had a hit and it dove for the bottom. "That's a togue."

"A what?"

"Lake trout. In Maine we call them togue. A brook trout will usually come to the surface and a togue will always dive."

After a half hour of playing it, "Your father caught an eight pound togue right here, I think this one will be heavier."

Another fifteen minutes has passed and he was able to bring it close enough to the canoe so when it rolled they could see it. "Yep a togue. And a lot more than eight pounds." Rascal dipped the net in the water and waited for Richard to bring the togue in closer.

As soon as he had it in the net the streamer fell loose. "Boy, was that a close one," Richard said.

Rascal brought it in and said, "I'd say at least ten pounds or better. Are you hungry?"

"I wasn't until you mentioned it, but yes, I could eat a horse."

A slight chop had developed on the lake and before they were back at the wharf the chops turned into white caps with a strong northwest wind. "I guess we won't be going out again today."

Richard carried his togue to the lodge where they weighed it. "Twelve pounds, four ounces."

"Is this the one you want mounted, Richard?"

"You bet I do."

"I'll make up a box big enough to add ice and sawdust and we can ship it this afternoon with the southbound train. While I'm making the box, Emma, would you telephone Jarvis that we'll be shipping this to him so he can pick it up at the depot this afternoon. And ask how much and tell him the money will be inside with the fish."

"In the meantime I'll put this on ice in the cold storage room."

An hour later he had the wooden box made and large enough so the sawdust would cover the ice and insulate it.

While they all were enjoying a cup of coffee with donuts it started to rain. Wind driven at first and then the wind died off. Leaving a good soaking rain. The grass in the old mill yard would spring back to life now with the rain.

Rascal put out the red flag so he wouldn't forget.

Belle helped Emma make some sandwiches for lunch with a fresh pot of coffee. After eating, Emma said, "If you two would like to lie down for a little you can choose any room upstairs."

"Thank you, Emma, that sounds like a good idea," Belle said.

"Were you planning anything special for supper, Emma? I mean they will be leaving tomorrow afternoon."

"I was thinking about beaver and frog legs with whipped potato, biscuits and a salad from the garden."

The engineer blew the train whistle and five minutes later it pulled to a stop at the platform. "What have you today, Rascal?" Tom Whelling the conductor asked.

"One box, Tom. For Jarvis Page and he'll pick it up at the depot."

"Wow, this is heavier than it looks. What did you find some gold?" Tom said while laughing.

"Nah, just a big fish."

"I'd say."

"Thank you, Tom."

The rain had stopped and as Emma was beginning to retrieve fixings for supper from the cold storage room, Rascal took his axe and went out into the woods to cut a couple of small beechnut trees and then chip those into small pieces to use in the smoker. He couldn't wait to try it out. He figured to take Emma fishing after Richard and Belle left the next day.

He put the wood chips undercover in the shed. "Rascal, take a bath and put on clean clothes."

"What about you?"

"I will after you."

"I have a better idea. The tub is big enough for the two of us."

He didn't have to twist her arm. "Okay, let's do it."

Afterwards, Emma put on her flowery print dress and Rascal his casual clothes. "I should start supper now.

"That rain cooled things off, how about you starting a fire in the fireplace?"

It would be good to warm the lodge before they went to bed. The nights were getting colder. He used some dry spruce slabs from the woodshed and then added a stick of hardwood.

When Richard and Belle came down for supper the lodge

was warm.

"The fireplace sure adds charm to this whole setting," Richard said.

Emma had not said anything to either of them what would be for supper. She wanted to surprise them.

"I don't understand how you can prepare meals like this when you have to ship your food in by train," Richard said.

"Well, none of this was shipped in, the vegetables are all from our garden. Now dig in," Emma said.

"What are these little apples?" Belle asked.

"They are spiced crabapples."

Belle bit into one and said, "Wow, this is good."

"I love these biscuits, Emma," Richard said.

Everyone had their plate full and Emma and Rascal were waiting for them to taste the beaver and frog legs.

Richard ate one leg and said, "Boy, this is certainly tender chicken."

Belle ate some of the beaver meat and dipped her biscuit in the gravy. "This beef is so sweet and tender." Then she picked up a frog leg and said, "Boy, this must have been some small chicken," and she ate it.

"Actually, it isn't beef or chicken." They both stopped chewing and looked at Emma. "The beef is actually beaver and the chicken is frog legs."

Belle coughed and then she and Richard began laughing. Then Richard said, "I would never have believed either one would taste so good."

They both went back for more. Belle said, "Your life out here is so different than what either of us are accustomed to. I'm not saying our way of life is better, by no means. It's just here everything is so different, relaxed, like there is no outside world. When I was caring for you, Rascal, I now understand why you talked about home with so much love. You two are wonderful people, living a wonderful life."

* * *

The next morning everyone was unusually quiet. Richard and his wife would be leaving soon and they were each finding it difficult to be cheery and talkative. Finally Richard broke the silence. "After being here and experiencing, let's say, Whiskey Jack, I can understand now why our folks enjoyed themselves so much. When my father first offered us this trip as our wedding present, I wanted to decline, but I was afraid of hurting his feelings. I think Mom and Dad could live here year round and be quiet content."

Before noon Rascal put out the red flag and joined the others for lunch and coffee. Even after they had finished eating they remained at the table talking and sipping coffee. Their luggage had already been brought down from the cabin.

The train whistle blew and they all looked at each other, knowing they soon would have to say goodbye. Rascal and Richard took the luggage out to the platform. When Emma and Belle joined them the two hugged. Rascal and Richard shook hands. Then Belle hugged Rascal and kissed his cheek and whispered in his ear. Richard and Emma hugged and he kissed her cheek. Friends they had become and saying goodbye was so emotional. The train came to a stop and then Tom, the conductor, helped them with their luggage. They just stood there looking at each other. "Do come again," Emma said.

"We will, I promise," Belle replied.

The train lurched forward and Richard and Belle stepped aboard.

* * *

"Leave the kitchen as is, Emma, and we'll change out of these good clothes and go fishing. I want to try the smoker."

Emma had her line out trolling on their way up to Jack Brook inlet and halfway there she hooked on to a nice trout that jumped clear above the surface and then came swimming towards her. She was busy stripping the line in trying to keep it taut.

When Rascal netted it, it still had enough energy left to keep struggling in the net. "That's a beauty, Em."

Once at the inlet, Rascal began fishing also. In an hour they had plenty of brookies to try out the smoker. While Rascal cleaned the fish and got the smoker going Emma walked up to the log cabin to change the sheets and sweep up.

Much to her surprise Belle had found clean sheets and the used ones were balled up on the bed. And on one pillow was a $50.00 bill and a note.

> Didn't want to insult you for being so nice to us by tipping you $50.00, so I found it easier this way and many thanks
>
> Richard and Belle

* * *

After breakfast the next morning Rascal checked the smoker and added more hardwood chips and another stick of beechnut.

The afternoon northbound stopped and two parties of two men each arrived for a weeks' fishing. Two from Portland, Harry Tilson and his cousin Finlay Gough, and two men from Boston, Tony Alberto and Myles Newman. "That's $100.00 each for the week. Supper is at 6 pm, breakfast at 6 am and lunch at noon. The $100.00 is payable now." Emma took their money and Rascal showed them upstairs to their rooms.

Rascal explained to the two groups not to keep more fish than could be eaten, as they were not able to freeze them so they would not spoil on the trip home. The sun was setting earlier and there was very little time to fish after supper, so Emma changed supper to 4 o'clock.

The four men waited until the next morning to go out. The two men from Boston seemed like genuine sportsmen, but the two from Portland seemed to be there for a good time. When the four did return from fishing they had enough fish for all of them to have for super. The two from Boston gave their string of brookies to Rascal and went back out in the canoe. "We're just going to do some canoeing and exploring. We'll be back for lunch," Myles Newman said.

They left and Rascal began cleaning the fish on the wharf. Harry and Finlay were still there telling Rascal about the huge bull moose they had seen and watching a doe deer with twin fawns feeding around the edge of the lake.

After supper Harry and Finlay started fishing from the wharf up the lake towards the upper end, staying close to the shore. They were taking turns fishing and paddling.

They went directly to the no name inlet. The doe and her two fawns were there feeding again. "I bet I could have me one of those deer with my pistol," Harry said.

"I'll bet you $5.00 you can't."

"Alright Finlay, I'll take your wager. Tomorrow when that other group goes back we stay out here and I'll show you."

The next morning Tony and Myles had six brookies, all about a pound apiece and they turned the canoe and headed back to the lodge.

The two from Portland watched them leave. "They'll hear the shot, Harry, even inside the lodge," Finlay said.

"Maybe, but how are they going to know it was us? All we have to do is say we saw someone on shore."

"I don't know, Harry."

"What are you trying to do, welch out of your bet?"

"Okay, okay, let's do it."

They had to wait quite a while for the three deer to come back out. It was close to lunch. Emma was fixing sandwiches with coffee and Rascal was checking the smoker when Harry fired his first shot. Tony and Myles were in their room upstairs and came down when they heard it.

Rascal ran for the lodge and grabbed his binoculars and ran down to the lake. He couldn't see anything from there so he hiked up to the point. They were across the lake near the small inlet.

"I told you I could kill me one," Harry said loud enough so Rascal could hear. "Here, you try it Finlay," and he handed him the .44 caliber pistol.

He took a long time lining up the sight before he pulled the trigger. Rascal was watching with his binoculars. And then came the second loud report and it echoed up and down the lake. Rascal saw the deer fall in the water. Then they fired four more shots. "What was that for, Harry?" Finlay asked.

"If anyone asks we can say we were just target shooting. Let's get back to the lodge, I'm hungry."

Rascal hurried back to the lodge and told Emma, Tony and Myles, "They just shot two deer. They're coming back. I'm going up and make sure the deer are dead. If they ask where I am, just say I had to go to the farm to check on things. Don't mention the shots, if they ask you about it or say anything, just say none of you heard anything. That you were probably in the cellar showing you two the cold storage room. Act as if nothing has happened, okay?"

"Okay."

Rascal had to walk the tracks up to almost Ledge Swamp before cutting down to Jack Brook. He was so angry he didn't look for a shallow place to cross, he waded through the water up to his hips.

Harry and Finlay tied the canoe up to the wharf and cleaned their four brook trout and brought them into the lodge and gave them to Emma. "Sorry we're late, ma'am," Finlay said.

"That's okay. There are sandwiches and coffee on the table."

Harry took his handgun up to his room. He returned to the cafeteria and sat down with Finlay and began eating. So far no one had said a word about hearing gunshots.

"What have you two been doing?" Harry asked.

"After we cleaned up Mrs. Ambrose showed us the cold storage room in the cellar and how they keep their food fresh."

"Where's your husband, Mrs. Ambrose? He usually eats with us."

"Oh, he had to hike into the farm to check on things. It's quite a hike and I wouldn't expect him back anytime soon."

Harry looked at Finlay and winked, so far they were as good as gold. When they were up in their room Harry said, "There is nothing to worry about. No one here heard the shots and her husband wasn't even here," Harry said. "And you owe me $5.00."

Finlay paid him and said, "We can't be doing that again. This time we were lucky and got away with it."

"Oh, you worry too much, Finlay."

When Rascal reached the small inlet he could see the two fawns lying in the water. He pulled them ashore and pulled the innards out and then put them in a crotch of a tree about four feet above the ground. They weren't very heavy. Then he returned the same way he had come.

The more he walked the angrier he was becoming. He had taken deer in closed season, sure enough. But it had always been for food. For he and Em or the Antonys. Never killed for the mere sake of killing. As he was coming close to the opening of the old mill yard he cut through the woods to the farm road. Then he had to sit down and cool his anger and clean the mud off his clothes.

Finally his breathing was slower, as was his pulse. He had stopped sweating and he now knew what he had to do. He stood up and walked calmly to the lodge. Emma met him at the door. "They're both upstairs in their room. Did you find anything?"

"Yes, two fawns," he whispered.

He placed a telephone call to Marcel Cyr. He wasn't long picking up. "Marcel Cyr."

"Marcel, this is Rascal. You need to take the morning northbound tomorrow. There's something you need to know."

"Yes, certainly. I'll be on the train."

"Is he coming?" Emma asked.

"Yes, in the morning. You know I don't like the idea of those two having a handgun in the lodge.

Tony and Myles came downstairs then. "We have noticed you have a smoker. Would you like some more fish to smoke?" Tony asked.

"We sure would and maybe some would be cured enough for you to take back with you."

Just then Harry and Finlay came down. Rascal walked over to Harry and standing in front of him he said, "I want your handgun Mr. Tilson. You two shot two deer today. I don't allow that in this lodge and I want your handgun."

"You go to hell," Harry said.

That was the wrong thing to say. Rascal hit him on the chin with the palm of his hand in an upward motion sending him backward and to the floor, screaming. Everyone heard his jaw break.

In between screams, Harry cried out, "You bastard you broke my jaw."

"I'll do more than that if you don't keep a civil tongue in your head." He looked at Finlay and it was clear he didn't want anything to do with Rascal.

"Em, you take Tony as a witness and go find Mr. Tilson's gun. Finlay you go get a towel from the kitchen and give it to your friend here. I don't want him drooling all over the floor. And you stay where you are."

Myles was taking all this in and was having the time of his life. This was even better than fishing. Finlay came right back with a towel and gave it to his friend. Emma and Tony came back downstairs and she handed the handgun to Rascal.

"It was under the mattress. It is still loaded," Emma said.

Rascal unloaded it. Then he looked at both Harry and Finlay and said, "Now this is what we're going to do. First, I'm going to bandage your jaw. Em, would you get me a pillowcase?"

While she was after that Rascal continued. "The game

warden is coming on the morning train and he'll haul you two out of here and more than likely to jail. I will not lock you in your room. There's no fear of you running off. There's nothing but miles of wilderness out here. If you were to try and follow the tracks let me tell you, you wouldn't live through the night. There is a huge bear near mile nine and another at mile twelve. I have had my run ins with them. That's why I have this limp. So you have no choice but to stay; we'll free you, as long as you behave. If you don't behave I'll tie you up and not feed you. Harry you'll have to drink soup through a straw."

Emma was back with the pillowcase. "Would you rip it into two inch strips?"

When she had finished Rascal began to tie them under Harry's chin to the top of his head and another one around the point of the jaw up behind his head. "There that should do. Is that better? Don't speak, shake or nod your head." He nodded it was okay.

"Where did you learn this, Rascal?" Emma asked.

"In the war. We had to do it quite often. It's only a temporary fix until he can see a doctor.

"All Harry will be eating is liquids for a long time."

"I'll make a soup for him tonight."

"There, you two are free to go to your room, outside or stay here. Just remember what I said about the two bear."

Tony and Myles followed Rascal outside. "Mr. Ambrose, is that true about the bear? I mean did they do that to your leg?"

"That was only to keep them from running off. I was shot in the war."

Emma made a tomato soup for Harry. The others had fish chowder and hot biscuits. After supper Tony and Myles went fishing again, and Rascal checked the smoker. The fish were cured, but he kept the fire going, in case the two brought back more trout that evening.

They came back with a dozen nice big trout and they helped Rascal clean and fillet them. He then soaked them in salt brine for a while before he hung 'em in the smoker.

"Hopefully, these will be cured for you by the time you leave Saturday afternoon."

When Rascal was back inside he asked Emma, "Have they been any trouble?"

"Haven't heard a word from them. They have been upstairs in their room."

"Good. Just in case I'll sleep out here tonight. Oh, what did you do with the handgun?"

"I put it in the silverware drawer in the kitchen."

* * *

Rascal only catnapped during the night. One thing he had learned while fighting in the war, never take your enemy for granted, always assume he will do the unexpected. He drank a lot of coffee and listened all through the night for any unusual sound.

Come morning, Harry and Finlay came to the breakfast table wearing long faces. Harry had more tomato soup.

When the train stopped Marcel came right to the cafeteria and the first thing he saw was Harry's bandaged head. "What in the world happened here, Rascal?"

"Yesterday this one and his pal shot two fawn deer and left them. I confronted them in here and when I asked him," and he pointed, "for his handgun he told me to go to hell. I won't take that from anyone and I didn't like the idea of him having a handgun in the lodge, particularly when there were other guests. And it was loaded inside. I had no idea they had brought it with them until I heard the first shot. Then I ran to the point of land with my binoculars and as I was watching I saw Harry pass the handgun to his cousin, Finlay Gough, and Finlay shot the second fawn. Before I confronted them about shooting the two fawns I hiked over and found them lying in the water. I gutted them and put them in a crotch of a tree. You have time, I could take you up there by canoe."

"Let's go. But what about these two? Emma will be here alone with them."

"Em will be okay. She still has their gun and she is a crack shot. Besides I told them about the two bear in either direction along the tracks. There's no place for them to go."

Rascal pushed off in his canoe and Marcel helped to paddle. "They were about here when they shot." He guided the canoe ashore and Marcel stepped out and pulled it in to shore and Rascal stepped out.

"Well, I see the gut piles are gone. The two deer are right there," and he pointed. Nothing had touched them.

"What caliber handgun?"

"A .44 caliber, 8 inch barrel."

"There are exit wounds in both deer, no wonder. Let's put these in the canoe and head back."

"Would you like deer steak for lunch?"

"That would be the icing on the cake."

Back at the lodge Marcel went to check on the two. "Emma, I'll take their gun now, and the shells."

"What are you going to do with us, officer?" Finlay asked.

"Take you to Beech Tree when the train comes back and then to jail for tonight. You'll be arraigned in the morning. From there it will be up to the judge."

Tony and Myles were back early with two four pound trout. "Can you clean and fillet them like I showed you? I'll help you as soon as I am through here."

With the hides pulled off he washed the meat in the lake and then took them to the kitchen and cut off enough steaks for everyone. Then he went out to make some salt brine for the two brook trout Tony and Myles had brought back.

Inside the cafeteria Rascal introduced Tony and Myles to "Marcel Cyr, the game warden." They all shook hands.

"This is a hellova way to meet the local warden," Tony said. "But personally I'm glad you're here."

Emma had fixed fresh deer steaks, biscuits and a variety of garden vegetables. And tomato soup for Harry.

"This is all so very good, Emma. Thank you. Rascal, we must have eaten one of those deer, would you like the other one?"

"Sure, but I thought you might like to have it."

"I would but I won't have time to take care of it. As it is now it'll be late 'fore I can call it a day and tomorrow I'll have to escort these two to court."

The train whistle blew reminding Rascal he had to put out the red flag.

The passenger car came to a squealing stop at the platform and conductor Tom Whelling opened the door. He noticed Harry's bandaged head and being escorted by the game warden and wondered what had taken place.

Emma said, "Ask for cell #1, it has the best bed." Even Marcel turned to look at her, and he grinned.

Rascal, Emma, Tony and Myles stood on the platform and watched as the train disappeared.

"Boy, am I glad they're gone," Emma said.

"Me too. We don't need people like that coming here."

Myles was usually so quiet but he spoke up now, "I've had a hellova good time. The fishing is great, the food is delicious and those two idiots just added a little excitement."

"Come on, Myles, let's go fishing."

* * *

By Saturday afternoon Tony and Myles were boarding the train and they were taking back with them twenty pounds of freshly smoke-cured brook trout. "I want to thank you both so much," Tony said.

"Me too," Myles added.

"This has been an interesting week to say the least," Emma said.

"I don't think we'll ever see Harry and Finlay back here."

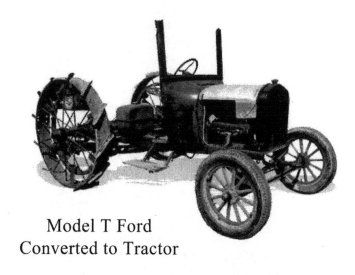

Model T Ford
Converted to Tractor

Cyrus Hay Mower

Chapter 11

The northbound train pulled to a stop at the platform on Sunday afternoon and Jeters stepped from the passenger car. Then the train moved forward to the ramp. "Hello, Jeters. We weren't expecting you," Rascal said.

"No, Mr. Hitchcock didn't have enough time to let you know I was coming and bringing a new tractor. We have to mow the hayfields at the farm. Come with me and I'll show you this new machine." Emma walked with them also.

"What is it?"

"It is a Ford Model T conversion tractor. The rear wheels are steel with steel traction cleats and the front wheels are rubber.

"Earl Hitchcock said there is a Cyrus hay mower in the big shed behind the barn that will attach to this tractor quite well. He wants you to ride the mower while I drive the tractor. When we have finished he wants the tractor left in the barn and you are to mow the fields hereafter."

"Well, it's too late to do anything today, so why don't you bring that tractor around to the old mill. You can put it under cover there."

While sipping coffee the three of them caught up with the goings on. "This new bandsaw is a big improvement over the circular saw, and it isn't anywhere near as dangerous.

"Only one family from here failed to transfer to Kidney Pond, and the brothers had to go to Quebec to find enough workers.

"The company has contracts for two railcars a day of sawn lumber and one pulpwood car. Right now they are having a difficult time filling the pulpwood car each day. You and Emma should come for a visit. It is a remarkable setup."

"I was planning on more deer steak as long as it is fresh. Any objections?" Emma asked.

Jeters looked first at Rascal and then at Emma wondering who had shot the deer. Rascal saw the puzzled look on his face and said, "Two sports from Portland shot two spotted fawns.

"You know it's too bad the mowing machine is at the farm. If it was here we could do this piece first. As it is we'll have to take them both back to the barn."

They had an early supper and Emma was saving a freshly baked apple pie for later. For now they all filled up on fresh deer steak, "My, this sure is tender."

"It is good isn't it? The trouble with shooting a small fawn, there isn't much meat."

As the sunset and twilight waned to night darkness, in the north was a brilliant display of green and yellow northern lights. "Oh my! Aren't those so beautiful tonight," Emma said.

"They sure are. I wonder what causes them? And then some nights, like tonight, they are so much brighter than other nights," Rascal questioned.

"I haven't a clue," Jeters said.

Emma went inside and served up the pie with some sharp cheese and brought plates out for Rascal and Jeters, and then she went back for her plate. They sat in silence while eating their pie and cheese and watching northern lights.

Rascal and Jeters wanted an early start in the morning and were up before the sun. As they were eating breakfast Emma said, "Now I don't want you boys playing with Bear today."

Jeters choked and spit up in his plate and he looked at Rascal. "I thought we weren't going to tell anyone?"

"Well—I kinda had to after Em met him."

"You mean Emma and Bear?"

"Yeup. We walked out to the farm to look things over and before we were through he came ambling up across the field within a hundred feet of us and stopped. I introduced him to my wife, Em. You take it from there, Em."

"And that son of a gun said *Hi* and reached out with his paw. I couldn't believe it. The noise he made sure sounded like he had said, 'Hi,'" Emma said.

"But that isn't all. We started walking backwards towards home and he kept keeping pace with us.

"Finally," Emma continued, "We started to run and Bear started running! He was right behind us now and he reached out with his paw and tripped Rascal. I helped him to his feet and we started running. And again he tripped Rascal. Then," and she started laughing, "then he head bunted him in the butt and Rascal went on his face. This time Bear jumped up on the roadside bank and—I'll be damned if he didn't start laughing. Then we all began laughing."

Now the three of them were laughing as if it had just happened. "How do you figure him?"

"I think you had it right, he gets lonely and wants a playmate."

"Yeah, but you know he could get rough."

"We know."

"What are you going to do about your hunters?"

"We'll tell them no hunting near Ledge Swamp and no one will be allowed to shoot any bear."

"They have a long lifespan, don't they?"

Rascal knew what Jeters was referring to.

"Well, we need to go to work, Rascal."

As they were going out the door Emma said, "Remember you two are supposed to be working and not playing with Bear."

"I'll show you how to start this tractor. It's a hand crank. Make sure the gearshift is in neutral, turn on the fuel, the magneto switch here and close the choke." Jeters inserted the hand crank and spun it real quick and the tractor came to life.

"It ain't always that easy. If you crank and crank and nothing happens chances are the sparkplugs have been fouled with too much gasoline. Then you'll have to take them out and dry them and put 'em back in and try again.

"Hop on back. You can stand on the drawbar and brace yourself. I won't be going too fast." He put it in gear and let the clutch out easy. No problem, Rascal was watching everything Jeters was doing.

"The gears in this have been changed so it'll have more power but less speed than the Model T auto. I find 2nd gear works pretty well. Have you ever driven anything, Rascal?"

"In the army, I had to drive a truck a couple of times, but I never got it out of 1st gear."

Once they were on the road where it was good going, Jeters gave it some gas speeding up to about 10mph. Already Rascal could see this was going to be easier than using a team of horses to pull the mower. At the farm, Rascal opened the barn door and Jeters backed in and up to the Cyrus hay mower.

"Have you ever been on the business end of one of these Rascal?"

"Yeah, on my father's farm. It was older than this one but basically the same function."

"Well hop on and we'll get started."

Rascal let the cutter bar down and as Jeters began driving around the outside of the field, Rascal engaged the cutter blades, powered by the iron wheels with knobs on the rims so the wheels would have enough traction to reciprocate the cutter blade.

The first pass around was slow, but then there after Jeters was able to drive along faster. The hay was good and dry and it was cutting and falling behind the cutter bar just as it was supposed to.

And no sign of Bear. Jeters was keeping a sharp eye out for him. He didn't want to be a plaything for a four hundred pound bear.

As they mowed row after row, hawks, foxes and even fisher cats were coming out to the mowed grass now to hunt for mice. By noon they were almost done so they continued for another hour.

Then all they had left was the outside row next to the tree

line. This was important to cut so to stop bushes from creeping out into the field.

"There, that went better than I'd thought. Let's go do the lodge field. You drive, Rascal. Your back must be sore from riding that machine."

Rascal took to driving the Model T tractor quite well. When they were back at the lodge they cut that also before stopping. "You know, Rascal, if I hurry I might be able to catch the southbound."

They walked over to the platform and the train blew its whistle. Rascal put out the red flag and they waited. "I guess you know what to do from here, Rascal.

"I really miss the village," Jeters said.

"Don't be a stranger," Emma said.

The train stopped and Jeters boarded and he stood on the car entryway watching behind him as the train disappeared around the bend.

"The fish in the smoker probably could be taken out tomorrow morning. Do you want to go and catch a few more?"

"Let's have something to eat first. You haven't eaten since breakfast.

"Did you see anything of Bear?"

"No. He might have gone back to Ledge Swamp. When the new grass and clover start to grow, he may be back."

"You know Rascal, even if he is a nuisance sometimes, I'd still hate to have anything happen to him."

"Me too."

They went fishing and just before dark they each hooked into one that would probably go four pounds or better each. That was enough for that trip. Rascal cleaned them and put them in the cold storage in a salt brine for the night.

In the morning he removed the cured fish and hung up the new fillets. He gave the cured fish to Emma to sample. "Wow, these are good. Wouldn't some wine and cheese go good with it?"

"Yes. Tomorrow is Monday. If no sports get off, let's go to Lac St. Jean for the day and buy some wine and some sharp cheese."

* * *

Monday morning when the train stopped the conductor handed Rascal a mail pouch. It was heavy. "We are going to Lac St. Jean Tom. I need to put this inside."

As they were going by the old beaver problem at mile twelve and a half, Rascal looked to see if they had come back. No beaver. He was relieved.

In St. Jean they had to be quick about their shopping. While Emma was getting groceries, Rascal went after four bottles of Emma's favorite wine and a fifth of ginger brandy.

"I bought more than I had intended and now we'll have to have a taxi to take everything to the depot."

Rascal put the wine and brandy in with the groceries. Emma had three wooden crates of food plus a bushel of freshly picked apples.

Everything was loaded into the freight car. A half hour later the train pulled out of Lac St. Jean. The train only slowed as they went through customs at the border.

At the lodge everything was set off onto the platform and carried inside from there. "Thank you, Tom," Rascal hollered as the train began to move.

"That was an easy way of shopping. Up and back in the same day," Emma said.

As Emma was putting everything away Rascal emptied the mail pouch.

"Em! Em!," Rascal shouted.

She came running up from the cellar, "What on earth are you hollering about?"

"Em, look at all this mail. I think it is a request for hunting this fall. At least this one is and with a $20.00 deposit."

"So is this one and another $20.00 deposit," Emma said. "I'll have to go get my reservation calendar."

As they opened each request, Emma marked it on her calendar. By the time they had finished every week was booked full except for Thanksgiving week. "I want to keep this week free, Em, to trap."

"Okay, that's five weeks and fourteen hunters each week. I'm going to need help, Rascal. I think I'll ask Anita Anthony if she would be interested." And then she added, "Holy cow, Rascal, that's going to take a lot of food to feed fourteen every day."

"These deposits come from Pennsylvania, New York state, New Jersey, a few from Boston and none from Maine. Apparently those advertisements are working."

After they had all of the deposits and reservations squared away Emma said, "That's a total of seventy hunters for five weeks and that'll net us $7000.00. I wonder now how much it'll take to feed them?"

"Anyhow," she added, "it's too late to cook supper. Let's have wine with smoked brook trout and crackers and cheese."

"That sounds good to me, I'll go down and get a bottle of wine and the fish," Rascal said.

Emma took one bite of the smoked fish and said, "Oh wow, Rascal. It's been a long time since I have tasted something so good. How much of this do we have?"

"Maybe ten or twelve pounds. That includes the two in the smoker now."

"Can we catch some more before the season ends?"

"We'll go out in the morning. Have breakfast outdoors tomorrow. We can take some bread dough and have some stick bread too."

"This wine is nice and cold."

"I put it on the ice. We'll have to remember to treat Al and Beverly to smoked fish next spring when they come."

They ate fish, cheese and finished the bottle of wine.

Emma didn't know why but each time she and Rascal had some wine—"Rascal, I'm horny. Let's go to bed."

* * *

Just as the sun was coming up over the treetops the next morning they were on their way to Jack Brook. There was a frost that morning and they could see their breath in the cold air. "In three weeks our first hunters will start arriving," Emma said.

After the ripples in the water had subsided and all was quiet, they began fishing. They caught several two pound trout and as many one pound. "Let's go ashore and eat, Rascal. I'm hungry."

While Emma started a fire and put the tea kettle on to boil water Rascal cleaned the trout. Four of the smaller trout Emma put on spits to roast and she wrapped some bread dough around two sticks. When the tea was ready Rascal poured two cups and gave Emma one. They walked down to the edge of the lake. Standing there sipping hot tea—". . . and I wonder what the rest of the world is doing?" Rascal said.

"I'm going to sit by the fire. I'm cold." She poured herself another cup of hot tea and sat down and turned the fish and bread sticks.

"How many more do you want?"

"I'd like to catch maybe two more big ones. That would give us maybe ten pounds today. And that should be enough to see us through 'til spring."

They ate their breakfast and enjoyed every morsel and had more tea. "Are you ready?" Rascal asked.

Emma dumped the rest of the tea on the fire and refilled the kettle and dumped that on also. "There that should do it. Let's do it."

They caught two more about a pound each and Rascal moved the canoe over next to the lily pads. "There, Em, cast in about halfway to shore. Let the fly rest on the water and just jiggle it some. Don't strip the line in or you'll get tangled up in weeds."

She cast out and let her fly rest on the water and before the ripples had disappeared a huge trout came up and took it and cleared the water. "Now, don't let it dive or it will surely tangle the line around the weeds. Try to keep it on top and strip the line in faster than you normally would."

She did just as Rascal had said and she brought the brook trout in on top of the lily pads. Rascal netted and brought it in. He took the fly out and said, "Do you think you can do that again?"

"Now that I know how, sure," and she cast out in the same spot and hooked on to another one almost as big.

After he had that in the boat she said, "Okay, that's enough. I'm cold and I have to pee."

Rascal turned the canoe and started for home. "If you don't hurry, Rascal, I'll have to pee right here." They both started paddling faster.

When they reached the wharf, Emma jumped out and ran for the lodge. After Rascal stopped and laughed, he tied the canoe off and cleaned and filleted the trout and put them in a salt brine for a while. The fish that were already in the smoker he figured would be ready to take out after another day.

* * *

Deer hunting season would soon be upon them. Anita had excitedly agreed to help until after Thanksgiving and they made up another room by moving around some of the stock in the old general store. There was a rug on the floor, bed and bureau, a nightstand with a lamp and Rascal had cut in a window for her and a lockable door.

A week before the first guest would arrive they went to Beech Tree and stocked up with food. Now with colder nights and the vent in the cold storage room open, food would last much longer. They purchased a good supply of baked beans. Anita had said she had a special recipe for beans with onion, salt pork and molasses.

Emma found something new also; very thin sheets of aluminum. She could see the possibilities of this new aluminum and she purchased four boxes.

Anita's main job was cooking and dishes. Emma would help out when she wasn't busy cleaning, making beds or doing laundry. "I sure am glad the Douglas's installed this gas cook stove."

Rascal had to tend to everything else the two women were not. He even found time sometimes to sweep the cafeteria floor. He was plenty busy though keeping the upstairs ram-down stove and the wood end-heater in the kitchen going, plus the fireplace. The weather had turned cold for the middle of October.

It was good to see the cafeteria full with people again and he listened to their chatter, stories and laughter. Anita, especially was enjoying this.

One Monday morning, Emma called the town office in Beech Tree and inquired how she would be able to vote without having to make it a two day trip.

"Why Mrs. Ambrose, I can send you and your husband an absentee ballot. You fill it out, seal it and return it."

"Would you send me three ballots then? One for my husband and one for Mrs. Antony, also."

She and Anita both were determined to use the right to vote as guaranteed in the passing of the bill, giving women the right to vote. "Yes, we are determined to vote," Emma said one morning at the breakfast table.

Two days later the absentee ballots arrived and both Rascal and Emma voted for Warren Harding. Not because they particularly liked Harding, but because his running mate for vice president was Kevin Cutlidge, born in Vermont. They both figured having someone in the White House from the northeast would be beneficial. Anita was not saying how she voted.

"It's supposed to be a secret ballot," she had said.

As the three were having supper Friday night, they all were a little nervous about the start of the deer season. There would be fourteen hunters arriving in the next two days.

Saturday morning eight of the fourteen arrived and it was apparent from listening to their conversations that they were businessmen and Rascal found he didn't have to entertain them like he had been worrying he would have to. Some of them had very nice and expensive rifles.

The next morning the other six arrived and two of them chose the log cabin across the cove, although they would be taking their meals with the others in the cafeteria.

After supper that evening Rascal stood up and said, "If I could have your attention please. There are a few lodge rules I'd like to explain to you. First there will be no foul language allowed inside the lodge. Number two, there'll be no loud disturbances from your rooms at night while everyone else is trying to sleep. Number three, the gasoline generator is turned off every evening at 8 pm. There is sufficient lighting with kerosene lanterns in every room and down here. Number four, there will be no hunting at all at Ledge Swamp, two miles up the tracks. And number five there will be no killing of bear. We want this to be a deer hunting and fishing lodge. Not a place to come to kill anything you see. Number six, there will be no loaded firearms inside the lodge.

"If you want to check your sights, I have set up a shooting range to the north side of the clearing.

"And now I'd like to introduce the two ladies who will be preparing your meals. This is my wife, Emma, and this is our good friend, Anita Antony."

Emma said, "Breakfast will be at 5 o'clock every morning. If you sleep in or late and miss breakfast you'll have to wait for lunch, at noon. Supper is at 6 pm. This should give everyone enough time to get back after the sun sets."

No one had asked for a guide yet. That was okay with

Rascal too. He could find plenty to keep him busy around the lodge. The smoke cured fish were all in cold storage now and he cleaned the ashes out from the fire pit.

Monday morning all the guests were ready for breakfast and that day's hunt.

A few hunters had gone up behind his cabin and the rest scattered out between the farm road and Rascal's hunting road. Two even went up to hunt the railroad right of way.

Come noon most were back for lunch and deer had been seen but no one had fired a shot. But they were jovial and excited to try again later.

The two that had gone up the tracks stayed out and didn't come in for lunch. And at 2 pm he heard two rifle shots from that direction, maybe a half mile up the tracks.

At 3 o'clock the two came back dragging a six point buck. They said there was another six point down and if Rascal would hang that one they would go after the second deer.

They were back about sunset, all of the other hunters had returned to the lodge and were all looking at the two bucks and excitement in their voices.

By the end of that first week the guests had only shot one more buck. An eight point. They all had seen deer and no one was bitter or discouraged.

They all boarded the afternoon train and Rascal, Emma and Anita sat in the cafeteria drinking a cup of coffee. "Well there goes week number one. Four more to go."

Anita was still jubilant about being asked to help out and she really liked people.

"Are we ready for tomorrow?" Emma asked.

"I think we had better be. Maybe we'll get more experienced hunters this week. Although they did all see deer and they were happy."

"I even took four deposits for next year," Emma said.

The next day all fourteen hunters arrived on the morning train and these men seemed a little older over the whole group.

And Rascal noticed that they did not have, that is most of them, new rifles. Which told him they might be more experienced hunters.

Sunday evening after supper and while they were all still in the cafeteria Rascal told them about the lodge rules. The week before there had not been any problems. By 8 pm most of them were already in bed and asleep.

* * *

By the end of the second week the guests had shot four bucks and one nice spike. And again, they all had seen deer.

By the end of the third week in Thursday's newspaper in big headlines on the front page, Warren Harding was the new president. When Emma made the announcement to the guests at supper that evening there were a few grumblings.

The next morning after the hunters had left Emma asked, "What do you think about asking Jarvis and Marcel and their wives here for Thanksgiving?"

"I think that would be a grand idea."

"So do I," Anita said.

Emma wrote them each a letter asking them to come spend Thanksgiving with them. Of course they would have to stay over one night and maybe do some hunting.

A few days later Emma received letters from Arlene and Rita and they would love to come.

By the end of the fifth week all three were tired and glad no one was coming Thanksgiving week. Of the five weeks, seventy hunters had shot twenty-five bucks, two spike horns and two does.

There was now eight inches of snow on the ground and Rascal decided not to trap. He was worn out, besides they had netted $7000.00 for five weeks of work. They gave Anita a bonus and they still had a lot of food left.

"We did okay, Rascal, financially. We gave Anita $200.00,

the food cost us $475.00 and we still have much of it left so I figure we grossed $6400.00 for five weeks plus $1200.00 from fishermen. You know this could be a good thing."

"Yeah, I agree with you, but I have never been so busy."

He did put out a few traps though, along the Jarvis Trail and across the tracks and Jack Brook and back up to his log cabin. He set eight traps. He only had a few days to trap and he tended every day until Thanksgiving morning when Jarvis, Marcel and their wives stepped off the train.

"It's too cold out here to stand around and talk. Come inside and I'll show you to your rooms and then we can have a fresh pot of coffee."

Jarvis noticed how well and happy Anita was looking. "You're looking good, Anita. Being back in Whiskey Jack must appeal to you."

"It does, Jarvis, and thank you. I do miss the town and the people and most of all, Silvio. But I have had a good fall here. I hope they'll want me back next year."

"Dinner won't be ready until 5 o'clock, so if you men want to go hunting, you can."

"Where do you want to go, Rascal?" Jarvis asked.

"Let's all three go out to that little valley and we'll leave Marcel on the road and you and I will hunt down to him. We'll go out beyond the Jarvis Trail." Rascal said and then he looked at Marcel for his reactions.

And it came, "You know about that trail?"

"For a while now. But I always wondered how Jarvis could just suddenly appear in town when no one saw him get off the train.

Rascal and Jarvis left Marcel sitting on the rock where he had stationed other hunters before him. And they walked a mile up along the valley almost to the farm road and then they started hunting, each following alongside the hardwood trees on the edges. There were many new and really fresh tracks in the snow and Rascal had no doubt someone would get a deer.

It soon became obvious that several deer had joined up and now traveling in the general direction of the road and Marcel.

Partway through Jarvis found a fresh bear track heading towards Rascal's position. Rascal saw the track also. "Oh no. Bear you are supposed to be hibernating."

If he had followed the tracks he would have seen where Bear had actually circled in behind him. Bear must have recognized Rascal's scent because it started following his tracks. Rascal heard branches breaking behind him and turned to look and when he did, Bear stopped and stood up and made that peculiar laughing sound that almost sounded like Bear was saying, 'Hi.'

Jarvis heard this sound and stopped and then he heard it again. Only a little different this time. When Rascal greeted Bear, he started coming up Rascal's trail toward him. Rascal said, "No, Bear, I don't want to play today."

Jarvis clearly heard this and wondered who Rascal was talking with.

Rascal turned around ignoring Bear and continued hunting. Jarvis started moving again, cantering towards Rascal. He could hear branches snapping. Then he saw Bear following behind Rascal. And he watched as Bear reached out and tripped Rascal and he fell in the snow. Bear laughed again and the hair on the back of his neck stood on end. Then Bear grabbed Rascal's hat in his teeth, that had fallen off, and he ran off.

Jarvis just stood there wondering what in hell he had just witnessed.

Rascal stood up and watched as Bear ran off and then he continued hunting. Jarvis went back on his original course. Time was passing and about a quarter of a mile from the road Jarvis and Rascal heard Marcel shoot. Just one shot was better than two or three. Jarvis stood still for a few minutes listening and suddenly a huge ten point buck stopped maybe forty yards straight ahead. Jarvis didn't waste any time, he sighted in at the base of the buck's throat and squeezed the trigger. The deer dropped in his tracks.

Rascal stopped and waited a few moments and went over to help Jarvis. When he arrived Jarvis had the deer almost cleaned. "Nice buck. I wonder if Marcel has one or if he was shooting at this one."

They grabbed the deer by the antlers and dragged it to the road, where Marcel had another buck, eight point, dressed off.

"Too bad there wasn't a third deer for you Rascal," Marcel said.

"If I don't get one, no big problem. Two of my guests only took the head and capes. They gave the meat to Em and me. So we have deer meat."

Jarvis looked at Rascal, "What happened Rascal, did you fall down? There's snow all over you. And where's your hat?"

Rascal felt the top of his head and said, "I must have come out without it."

Jarvis let it alone from there. But he was more curious now than ever. If he didn't know better, it looked to him like that Bear was playing with Rascal. And then he thought, *If I had a bear for a playmate I don't think I would tell anyone either.*

"Back there a ways, I cut a real fresh bear track. A big brute too. You must have seen it, Rascal; his tracks were heading towards you."

"That must have been the noise I heard behind me."

Jarvis didn't say anymore. He turned around so Rascal wouldn't see him smiling. On the inside he was laughing, and boy would he like to know the whole story.

They walked back to the lodge and went back after the two deer with the crawler. "We can put them both in the bucket."

There was still a few minutes before dinner would be ready so the three men sat in the living room area of the cafeteria with a pot of coffee, talking.

"Did you have any more problems with your guests

bringing loaded guns inside the lodge or shooting animals for fun?" Marcel asked.

"No, actually they were all very good. After supper on Sunday evenings, I explain the lodge rules and that seems to work pretty well.

"What happened with those two you took out of here?"

"Judge Hulcurt said the usual fine would have been $50.00 but considering the wanton act and the fact that when you asked Harry about the handgun and he told you to go to hell, Hulcurt fined them each $100.00 and two days in jail."

"What about Harry's jaw?"

"I had to take him to the hospital and the doctor wired his jaw closed and for six weeks he'll have to eat through a straw."

"I'm glad he didn't come as a hunter," Emma said. "You can carve the turkey now, Rascal."

"With the village gone now, Emma, don't you ever get lonely?" Rita asked.

"Not yet, we have been busy enough so we haven't had time to be lonely. It may be different this winter with no one else around. If we do, we'll come out and visit you, Rita."

After they had finished eating, it didn't take the four women long to clean up. While they were doing that Rascal started the fire in the ram-down heater upstairs and filled all of the wood boxes.

After everyone had gathered in the living room, Emma said, "I think this is a special occasion and I think it requires something special."

She left and came back with a tray of seven glasses and two bottles of wine. There wasn't one word spoken about prohibition.

Once Emma had filled their glasses she raised her glass and said, "Here's to good friends."

Everyone now raised their glass and said all together, "To good friends."

Rascal disappeared then and came back with some sharp cheese and smoked brook trout.

"Oh, wow, is this good," Arlene said.

"Did you smoke this, Rascal?" Jarvis asked.

"Em and I did."

They stayed up into the night sampling smoked trout, cheese and washing it down with wine. Again strange thoughts were going through Jarvis' head. He knew it had been Emma who had written the letter to Sheriff Burlock about the making of brandy. And the men had all spent one night in jail, all because of Emma. And here she was now serving wine. Boy, what a juxtaposition she was. And then there's Rascal and the secrets he was keeping. He burst out laughing then and everyone looked at him and he pretended he had choked on some cheese.

It was midnight before they all went to bed.

Emma was tired and she wanted to go to sleep but Rascal was still thinking about Bear and he wanted to tell her about it. "I had another run in with Bear today."

"Did anyone see you?"

"I don't think so. Jarvis and I were hunting alongside the valley towards the road where you shot your deer when I came across the bear track that Jarvis must have spooked. Then I heard something behind me and it was Bear. He came up behind me and tripped me like he did when you were with me. He took my hat in his teeth and ran off."

Emma began laughing so hard she began coughing. "I hope he doesn't follow you home like a little dog."

"Yeah, me too."

* * *

During the night Anita decided to return to Beech Tree and her sister, so when Emma saw her bags were packed she was surprised. "No, it's better this way, Emma. My sister is older than me and we'll be good company this winter. I would like to come back for next year hunting season if you should need help with the sport fishermen, just call."

"I'll do that, Anita, and thank you."

Goodbyes were said and they boarded the train for Beech Tree, leaving Rascal and Emma by themselves until spring fishing.

It was cold standing on the platform. There was a cold wind from the north blowing clouds of snow down along the frozen lake. Emma went inside and Rascal had traps to tend.

With all the excitement of their first year running the lodge and as busy as he had been, his heart wasn't into trapping. He pulled all his traps that day and did have four martin, one bobcat and a lynx. "Not bad for one day's work." He explained to Emma why he had pulled everything.

"We should get two more bottles of propane gas."

"And maybe more gasoline, just in case," Rascal said. "And we should take some of the money we have to the bank."

* * *

They left some money in the safe and they rented a safe deposit box in the Beech Tree Bank and put some money in that and the rest in their bank account.

That winter they made plans for the coming spring fishing and they made some improvements to the lodge. When the ice was about sixteen inches thick Rascal spent a day cutting ice for the cold storage during warmer months. He used the new crawler with the bucket to haul the ice blocks to the cellar entrance.

To keep the chickens warm during the winter Rascal found a new kerosene heater in the old general store. Turned on low and it provided enough heat to keep them warm. They were beginning to lay eggs now and Rascal let the rooster breed one chicken so they would have chickens to eat as well as for eggs.

President Warren Harding took the oath of office soon after the first of the year.

On one trip to town, Emma insisted that they purchase a new console radio. "When you're out working somewhere,

Rascal, I need to hear people talking, even if only on the radio."
He didn't refuse. In fact in the evenings they would sit by the fireplace and listen to the local and world news. Emma would listen to the music channels as she worked all day inside.

Rascal waited until early March to sell his fur to Jarvis and for the five pieces Jarvis paid him $250.00.

The economy was better, even before the outbreak of Europe's War. There was now a wider selection for goods and it seemed as new inventions were being revealed every day.

By mid-March requests for fishing started arriving. Not so many that any week would be a sellout, but the fishing end of the lodge was beginning to look better.

In April during the mud season, Jeters arrived to visit for two days and Emma was as glad to see him as Rascal.

Rascal had to build a bigger smoker. Now all of the fishing sports wanted to take home some smoke cured trout. And there was the occasional large brookie or togue that the sport wanted mounted. And this was good business for Jarvis as well.

Rascal and Emma saw very little of Marcel. He knew Rascal wasn't going to ruin the reputation of the lodge and he knew Rascal was quite capable of keeping their guests in check. On occasion he did take the train to the border and look for new signs of Canadian hunters. But most of his time now was being spent around Hitchcock's new village and farm at Kidney Pond.

In mid-July Rascal received a telephone call from the station master in Beech Tree that beaver were a nuisance again at mile nine.

"What are you going to do?"

"I'll have to take care of it."

"What about Bear?" Emma asked.

"Maybe he won't be around."

"Can you walk down and back again?"

"I think I'll be okay."

"I think I should go with you. We only have four guests this week and Anita can take care of things while we're gone.

"Okay, we leave after breakfast tomorrow."

With a full pack basket, axe and Emma insisted he take his .45 handgun, they started walking the tracks to mile nine.

They were all day catching beaver. When the afternoon southbound went through the engineer blew the whistle. They removed six beaver and Rascal was sure that that was all there was. And there was no sign of Bear until they started to leave. They were just beginning to walk between the rails when Bear came out to the cleared right-of-way and gave them his usual call of hello and when Rascal answered him, he walked back into the woods to finish eating beaver carcasses that they had left.

"Well, at least he didn't chase us or trip you or run off with your hat this time."

The next morning Rascal called the station master and told him the beaver were all gone. "The track crew will be up probably tomorrow to clean the culvert. I'll send you a check for $50.00 Rascal."

"How is it, Rascal, that Bear always seems to know where you'll be?"

"I have never thought that much about it, but I think you're on to something. I wish I knew, there's no evidence of him staying around the clearing and watching for me to leave. I wish you hadn't said anything. Now I'll be looking for answers."

"He seems to have formed a bond with you."

* * *

In the dog days of summer in August there were not any late reservations and Rascal, Emma and Anita breathed a sigh of relief.

On the front page of the newspaper on August 3rd, 1923, in big bold letters:

President Warren Harding Dies of a Heart Attack

Rascal jumped up from his chair in the living room and turned the radio on. It was on the news. "Hey, Em, Anita, you'd better come and listen to this!" he hollered to them out in the kitchen.

"What in the world are you hollering about, Rascal?"

"You'd better listen to this."

The broadcaster repeated the news again, "While on a western speaking tour, President Harding died from a heart attack yesterday on August 2nd while in San Francisco. Vice President Kevin Cutlidge was visiting his family in Plymouth Notch, Vermont when he received word by messenger. At 2:47am, the elder Cutlidge, being a notary public and a justice of the peace, in the illumination of a kerosene lantern, in the family parlor, administered the oath of office to his son and now President Kevin Cutlidge."

Rascal switched the radio off and the three of them sat speechless at the table.

The next day things returned to normal at the lodge. In September there were two parties of man and wife the first week and two single men each for the last two weeks.

At breakfast one morning Rascal said, "If you can, Em, I need your help today mowing the hay field at the farm."

"Will you be okay, Anita, alone?" Emma asked.

"Sure, you go ahead."

"I'll fix some sandwiches to take with us and some water."

While Emma was fixing a lunch to take, Rascal started the model T tractor and hooked onto the mower.

"I think you'll be more comfortable riding on the mower out to the farm."

It took them fifteen minutes by tractor where they would have been a half hour walking. Emma put the sandwiches and water on the farmhouse porch. The first trip around was slow, but after that the mowing went better. By noon they had half of the field down and decided to break for lunch.

When they had finished eating, Rascal said, "Your turn

on the tractor. You've seen how I have been doing it. Just do the same. I know it is a little dusty on the mower." Emma didn't argue with him.

Rascal started it for her and the tractor jumped a little when she first let the clutch out.

"Rascal!" she hollered with alarm. "Bear! That SOB is in the middle of the field."

"Just keep going, Em. Maybe he'll wander off."

But he didn't wander off. He sat there in the middle watching as they went round and round mowing strips of hay. Coming closer with each pass.

They were coming close now. Only four more passes. "He hasn't moved, Rascal. What do we do?"

"Keep mowing. I think he'll eventually move on."

Move on he did; he stepped in behind the mowing machine and began following. Once in a while he chewed on a mouthful of freshly cut clover.

When the last swarth had been cut Emma asked, "Now what? He is still following us."

"Don't stop. We still have to mow the outside strip."

So she set over and began the outside. She had to go slower because of the overhanging tree branches and other obstacles. Bear continued following. "You know!" Emma hollered back, "I really think he is lonely."

When they had finished that last strip, Emma asked, "Now what?"

"We go home, but I need to bring the cutter bar up and bolt it."

"Good luck with that."

Emma stopped and Rascal climbed off the mower machine seat and lifted the cutter bar, all the while keeping an eye on Bear. He bolted the bracket that holds the cutter bar up. Bear was still standing behind the mower.

"Well, Bear, we need to leave now and go home," and he climbed back on the seat.

"Okay, let's go."

Emma started for home and Rascal turned to look at Bear. "Goodbye, Bear."

Bear stopped following and stood on his hind legs and reached out with his paw and made that same sound. Rascal tried to mimic the same sound. "You talking to Bear again?"

Emma turned around to look. Bear was still on his hind legs. "Goodbye, Bear," she said.

Bear reached out with his paw again. "He's waving goodbye, Rascal." She waved back. Bear stood there watching them disappear.

"Do you want to do our field now, Rascal?"

"Might as well."

"Do you want to take over driving?"

"You're doing a good job."

That night as they were lying in bed, Emma said, "I would sure hate to have anything happen to Bear."

"Yeah, I know what you mean, me too."

Chapter 12

During the deer season that year each week there was a hunter who would get lost from the lodge. They were all novices to the woods and although they each carried a compass, not one of them knew how to use it.

A few does were taken that year and two fourteen point bucks, that weighed 235 pounds. Those two hunters wanted the head mounted and they gave the meat to the Ambroses and Anita.

At the end of the season, Emma and Rascal asked Anita to stay on at the lodge permanently, and without any hesitation she said, "Oh yes, I'd love to and maybe go out and visit my sister when we aren't busy."

Again this year Jarvis, Rita and Marcel and Arlene joined Rascal, Emma and Anita for Thanksgiving and this time instead of taking the train back with them Anita was staying on. Every year after that the group of friends would meet at Whiskey Jack Lodge for Thanksgiving and some late-season deer hunting.

In December, Rudy and his wife, Althea, came for a visit and to inspect the old mill and the farm.

They were surprised with what Rascal and Emma had done to the old hotel. "It really looks like a sporting lodge. How has your business been?"

"We don't know what we would do if we were any busier," Emma said.

They were happy to learn that Anita was working there. "She lives with us now. Anita is part of our family," Emma had said.

Rudy was quite satisfied how Rascal had been taking care of things. The bushes and weeds were even cut back around the old mill, the farmhouse and outbuildings.

"Everything looks in perfect order, Rascal. I couldn't have asked for a better man for the job."

They left two days later feeling confident that things were being well looked after.

In the 1924 presidential election, President Kevin Cutlidge won a landslide victory against John W. Davis, taking thirty-five states, while Davis only took twelve.

The economy was good and businesses and workers alike were making money, so the general outlook was why change presidents when everybody was doing so well.

After his inauguration in 1925 President Cutlidge had big plans for the United States. But it was going to take a lot of secret behind-doors kind of work to pull it off.

One evening in early May of that year he had invited Raymond Butler, the head of his Secret Service, to join him in his private study at midnight.

"Come in, Raymond, and please sit down. I need to ask you to perform a very special detail for me."

"Yes, Sir."

"And I must have your complete cooperation and secrecy. Do I have it Ray?"

"Yes, Mr. President, you do. Always, Sir."

"Good. Tomorrow you officially go on vacation. A fishing trip to northern Maine, at a hunting and fishing lodge at Whiskey Jack Lake, north of Beech Tree. You'll take the train to Portland and switch to the Canadian and Atlantic Railroad and purchase passage to Whiskey Jack Lodge. You are to travel in attire that you are going fishing, with fishing gear. No suits and ties.

"At Whiskey Jack I want you to reserve the entire lodge for the full week of November 8th. You'll have government vouchers to pay ahead for this.

"When you make the reservation you are only to say that a government official is requesting this. I do not want them to know it'll be me until the day I arrive.

"This lodge is only accessible by railroad. There are no roads within miles of what was once a lumbering village. All that remains now is the lodge.

"After you have everything squared away at Whiskey Jack Lodge, I want you to return to Beech Tree and confidentially locate Jarvis Page at Page's Furrier. Mr. Page is a retired Game Warden and probably by far the most capable officer in the entire state. I have done my research, Ray.

"You are to talk with Mr. Page only, and you must have his confidentiality about this. I don't want him even telling his wife what he will be doing.

"When I leave here, Ray, you and two other secret service men, at your choosing, will accompany me to Beech Tree. All four of us will be dressed as hunters. I will be using the name, David Elliot.

"Mr. Page will accompany me to Whiskey Jack from Beech Tree. You and your men will remain in Beech Tree and make sure no one boards the train for Whiskey Jack. I figured it would be best if I was with someone the locals know. Less questions that way."

"Yes, Sir."

"Inquire from Mr. Page about a capable guide for the week. Let the choice be his and his responsibility that all this is kept confidential."

"Yes, Sir.

"When you have things squared with Mr. Page, I want you to talk with Sam Grindle, the Canadian and Atlantic supervisor there in Beech Tree. His office is upstairs at the main depot. Without telling him much, be sure he understands no passengers will be allowed to board the train for Whiskey Jack during that week.

"Are you okay with this so far, Ray?"

"Completely, Sir."

"Good. At the end of the week on Saturday, Mr. Page and I will meet you at the depot.

"Now, I am spending the week hunting and meeting with a very important person and if this goes as I hope, our country will definitely benefit from our meeting. But this must remain quiet and under wraps until I am ready to propose it to Congress."

"Yes, Sir."

"Any questions?"

"Yes, Sir, one."

"And?"

"This all seems like a thorough plan, but how are you going to explain your absence?"

"I'm going to have to work on that. I may have to bring the VP in on this for a diversion.

"Now here are enough vouchers for you to take care of this business."

"I won't fail you, Mr. President."

* * *

"Emma?"

"Yes, what is it?"

"Did we have any sports scheduled for this week?"

"No, why?"

"Well, one just stepped off the train and he appears to be well equipped."

The train left and Rascal went out to meet their new guest. "I understand this is Whiskey Jack Lodge and famous for fishing. I didn't make a reservation but I hope you have room for me?"

"Certainly, come in. The ice just went out of the lake. It's usually a little early for fishing but you never know until you try."

"That's okay, my name is Raymond Butler."

Emma booked him and said, "Your room is at the top of the stairs and the first door on the right."

"Thank you." Butler went up and left everything there and then came back down. "What time would lunch be served?"

"Noon."

"I've been cramped up on trains for too long, I think I'll walk about and stretch some muscles and breathe in some of this fresh air."

He left and wandered around outside checking things over and making sure no one else was there except for the three of them. Although he had only seen the man and woman so far, there was supposed to be an older woman, the cook.

The president had been correct, there was no way into this area except by train. He had chosen well. He returned by noon and food was already on the table.

"Fish chowder with egg salad sandwich, Mr. Butler."

"It smells delicious. Do you do all of your own cooking, ma'am?

"My name is Emma, not ma'am. There is an older woman and friend who does most of the cooking. She is out visiting her sister now for a few days."

"Doesn't it get lonely out here, I mean just the two of you?"

"You get used to it. We do miss the village that used to be here."

Rascal told him all about the Hitchcock Company and the village.

"How is the hunting here?"

"Excellent."

"I take it we are here alone," Butler said.

"Yes, and why?"

"I have come for a special reason from Washington DC. I have no intentions of fishing."

"Maybe you had better tell us what you want Mr. Butler, if that is your name," Rascal said.

"On November 8th, an individual from Washington will be arriving here for the week. There will be a highly classified meeting between two men. They both will pose as hunters. I need to secure your full compliment for that week. At this time I am not at liberty to tell you who the two men will be. But they each will be traveling with guards at all times.

"Now that you understand this what is your full compliment?"

"Twelve here and two or four more across the cove in our cabin," Rascal said.

"How much per hunter for a week?"

"$125.00 each per week. We had to increase our fee this year as the cost for everything we need here has increased."

"So that's $2000.00 for the week. Here is a government voucher for that amount, redeemable at any bank."

They took the voucher.

"During that week no one will be allowed into Whiskey Jack and the Canadian and Atlantic superintendent will be told not to make any unauthorized stops that week.

"Are you okay with this so far?"

"Yes."

"You will not know who is coming until the train arrives on the morning of the 8th. Everything I have said to you must stay confidential. You are not allowed to talk with anyone until after that week. Not even Mrs. Antony. There will be no need of her knowing anything until November 8th. It will be a penalty of law if you violate this trust.

"Do you have anyone already booked for that week?"

Rascal turned to Emma, "No, so far only the two weeks in October."

"Any questions?"

"Will these two men require any special food?" Emma asked.

"No, I'm sure whatever you serve your guests will be sufficient."

Rascal just had to ask, "Mr. Butler, do you know what these two men will be discussing?"

"No, and even if I did I am not allowed to say.

"I must say you two have a very unique arrangement here and no roads into this lake. Very unique indeed.

"We have covered a lot; are you sure you understand everything?"

Rascal and Emma looked at each other and both said at the same time, "Yes."

"Good, when does the afternoon train come through?"

"When it has to stop here it usually departs at 2 pm."

"It looks as if I will be able to make the afternoon train. I still have to talk with C&A's superintendent. But that may have to wait until tomorrow.

"And now Mrs. Ambrose could I trouble you for another bowl of that delicious chowder?"

"Certainly, and would you like a biscuit with it?"

"Yes, please."

While Emma was warming another bowl of fish chowder Rascal and Raymond Butler kept talking. Butler was particularly interested how the lodge came to be, "I mean, it is apparent, Mr. Ambrose, that there was a mill here once."

"Please, drop the mister, everyone calls me Rascal."

"Okay, somehow I believe that name suits you very well."

"It does, or at least my grandmother thought so. She gave it to me."

Then Rascal told him all about the Hitchcock Company, the village, the people, the farm and even about the old retired game warden, Jarvis Page. "You didn't get along with Page?" Butler asked.

"He is probably the best friend I ever had. He's had me in court and in jail and he has eaten at our table and slept in our home. He was a man with a big wilderness to patrol, and all alone. He did his job and there will never be another like him. And I'm proud to call him my friend. Every Thanksgiving

Jarvis and his wife, Rita, and the new game warden, Marcel Cyr, and his wife ,Arlene, come for dinner and stay over a couple of nights now.

"Jarvis even took Emma to jail once for shooting a deer in closed season."

"And the two of you still stay friends with him? Unbelievable. I wish I could have been around here then."

Rascal got up and put out the red flag, for the train to stop, and Emma brought Butler another bowl of chowder and a biscuit and a cup of cold milk.

"How in the world do you keep milk this cold way out here in the wilderness?"

"We have a cold storage room in the cellar and Rascal cuts ice in the winter and buries it in sawdust in the room. The ice usually will last until about December. We do have electricity here, Mr. Butler. We have a small generator. We also have mail service every day and a telephone."

"Not so backwards as I was thinking. My apologies.

"These are the finest tasting biscuits I have ever eaten."

"Thank you."

The engineer blew the engine whistle. "What was that?" Butler asked.

"The train is approaching. You better get out there, Mr. Butler. The engineer likes to keep on schedule."

"Emma, it has been a pleasure meeting you."

Rascal waited on the platform for Butler. "Rascal, I have enjoyed talking with you and thank you." He boarded the train and the engineer blew the steam whistle again and the train lurched forward.

When the train was out of sight they walked back inside not saying a word, until they sat down opposite each other at the table.

"What do you think of that, Rascal?"

"If I had not been here I would not have believed it."

"Who do you suppose is coming in November?"

"The president wouldn't come all the way up here from Washington, would he? Congressmen maybe, governors? I haven't the slightest idea," Rascal said.

"Maybe a couple of generals? Whoever it is must be very important to take all of these precautions," Emma said.

"And maybe it is best if we just forget about it until then."

* * *

Raymond Butler was able to catch Sam Grindle still in his office. He identified himself and told him of the president's visit. Only he used a pseudonym name, David Elliot. Mr. Grindle said there wouldn't be any problem and Butler also swore him to secrecy with the penalty of a violation if he leaked any information.

It was now evening and Butler didn't want to impose at this hour so he found a hotel and would talk with Jarvis Page in the morning.

"Hello, are you Jarvis Page?"

"Yes, what can I do for you?"

"My name is Raymond Bulter and I must talk with you. It is extremely important that we can talk without interruptions. Is Mrs. Page here?"

"No she isn't. And what is this all about?"

"Mr. Page, I am from Washington and Chief of the Secret Service Agency. Now, can we talk privately?"

"Mrs. Page is shopping and I don't expect anyone soon."

"Good, I'll get right to the point. On the morning of November 8th there will be an important individual coming to Beech Tree on the train and switch trains for Whiskey Jack. I and two of my associates will be accompanying a David Elliot. We will be remaining here as part of our detail and you have been asked to accompany Mr. Elliot by train to Whiskey Jack where he will meet another important person. You are to be Mr.

Elliot's personal body guard during that duration. Can you do this?"

"I can, but tell me more."

"I have no idea what will be discussed at this meeting but it is obviously important. Mr. Elliot and his counterpart both expect to deer hunt while they are there and I have been asked also to inquire about two guides. I understand, Mr. Page, that you are a retired Maine Game Warden. Those credentials will certainly suffice as one guide. And I am sure you are already quite familiar with that wilderness. What I need from you is your recommendation for a second guide. Do you know someone who would fit the bill?"

"Hell yes, the owner of the lodge, Rascal Ambrose. He is without question the best guide in this entire area."

"Then that will be ideal. Now, Mr. Page do you have any reservation about being Mr. Elliot's personal guard for that week?"

"No, I would enjoy it."

"There is one stipulation, Mr. Page, if you accept this job."

"And?"

"Because of the nature of this you will be under oath not to divulge a word of this to anyone, not even your wife. Do you think you can go to Whiskey Jack for a week without telling your wife the real reason behind your going?"

"That won't be a problem."

"Good, then here is a government voucher for $200.00. That should cover your expense and a fee as guard and guide. By accepting this you agree under oath the conditions I have set forth."

"I accept."

"Good. You will not hear from me again. Be at the train terminal the morning of November 8th. We will all be dressed as sport hunters."

As Butler was leaving Rita returned and she asked, "Who was that gentleman, Jarvis?"

"Oh him, he was a fur buyer from Canada. I told him we sell our fur pelts on the Ontario fur auction."

* * *

Three days later, Raymond Butler reported back to President Cutlidge. "How did it go?"

"Very well, Mr. President. Everything on that end is all in place. All you have to do now is make sure you are at the Canadian and Atlantic train terminal in Beech Tree before 7 am on November 8th.

"I have no idea what you are planning sir, but you could not have picked a more isolated and convenient place, safe from intruders."

"What did you think of Rascal and Emma Ambrose?"

"Two very unique people, Mr. President. Retired game warden Jarvis Page highly recommended Rascal as the second guide. Although he does have a limp, apparently he doesn't let it slow him down."

"He was wounded twice in France, Ray, and almost died."

"I didn't know that sir."

"Thank you for your work, Raymond. That'll be all."

Chapter 13

Emma and Rascal went back to work trying not to think too much about their guests on November 8th. This year, the first in three years, Rascal was able to pick a huge mess of fiddleheads along Jack Brook. Some Emma kept near the ice to keep them fresh as long as possible and she canned most of them. She dill-pickled four quarts the same as she would cucumber pickles. The field behind the lodge had turned yellow the year before with dandelions, so after the fiddleheads Rascal picked and cleaned and Emma canned.

They were having regular fishing guests in every week now and Anita had returned from visiting her sister a week after they had talked with Mr. Butler. Many of the guests were now regulars and didn't need or want a guide. Except for Al and Beverly Cummings. They were making this a yearly trip now as much to visit with Rascal and Emma as it was to fish.

Before the woods dried out from the spring thaw, Jeters came to visit and fish. He stayed two nights and left on the third morning. They told him about the antics of Bear. "He knocked me down while I was hunting and then he ran off with my hat. Never did find the hat."

"And when we mowed the farm field he stayed in the middle of the field the whole time watching. When we started to leave he followed behind us for a short distance. Then Rascal said goodbye to Bear and he stood up and waved goodbye and made that same sound."

"I also had to remove beaver again at mile nine, and when I was done he followed me up the tracks for a ways."

"I sure would like to know why he does that," Jeters said.

"Well, I think you got it right when you said he's lonely."

"It's still odd don't you think? I mean a wild bear—and a big one—picking a human to befriend?"

"No one in this entire world would ever believe it."

"We see him in different places now, not just at mile twelve. But he stays clear of the lodge. We see deer in the field all the time, and an occasional moose."

"As I see it, he will always remain a mystery," Jeters said.

* * *

Rascal was smoking fish almost every day now. If not for the sports to take back with them, then for he, Emma and Anita.

Anita was the happiest now that she could ever remember. Her living quarters were nice and she looked at Emma and Rascal as her children.

In June a crew of four arrived on the morning train to make repairs to the tracks a half mile north of Whiskey Jack. They also unloaded a hand railcar for the crew. There were two empty rooms in the lodge and the other two stayed in the log cabin and took their meals in the cafeteria. Each morning Emma would put up a lunch for the crew to take with them.

Four days later before they left on the southbound train, Emma gave the foreman an itemized invoice for room and meals. It wasn't as much as the sports had to pay.

When he could Rascal would go frogging. Emma wanted a good supply of frog legs to serve to their two special guests in November. And each day he went frogging he would also catch one or two large brookies that were excellent for smoking.

This year when they mowed the farm hayfield, Bear was again in the middle of the field. And at the far southwest corner in the knee-deep clover was a mother bear and two cubs. "Those have to be his offspring." Rascal said.

"He looks like he is in the middle watching over them," Emma said. "What do we do about the mother and two cubs?"

"When we start for that corner, my guess is she and the cubs will leave."

"I hope you're right, I wonder if he is here safeguarding his family?" Emma said.

"Maybe, but that doesn't explain his attachment to me."

"You know, Rascal, maybe that's his way of thanking you for all the beaver carcasses you have left for him. And now the many deer innards left when our guests shoots a deer." She had to stop talking and pay more attention to what they were doing.

Bear stayed in the middle of the field until they were only one pass away and he begrudgingly stood and stretched and stepped aside to let them pass and then he stepped in behind them and followed as they mowed the outside swathe. When Emma stopped the tractor Rascal climbed off the machine and lifted and bolted the cutter bar in place and then climbed on the seat and he turned around and said to Bear, "Bear, sure would like to know why you are so friendly."

Bear stood up on his hind legs and reached out with his paw and making those same noises. "He's talking to you, Rascal."

"Emma, I've just gotta try something." Without asking what, she knew what he had in mind.

He climbed off the mower and started walking around the tractor towards the road. And sure enough, Bear was following. Then Rascal started running and Bear gave chase. Rascal couldn't run very fast because of his leg. And Bear surely could have out distanced him. But he didn't, he kept close behind Rascal. Emma followed with the tractor.

It wasn't long before Rascal began tiring and slowing down. This is when Bear took advantage and tripped him. Rascal fell in a heap, all while laughing. Bear sat down on his butt about ten feet away and Emma was sure Bear was also laughing as he made that noise again.

Rascal picked himself up and said, "Okay, Bear, that's enough. I'm too tired to play anymore," and he climbed back on the mower seat. Bear sat there watching as they disappeared down the road.

Before driving out into the field at the lodge, Emma stopped and turned around in her seat and looking at Rascal, she began to laugh almost hysterically. Rascal sat there with a big grin on his face. Finally she said, "You're a clown, Rascal. No wonder Bear likes to play with you."

They waited until the next morning to mow the field. Now it was time to work on firewood. There were two cord of wood left after the cold winter months. But Rascal intended to work up just as much, just in case.

Using the bucket he could lift the logs up off the ground some so he didn't have to bend over as much. He figured he had two months to finish the firewood.

By the end of September they saw the last of the sport fishermen, the firewood was done and Emma figured they now had twenty or twenty-five pounds of smoked trout. The frogs were already hibernating in the mud but Emma had actually canned ten quarts this year. "I wish we had some beaver for our special guests while they're here."

"Well, maybe just before the deer season opens, I can go up behind the log cabin and trap."

* * *

He left home one morning a week later with his pack basket, traps and paraphernalia and headed out behind the log cabin. He had seen a new colony out there two years ago but had not been able to trap it. There was a chill in the air and Rascal was feeling good. The flowage was much bigger now and he went to work setting four traps in troughs on the dam, in two runs and one in the small inlet stream. When he had finished setting he went back to the dam and had three beaver.

At the end of that day he had taken seven extra-large beaver. This would be enough. He was up late that night putting all the hides on drying boards. The next day they canned sixteen quarts of beaver meat. "This we will not serve to our guests. It will be for the two coming in November whoever they are. The rest will be for us this winter," Emma said.

There were more beaver there but he had taken enough for what he wanted. He had thought about setting some land sets, but the next week they would be busy with hunters so he decided against it.

They no longer saw very much of Marcel Cyr. As he had said before, most of his work was now around Kidney Pond. Rascal was beginning to wonder if he was patrolling the border for illegal hunters like Jarvis used to do. If he was traveling back and forth by train he wasn't even stepping off long enough to say hello. And then perhaps the two poachers Jarvis and Marcel had arrested and taken to Beech Tree had stopped the poaching in that area.

The first week hunters were usually mostly novices who had no experience in the woods, let alone so far in the wilderness as Whiskey Jack. The first two weeks of hunting never produced big deer—hardly. And the more experienced hunter was aware of this and booked their hunt in November, only this year the week of November 8th, the fourth week, was already full up and many hunters wanting that week found it difficult to accept.

That first week there were two lost hunters. Two friends hunting didn't return to the lodge for supper and Rascal spent most of the night looking for them out at the farm. These two when found were so shaken up by the experience they didn't leave the lodge for the rest of the week.

No one made fun of them or ridiculed them. As they, too, were uneasy about how expansive this wilderness was. For many it wasn't what they were expecting.

* * *

The southbound train stopped at the lodge without a red flag being displayed, and this time the engineer, Luke Davis, climbed down from the engine. Rascal walked over. "What can I do for you, Luke?"

"A half mile up the tracks I hit a big cow moose. There was a calf with her but the calf is okay. The cow though was clipped in the head and she's dead. The whole moose should be salvageable. If you go after it, Rascal—well, me and the boys sure would like some."

"I'll go up now, Luke. You stop here tomorrow and I'll give you half. How's that?"

"I'll stop. See ya tomorrow."

Rascal went inside to tell Emma. "Looks like we'll have some fresh moose meat for next week also. The train just hit a big cow in the head and I'm going up with the crawler and bring it back."

He put a chain and axe in the crawler bucket and he always had his hunting knife on his belt. Walking the crawler up the left side of the tracks wasn't a problem he was just glad the moose wasn't on the other side, where there were wet holes and peppered with boulders.

He saw a flock of ravens circling up ahead and knew they must have seen the dead moose already. He looked around for the calf and it had already run off. "I hope it'll be okay." His first thought was to quarter it and put everything in the bucket but the bucket wasn't big enough.

He pulled the innards out and hooked the chain around the neck and then to the bucket. When he lifted the bucket only the hind legs now would drag. He was a lot longer backing all the way to the lodge.

The game pole at the lodge was rugged enough to support the weight of the moose, plus it was in the shade. It didn't take him long to skin it. He split open the brisket and removed the heart and liver and took those to the kitchen. "Oh my, Rascal," Anita said, "there's enough to feed heart, liver and onions to everyone for supper."

Rascal split the body, down the backbone into two halves. It was cool enough so the meat would not spoil.

He made two wooden boxes from slab wood to put one half of the moose in for the train crew.

That night the temperature really dropped and while the moose meat was still cold he sectioned it off and put it in the cold storage room. He would cut the steaks from it later.

It was now Friday the 6th of November and Emma was becoming nervous and anxious about their two special guests who would be arriving in two days.

Rascal kept walking around, inside and outside the lodge and up to the log cabin, making sure everything was picked up and cleaned and ready. He even collected fresh eggs twice that day. Anita saw that both Rascal and Emma were acting nervously and wondered why.

Saturday afternoon all the guests left on the afternoon southbound. As the three were eating supper, Anita asked, "Alright you two, what is going on? For three days you both have been walking around inspecting everything and as nervous as a cat with a long tail laying under a rocking chair. What's up?"

"We have been under strict orders, Anita, not to say anything until now." Anita looked at each of them quizzically.

"Tomorrow morning, Anita, two very special people are arriving and they will be the only guests we'll have all week."

She asked the obvious question, "Who?"

"We don't know. This was all arranged six months ago and we don't know who is coming. So in the morning, Anita, I'd like you to dress up a little." She turned to Rascal and said, "You too, Rascal."

"And I suppose you expect me to take a bath tonight, too?"

She didn't answer him. She only looked at him. That told him all he wanted to know.

* * *

President Cutlidge had to tell the Vice President Charles Dawes where he was going but not why. "This is a very important meeting, Charles. I'll leave you a telephone number and that is all. I have said nothing until now because this meeting, until it is over, must be kept in the strictest confidentiality. It will become clear when I return. As far as anyone knows, my wife and I are spending several days at Camp David, by ourselves. The Director of Secret Services and two others will be accompanying me.

"We leave for Camp David tomorrow morning and I will leave at 10 pm tomorrow night for my meeting."

"Yes, Mr. President," that's all he could say.

President Cutlidge had to tell his wife something, but only as little as he had to. When he left Camp David in escort with three Secret Service Agents no one's curiosity was aroused.

On the way to the train station, the president put on a wig and mustache to hide his real identity.

When they boarded the train as far as anyone could tell they were three hunters traveling north.

* * *

Jarvis had told his wife, Rita, that Rascal had asked him to guide the week and he would be back the following week.

At 6 o'clock on the morning of November 8th Jarvis left the house dressed in hunting attire, rifle and a traveling bag. He knew he would be early but he hated the idea of having others wait for him.

The train pulled in right on schedule and Jarvis met Agent Butler inside. "Jarvis Page, this is your charge David Elliot. Now the three of us will take our leave." And Agent Butler and the two others left.

After the train was moving Jarvis checked the other passenger and freight car to make sure they were traveling alone.

"Is everything satisfactory, Mr. Page?"

"Yes, we are alone."

"Good," and President Cutlidge removed his wig and mustache.

Jarvis grinned and said, "I knew Mr. Elliot must be an important person, but I never expected the President of the United States."

"Now that you know who I am, do you have any reservations about your duties?"

"No, Mr. President, not at all."

"Good, let's talk."

"Yes, Sir."

"Tell me about Rascal and Emma Ambrose. Rascal seems a rather odd name for an adult man."

"Not for Rascal, Sir. His grandmother gave it to him when he was young and he is proud of it."

"I know Rascal was in the war and was wounded twice, but I want to know the man."

"Well, I think of both Rascal and Emma as family. I have always believed there is nothing either one of them wouldn't do to help out a friend. Even if it was to kill an illegal deer for someone who couldn't afford meat. Or get caught with two limits of trout. One being meant for an elder couple."

"Did you ever catch him for anything?"

"Yes, Sir. Once of two limits of trout, and as I said one limit was for the Antonys, and five years ago I charged him with selling two deer to sport hunters. When I was the game warden they would invite me for supper and let me sleep there.

"I arrested his wife Emma once also for shooting a deer in closed season that was eating her lettuce. Rascal and I were standing on the dam when she shot. And he insisted I take her to jail." Jarvis started laughing then. "I believe, always have, that somehow Rascal planned the whole thing. Except I could never understand how he planned for Emma to shoot a deer when I was in the village. I was there purely by chance that morning.

Anyhow I figured he did it to get back at his wife because she had sent a confidential letter to Sheriff Burlock telling him that her husband and some friends were making brandy. I came up with Sheriff Burlock when the four were arrested."

"That's odd. Any animosity between them now?"

"None at all. Like nothing ever happened. And Sir, I'd appreciate it if you didn't bring it up either."

"Of course not. But they both sound like delightful people."

"You'll understand when you get to know them. Anita Antony lost her husband the last winter the village was here, and now she lives with Rascal and Emma and she does much of the cooking. A marvelous cook too.

"Every Thanksgiving since they started operating the old hotel as a sporting lodge they have invited Rita and I and the new game warden, Marcel Cyr, and his wife, Arlene, for Thanksgiving dinner and we stay over one or two nights and we hunt and usually get a nice buck."

"From what you have told me, Mr. Page—"

"Please, just Jarvis."

"Okay. Jarvis, from what you have told me, I can't wait to meet them."

The train blew the steam whistle. "Well Sir, you are about to."

Anita, Emma and Rascal were all standing on the platform in nice clothes. Emma had cut Rascal's hair and made him shave. She and Anita were wearing pretty casual dresses. The passenger car came to a stop. The door opened and Jarvis stepped out. Rascal looked surprised, as did they all. "Jarvis, you aren't supposed to be here."

Jarvis didn't answer. He looked all around with a real serious expression on his face. Then he asked, "Is there anyone here but you three?"

Rascal gave him a short answer, "No."

Jarvis turned and looked back inside the car and nodded

his head and then he stepped back out of the way. President Cutlidge stepped down onto the platform happily. Jarvis then stepped up and said, "I'd like to introduce you, President Cutlidge, to Rascal and Emma Ambrose and Anita Antony." Both women curtseyed. The president shook Rascal's hand and he took Emma's hand instead of shaking it he kissed the back of her hand and then he did Anita's also.

Jarvis retrieved the president's luggage and waved they were all clear and the train left. "You must be tired after your trip, Mr. President, won't you come inside. Anita has just put on a fresh pot of coffee."

Rascal and Jarvis carried his luggage inside. "Upstairs, Jarvis." He followed Rascal up and to the first room on the right. "I guess you are the Secret Service special agent assigned to this detail, Jarvis?"

"Yes."

"Then your room is across the hall. Who is the second person, Jarvis? Do you know?"

"I have no idea. This has all been a mystery."

"You can say that again," Rascal added.

They returned to the cafeteria where Anita and Emma had coffee and donuts on the table.

"I like how this looks. It gives one a comfortable feeling."

"When will this second person arrive, Mr. President?" Rascal asked.

"This afternoon." That meant whoever it was was coming from Canada or perhaps via Canada. That could mean this second person could possibly be anyone.

"I noticed a nice log cabin across the lake. Whose cabin is it?"

"That is ours, Mr. President. When we started this lodge we decided to live here. We have it fixed up for guests and married couples and we thought that might be a better place than here to have your meeting."

"That is very considerate. Thank you. Indeed it will be.

"What about the cabin up beside the tracks?"

Anita answered this one. "That was my husband and my home before he passed away. Now we keep chickens there, Mr. President."

"I have many more questions, but right now I need to lay down for a couple of hours. It has been a long journey here."

"Certainly, Mr. President. We'll call you for lunch," Emma said.

"That would be good."

Jarvis stood up with the president and went upstairs with him and sat in a chair in the hall while the president rested.

"I'm going to change clothes," Rascal said.

"Oh no you're not. We still have one special guest coming and none of us were expecting President Kevin Cutlidge, or, who might the person be that he is waiting for? The Queen of Scots? Who knows. But you aren't changing your clothes, Rascal. Not yet ,anyway." Emma had spoken.

Rascal smiled and walked off.

Anita had to muffle a laugh.

Everyone was working, even Jarvis, but there was nothing he could do without getting his nice clothes dirty. So he sat on the platform in the cool sunshine with yesterday's newspaper.

He tried reading a few articles, but his mind enviably started wondering who was coming in on the southbound train. There was nothing he could do wearing these clothes. He moved back into the cafeteria and sat in the living room with his newspaper. He would like to go upstairs and talk with Jarvis, but he didn't know if he would be allowed to do that. Jarvis was working.

After two and a half hours, Emma said, "Okay Rascal you can tell Jarvis to awaken the president. Lunch is almost ready."

Jarvis heard Emma and he was already knocking on his door. "Mr. President."

"Yes."

"It is time to get up. Lunch is almost ready."

"Okay, I just need to splash some water on my face."

A few minutes later President Cutlidge and Jarvis joined the others. "Sit anywhere you wish, Sir," Emma said.

Anita joined them also. "This chowder surely smells delicious. Hum, and it tastes as good as it smells."

He had a second bowl of chowder and marveled at the fine texture and taste of Emma's biscuits.

"When does the afternoon train arrive?"

"2 o'clock, Mr. President."

"Then I have time for a short walk. I need to walk off some of this fine chowder and biscuits. Maybe I could walk up and look at your log cabin?"

"That would be fine, Mr. President."

"Perhaps, Rascal, you might join Jarvis and me."

"Yes, Sir."

When the three men had left the cafeteria, Emma turned to Anita and said, "We did it. He loved your chowder and my biscuits. How about an apple pie, Anita, for dessert with coffee after supper."

"I'll get right on it. What are you planning for supper, Emma?"

"Moose steaks, baked potato, fresh tomatoes and pickled fiddleheads and biscuits and instead of coffee, maybe cold milk would be a good substitute.

"Wednesday, I want a smorgasbord of different meats and vegetables. You know, Anita, next year we'll have to try and pickle some cattail stalks, when they're young. I have always heard they are good."

As they were walking by the old mill, the president asked, "Will the company ever come back and restart the mill?"

"The company is at Kidney Pond now and Mr. Hitchcock said there are designers working on a special design for the military and much of the planes will be made from a special aircraft quality plywood. And there are a lot of real nice hardwood trees on Hitchcock's property. So he said once these planes' designs are approved and tested, there'll be a big demand for high quality hardwood and he expects to come back in then.

The president liked the coziness of the log cabin and said, "This will make for a great place for our meeting. This is really nice.

"Where does the road go over the hill?"

"The road only goes about a quarter of a mile and stops at an old log yard. We probably will be hunting up there before the end of the week."

They walked back to the lodge and just as they were crossing the dam they heard the train whistle. "We're just in time," Rascal said.

Everyone was on the platform to welcome the new guest. Whoever it would be. The passenger car stopped and the door opened and just like President Cutlidge's arrival, a man dressed in a dark suit stepped off first and casually surveyed the old terminal and he turned like Jarvis had done and nodded, and a stately looking gentleman stepped onto the platform. President Cutlidge stepped forward to greet this new arrival.

"Mr. Prime Minister Kingsley, it is a pleasure to see you. May I introduce our hosts for this week. This is Rascal and Emma Ambrose." Like President Cutlidge had done, Prime Minister Kingsley shook Rascal's hand and kissed Emma's.

"And this is Anita Antony." He kissed her hand also. "And this is my personal escort while we are here, Retired Maine Game Warden Jarvis Page." They shook hands.

"And this is my escort, Francois Dubois." Mr. Kingsley had more luggage than President Cutlidge. Rascal helped Francois with the luggage and showed him to their rooms. Francois spoke perfect English as did Prime Minister Kingsley.

Everyone was in the cafeteria and living room and Emma said, "Supper won't be until 6 o'clock, would anyone like a cup of coffee and a donut or a biscuit?"

"Prime Minister, you should try her biscuits. I have never

tasted such a delight," President Cutlidge said.

Everyone had coffee and biscuits and while the two gentlemen conversed in the living room the others gave them some courtesy and sat at the cafeteria table.

While in the living room the two gentlemen agreed to talk socially and a little shop, but when Prime Minister Kingsley asked, "What is so important that we had to meet covertly?"

"Prime Minister, I understand your curiosity but let us enjoy this day and surroundings and take this day to know each other. Tomorrow we talk business. And the Ambroses have given us the use of their log cabin across the lake."

They finished their coffee and biscuits and President Cutlidge said, "Do you feel like going for a walk, Prime Minister?"

"Yes, I was going to suggest we do."

"Would it be okay, Rascal, if we walked out to the farm?"

Jarvis noticed Rascal look towards Emma before answering. She ever so slightly nodded her head okay.

"Yes, by all means."

The four men stood up to leave, "Rascal, I'd like you to come with us to tell us all about the farm."

"Yes Sir, but I must change my clothes first," and he went into the bedroom and returned shortly. Jarvis was taking all this in. Why did Rascal have to change into working clothes when the others were still in casual clothes.

Rascal was asked to walk with the president and the prime minister while Jarvis and Francois knew their duties and stayed about twenty feet in the rear.

Both men were very interested with the Hitchcock Company. The mill, the village and the farm. But they could see the value in the high grade hardwood trees they could see along the road.

Jarvis noticed how Rascal kept looking at the ground. It was something he often did and he doubted if the other three realized what Rascal was doing. He even stopped once near the field and knelt down to look at tracks. He brushed away the dry leaves and there was a bear track. But not big enough for Bear. "What are you looking at, Rascal?" President Cutlidge asked.

"Bear tracks. I think it is a sow. When Em and I mowed the field here, there was a sow with two cubs down in the further corner. I think this is her track."

"I'd like to shoot a nice bear," President Cutlidge said.

"Not here, Sir. We do not allow any of our guests to shoot bear."

"Why is that, Rascal?"

"Em and I both want Whiskey Jack Lodge to have the reputation for good fishing and deer hunting."

"I guess I can understand that."

"Where did the name Whiskey Jack come from Rascal?"

Rascal explained that there was a man named Jack who, before Hitchcock had built the village, made whiskey and he sold it in Canada as well as shipped much of it south on the train. Then one day the still blew up and Jack's body was never found. Everyone assumed he had been killed in the explosion and his body burned in the fire.

They stopped at the edge of the field and Kingsley said, "What a beautiful location. Could we go inside?"

"I'm the caretaker; I don't see why not." He pulled the nails that held the 2x4 across the door and opened the door. "Jarvis, you can take them through the house."

Jarvis entered first, but he was thinking that this was another oddity about Rascal. If he had not been a game warden and trained investigator he probably would have not noticed. But he did, and this was beginning to bother him.

From the upstairs window he could see Rascal in the field looking for something. What? What was he expecting?

Jarvis caught up to President Cutlidge and Prime Minister Kingsley and Dubois in another bedroom at the other end of the upstairs. When the president looked out of the window he exclaimed, "Good heavens! What is Rascal doing with that bear?"

They all rushed to the window to see. Rascal and Bear were standing about fifty feet apart and Bear was slowly moving towards him. The four men rushed downstairs and outside. "Good heavens, Jarvis, shoot the bear," Cutlidge said.

Many memories were going through Jarvis' head just then. Changing his clothes, the bear running off with his hat, chasing he and Elmo on the handcar. "This is beginning to explain many things, Sir. I don't think we'll have to do anything. I may be wrong, but I don't think so."

Just then Bear stopped and stood on his hind legs and reaching out with his paw, and Rascal doing the same, Bear made that same noise. And so did Rascal. "My word, man!" The prime minister said," I believe that bear just said hi."

"It sounded that way to me, Mr. Prime Minister," Mr. Dubois said.

Then Bear dropped down to all four feet and began running towards Rascal. "Good heavens, Jarvis, do something! He'll maul Rascal," President Cutlidge said.

"Wait. I don't think so."

Rascal began running towards the trees away from the others. Bear soon caught up to him and he tripped Rascal and he went sprawling on the ground. Bear sat on his haunches and made what sounded like he was laughing. Rascal got up and started running again. And again Bear tripped him and sat down laughing. Rascal was close to the trees now and he started running and Bear bunted him in the butt with his head and Rascal went down face first on the grass. And Bear wandered over to the trees and sat on a little knoll and turned to look at Rascal.

Rascal stood up and Bear raised his paw and Rascal raised his arm. The game was over.

The four men stood there not so much surprised but in total disbelief. Shocked.

Rascal dusted himself off and walked over to the others knowing he had a lot of explaining to do.

Before he could say a word Jarvis said, "It was that bear

that ran off with your hat wasn't it?"

"You saw that, did you?"

Rascal looked at the four of them and said, "I know I have a lot of explaining to do, but I'll wait until we're back at the lodge. Em is part of this."

All were quiet then and the only thing Rascal could think to say was, "Nice day."

Everyone broke out laughing, even Rascal. The prime minister and the president were laughing so hard they started coughing.

As they walked back to the lodge, when Emma looked at Rascal and his messed up hair and grass stained pants, she said, "You were playing with Bear again, weren't you?"

Again everyone burst into laughter. Even Anita although she didn't know why.

"We have some explaining to do, Em. Do we have time before supper?"

"We'll be alright."

He looked at everyone first and then he began. "It all started the first summer I was back from the war. Jarvis had asked me to speak with the station master, Greg, about beaver flooding the tracks at mile nine. Greg said he would have Elmo Leaf help and we took a handcar down. We had caught several beaver, ate our fill and started back with a pack basket full of hides, meat, tails and castors. Just as we had the handcar moving Elmo screamed about a bear that was coming towards us from the woods. We started pumping the handcar as fast as we could and that bear began running after us between the rails. I thought sure once we were close to the village the bear would break off. But he chased us right through the village about twenty feet behind us. Everybody came out to see and were hollering, but that didn't bother the bear none. When we went by Anita and Silvio's cabin, Silvio hollered the bear was gaining on us. So we pumped harder. That bear chased us all the way to Ledge Swamp at mile twelve. When another bear stepped onto the tracks. Elmo was really screaming now. I was scared also. The second bear left the tracks and went up on the bank and our bear finally broke off and began fighting with the second bear. We changed directions back to the village."

"He chased you for three miles?" the prime minister asked.

"Yes, if it hadn't have been for that second bear he probably would have chased us right into Canada."

"Then what happened, Rascal?" Jarvis asked.

"Well, that fall I set traps all around the swamp. It's the best trapping grounds around. Well, when I went back to tend, every trap—even the water sets—were buried. I've had a trap buried before but not the entire trap line. I went back again and they were buried and I picked up. As I made my way around the swamp something was following me, but I could never get a glimpse of it until I was back on the tracks. And this bear came out onto the bank and he stood up and waved and began laughing at me. The only thing I could think to do was raise my arm and laugh back. I left the tracks and hiked down to my canoe and I didn't see him again until a year later when there were nuisance beaver at mile twelve and a half. Elmo Leaf refused to go with me again, so Jeters said he would go."

"Say that name again," the prime minister said, "I have never heard it before."

"Jeters, Jeters Asbau. He worked for the Hitchcock Company in the boiler room.

"We took the handcar up and sure enough, Bear came out and sat between the rails watching us. We were there most of the day and we had caught many beaver. We started a fire and roasted beaver meat and made some tea. We left with a pack full of hides, meat, tails and castors. Bear was still between the rails. Jeters wasn't liking this.

"When we started moving the handcar towards him for home he stood up, raised his paw and we both swore he was laughing. He let us pass and didn't follow. We left traps set and had to return the next day and Bear was there. We only had a few beaver and we left the carcasses for Bear beside the tracks. He followed us for a short distance and stopped and raised his paw and laughed.

"That's when Jeters said he must be lonely and looked towards us as playmates. We took an oath not to ever say anything to anyone because people would think we were crazy."

"Probably," Jarvis said.

"I'll let Em tell you the next time we both encountered Bear."

"It was the first time I helped Rascal mow the farm field. Rascal drove the Model T tractor out to the farm and the first few passes around the field, and then we switched and I drove. It wasn't long when I saw Bear following us. He kept following us until the field was mowed. When Rascal climbed off the mower and lifted the cutter bar and bolted it upright, Bear raised his paw and Rascal introduced him to me," she said and the others began laughing.

She continued, "And Bear made a sound that I swear to God he said, 'Hi.'

"I didn't know until that day that Rascal was talking with him.

"One evening we hiked out to the farm to go through the farmhouse and make sure things were alright. When we were about to leave, Bear came wandering in and started following us. When we started to run he ran behind us and twice he tripped Rascal and then he bunted him in the butt with his head and he went facedown. Bear then went off the road onto a little grassy knoll. Stood up again and waved and made that same noise. Rascal did also, and then we were allowed to go home."

"You left something out didn't you, Em?"

"Rascal! Behave yourself."

Now everyone was waiting and looking at her. "All right, all right. I was so scared when he was chasing us he made me pee my pants."

"It seems now whenever we go out to the farm, Bear is always there. We did see a sow and two cubs this summer when we mowed the field and Bear was already there in the middle of the field. Like he was watching over the sow and cubs.

"I trapped beaver in the winter twice at Ledge Swamp, but I was sure he had hibernated. We do not allow any of our hunters to hunt at Ledge Swamp and that is why we won't let anyone shoot bear."

"Has he ever offered to play with you, Emma?" Jarvis asked.

"No, it's only Rascal. For some reason I think Bear thinks of Rascal as a toy, a playmate."

"Extraordinary," President Cutlidge said.

"Simply unbelievable," the prime minister said and then laughed.

"Have you ever seen him or tracks around here?" Jarvis asked.

"I keep checking and no. Somehow I think he understands."

Emma and Anita went back to the kitchen. "Anita, if you want to start frying the steak, I'll set the table."

When the table was set, Anita came out with a heaping hot tray of moose steak. Emma brought the baked potatoes and biscuits and Anita went back for the vegetables. "Rascal, would you go downstairs for the milk."

He came back with a pitcher full. "Sit down, please; everything is ready."

"It sure smells delicious," President Cutlidge said.

"And more hot biscuits," the prime minister said.

After one bite of steak Jarvis knew what it was and wondered how he came by it.

"Humm, this steak is so tender and good," the prime minister said. "What kind is it?"

Rascal spoke up, "Moose. The train stopped here four days ago and the engineer said he had hit a moose in the head.

He asked if he and the crew could have some. I went up with the crawler and brought it back and gave half of it to the train crew the next day. It is good, isn't it?"

"How on earth do you get and keep fresh milk out here?" President Cutlidge asked.

"We have it shipped up in large milk cans and we keep it on ice in the cold storage room in the cellar," Emma said.

When they had finished eating, the moose steak and biscuits were gone. "I can't remember when I have eaten so much," President Cutlidge said and then he excused himself and went upstairs and came right back again.

"Madame, would you have seven clean glasses? I think this calls for a little after dinner brandy," the president said.

He saw everyone's face and added, "Don't worry, this is an old bottle that I have been keeping for just such an occasion."

"I am glad to hear that, Mr. President," the prime minister said, "for I have brought a little brandy and some wine for the ladies, if they prefer."

Emma came right back with the glasses. "I think tonight I would like some brandy."

"I will also," Anita said.

When the glasses were filled, President Cutlidge said, "I'd like to make a toast," and he looked squarely at Prime Minister William Kingsley. "May we have a successful week, Sir."

Everyone said, "Hear, hear," and held their glass up and then took a sip.

Emma and Anita excused themselves and cleared off the table and kitchen dishes and then rejoined the men. And had a little more brandy, "My, I never knew brandy could be so good," Anita said.

The wind started blowing and the temperature was dropping. "Listening to that wind has made me sleepy," Prime Minister Kingsley said.

"Did you want to hunt at all tomorrow or will the two of you be in conference all day?" Rascal asked.

"I think we need the morning to start our discussions but I'd like to hunt the afternoon," President Cutlidge said and looked at the prime minister.

"Yes, that sounds excellent. Now I really must get to bed. It has been a long day," the prime minister said.

"Yes, I agree," and they walked upstairs to their rooms.

There had to be a security in the hallway all night, so Dubois and Jarvis made up a schedule for the two of them.

Rascal, Emma and Anita also called it a day and went to bed.

"This has been quite a day, Rascal. I mean we have the President of the United States and the Prime Minister of Canada here in our home, i.e. sporting lodge. Who would have ever guessed?" Emma said.

* * *

The temperature had dropped below freezing during the night and there was a thin coating of ice in the cove. Rascal was up early and went up to the log cabin and started a fire in the ram-down stove and the kitchen cook stove. And then he put in the fixings for a pot of coffee but didn't put it on the stove. He would let the two of them do it when they came up for their meeting.

By the time he was back at the lodge everyone else was up and the inside was warm and he could smell fresh coffee and bacon.

"Emma, after this week do you suppose anyone will know two world leaders were here?" Anita asked.

"I don't know, Anita. So far everything has been kept very quiet. We'll just have to wait and see."

The two world leaders walked up to the log cabin. Jarvis in the lead and Dubois in the rear. After both men were inside Jarvis and Dubois positioned themselves outside.

"Mr. President, Rascal said all we had to do was put this

pot on the stove to boil, and he set it over on the hot stove lids.

"You know it's just the two of us now, let's knock off the Mr. President and Mr. Prime Minister. My first name is Kevin," and he extended his hand to shake.

"That sounds fitting to me; my name is William," and he shook Kevin's hand.

Once the coffee was done and they each had a hot cup and they sat at the table. "Now, Kevin, why don't you explain what you have on your mind."

"There is no reason in this universe or this time in our history that our two countries should not combine into one country. We are all Americans. We are both part of the North American Continent."

"This is true. Continue, Kevin."

"Both countries have similar forms of government and economy. A very similar history. There's no reason why two countries with this much in common lying side by side should have to exist individually."

"Oh I agree with you, Kevin. Have you talked to anyone else about this?"

"No. So far I've kept this idea to myself. I didn't want politicians knowing a little about the idea and blowing everything out of context and proportion.

"Each country independently has much to offer the other. Let alone our world security."

"I agree with you, Kevin. I can understand why Canada didn't take a stand against England during the American Revolution. There were those in our government who loyally supported England. Some might say they owed England, but our country perhaps was too young to take that stand, but in the War of 1812, instead of Canada remaining neutral we should have joined forces with the United States and driven England's dormancy from North America forever. We had our chance and we didn't do it."

They each became so interested with the new idea, the

coffee in their cups was cold. The fire in both stoves had gone out and the coffee pot was now cold.

Francois Dubois was quite content to remain stationary at the back door, while Jarvis would walk around the cabin and the perimeter occasionally, more to stretch his legs and break up the monotony.

At 11:30 President Cutlidge said, "Why don't we leave it there for today. It is obvious we both have strong ideas about this. Let's have lunch and go hunting."

The weather had warmed during the morning and the ice in the cove was gone.

As everybody was eating lunch, President Cutlidge asked the prime minister, "What do you think? Let these good people know what we are talking about?"

"Let's do it and see what their reactions are like."

Everyone was now looking at President Cutlidge and waiting. "Prime Minister Kingsley and I have been discussing the possibility of our two countries coming together to form one country. How do you people feel about this?"

Rascal spoke first, "In my opinion, the only difference between our two countries is that damned border."

Jarvis was next, "For years I have had to work the border for illegal Canadian moose and deer hunters. And as Rascal said the only difference is that boundary line that separates us. The moose a Canadian hunter shoots and gets arrested because he is on this side of the border. Who's to say that that same moose didn't come from Canada to begin with. Or the deer?"

"That is a very good point, Jarvis," the Prime Minister said.

"Emma, how do you feel?"

"I'm all for it, I agree with Rascal that the only difference is that line."

"Anita?"

"I think we could all be good friends and neighbors. And I think we each would benefit from the alliance."

"A very good point, Anita," President Cutlidge said.

"Mr. Dubois, what about you?"

"I have always been in favor of one country on the North American continent. But I think perhaps Lower Canada may not have the same feelings."

"That is a good point," the prime minister said. "We'll have to talk some about that."

After eating lunch, Jarvis and President Cutlidge went hunting out the road to the valley and Rascal and the prime minister went up and behind the log cabin. Francois Dubois was neither hunter nor guide so he stayed back at the lodge talking with Emma and Anita.

Rascal stopped at the game trail that he also used for trapping and looked for tracks. He pointed to tracks traveling in both directions. He checked the wind direction and it was coming towards them from the north-northwest.

Rascal had him go in front of him following the trail. "Hunt your way through and take your time."

Rascal didn't have his rifle, only his .45 handgun at Dubois' insistence. This trail was being used more now than since Rascal had trapped along it three years ago. He was liking what he was seeing for signs.

Just as Jarvis and President Cutlidge were nearing the deer crossing in the old road two deer ran across running into the wind. The first one was a doe and the second one was a buck following her scent. Jarvis had figured on having the president sit on the rock and watch the crossing.

Rascal and the Prime Minister had hunted through to the big rock where his trap line turned towards the lake. This was as good as a place as any to sit for a while. No sooner had they gotten settled and a big cat screamed not more than fifty yards in front of them. Rascal touched the prime minister's hand and when he looked at him, Rascal touched his eye and then made a scanning motion with his hand. The prime minister understood and started looking beyond where the cat had screamed.

261

An hour later they could hear two deer running into the wind, just beyond where they could see.

On the way back to the lodge, Kingsley asked, "Was that a mountain lion that screamed?"

"I think so. Three years ago there was a mother and cubs here that had killed a deer and then a male cat came too close and the mother tackled it and tore a piece of hide from its shoulder. The village was still here then and I was afraid the cats might attack a human or carry off a small child, so I set traps for them and caught the two adults. I never knew what happened to the cubs. Maybe that's what screamed. But with a cat up here the deer are going to be pretty spooked."

While the men waited for supper they swapped hunting stories. Jarvis was particularly interested in the big cat.

Anita had been roasting a pork shoulder all afternoon and Emma made another batch of biscuits and an apple pie.

It was obvious to everyone that the two men were extremely tired, so right after supper they excused themselves and went up to their rooms. Tonight it was Dubois' first watch. Jarvis would relieve him at 2 am so he went to his room also.

Rascal, Emma and Anita stayed up for a while sitting in the living room with the glow of the fireplace, talking.

* * *

Right after breakfast the next morning the two men adjourned to the log cabin and Rascal had already started the fire and the coffee pot was ready to put on the stove.

"With our two countries coming together as one, just think of the savings. Right now both of our countries have our own custom officials securing our borders. If our two countries come together then both countries can do away with all that hoop-de-la. There are ten states that border with Canada with manned custom agents and equipment. How many provinces are there?"

"Seven provinces. I see what you are getting at. In five years we would be saving millions of dollars that could go to more useful projects."

"Exactly. There would be no more quarreling across the border about unfair trade practices, no more tariffs on goods and products going both ways. The advantages of one country are clear and numerous."

"I agree wholeheartedly. And I don't think there'll be any problem with Upper Canada. But I'm not so sure about Lower Canada. Remember, many settlers loyal to the crown moved willingly from the colonies to Lower Canada, and some were expelled; and many in Lower Canada I believe would want to remain loyal to the Commonwealth. It's hard to say without a popular vote. I know that there were many disappointed settlers in Lower Canada who wished to have been on the Maine side or to the west of the boundary line when it was finally established by the Webster-Ashburton Treaty of 1842. Many settlers from Scotland had had enough of British domination and that's why many settled in Nova Scotia. There were also some English settlers who were tired of England's domination and would have preferred if the boundary line had come further to the east than it did.

"But to begin with, I believe Canada would have to petition England for complete autonomy before we could even consider sending this idea for a public vote. Although Canada has had a more or less democratic form of government, England still sets foreign and defense policies.

"When I return to Ottawa I will check with our judicial minister of law. He may be able to find a way around petitioning England, but I doubt it."

"It would have to go out to popular vote in the states also. But I don't look for any problems. The benefits that both countries would gain would surely outweigh any negative arguments."

Hunting that afternoon, Jarvis took the president back

to the same valley and Rascal took the prime minister out to the farm to hunt down through the old choppings to the road the president would be on.

"Do you think your friend Bear will still be at the farm?"

"I hope not."

When they came to the field they stayed to the left hand side and next to the tree line. Hoping that if Bear was there he might not see them. The little breeze was in their favor though. As they began the downhill slant, there were numerous deer feeding on clover next to the tree line. Rascal stopped and pointed. There were five adult deer and two fawns, and two of the bigger deer had a nice set of antlers. The prime minister raised his rifle, but Rascal pushed the barrel down and whispered, "Too far, let's see if we can get closer."

Down on their hands and knees they began crawling to the corner of the field. So far the deer were not alerted. The wind was still blowing in Rascal's face, which was good. He knew the deer would not be able to wind them. But with those big ears— well, Rascal knew they would have to be extremely quiet.

They were about a hundred yards out now. Maybe a little less. Rascal turned so the prime minister could steady his rifle across Rascal's back. Rascal wanted to cover his ears—'cause he knew the rifle blast would be deafening. And his knees were beginning to ache. Just then the prime minister fired.

Rascal didn't see if a deer had fallen or not. The others ran off though.

As they walked down to where the deer had been the prime minister kept his rifle ready in case he had to shoot again. There was a small pool of foamy blood not far from where the deer had been. "I'd say you hit him in the lungs. He'll not go very far."

"How do you know that, Rascal?"

"This blood is foamy because it is mixed with air. That always indicates a lung shot. All we have to do now is follow the blood trail."

The buck lay in a heap down over the bank at the edge of

the field. "That's a nice buck, Mr. Prime Minister. A twelve point and not yet in rut. The meat will be good and tender."

After he had finished cleaning out the innards, leaving the heart and liver, he said, "We'll have just about enough time to get back to the lodge before dark." And they started dragging.

"Is Bear apt to follow this blood trail to the lodge?"

"Not likely. If anything he'll find the gut pile and eat that. Probably tonight.

* * *

When Jarvis heard the rifle shot and only one, he figured the prime minister had probably shot his deer and the two of them would be dragging it back now.

Shortly after they had arrived at the valley crossing, they could hear a bull moose smashing his antlers against some bushes. This went on for ten minutes and then all was quiet.

When everyone was back at the lodge and the prime minister's buck hanging, and the liver and heart soaking in a pan of water, the four men cleaned up for supper and then came down for supper.

"We see deer each afternoon but nothing to shoot at," Jarvis said.

"I have found that the best time to hunt that valley crossing is in the morning."

"Then by all means, the prime minister and I will have our meeting after lunch tomorrow."

"How much did your deer weigh, Mr. Prime Minister?" Emma asked.

"225 pounds. But while we were dragging it I thought sure it would have gone closer to 300 pounds."

"Would you like to have the head mounted, Sir?" Jarvis asked.

"That would be nice. My first white tail deer. Do you know someone who does that sort of work?"

"Yes, Rascal sends him a lot of work through me. After supper while it is still warm Rascal and I will skin it. The hide will come off much easier than if we wait until morning when it is cold. Then we can box it up and when I leave, I'll take it with me and when it is finished I'll send it to you."

"That would be excellent. How much should I give you?"

"$75.00."

The prime minister handed Jarvis the money and said, "Before I forget to pay you."

The next morning for breakfast Emma and Anita fried slices of heart with onions, scrambled eggs and biscuits. "I never would have imagined eating fresh heart with eggs for breakfast, and being so delicious," the president said.

"Jarvis do you want to go out with us?"

"I think I'd better. I was told not to leave the president's side."

"What do you need, Rascal? Maybe I can help," the prime minister said.

"Well, what I have planned would work better with another person with me. I was planning on making a short drive down the valley. If there are any deer in that valley we'll push 'em towards the road."

"I'm game. You'll be with me, correct?"

"Yes. You'll never be out of my sight."

He looked at Dubois and asked, "You don't mind do you, Francois?"

"No, not at all."

When they came to the cut off for the big beech tree, Rascal stopped and said in a low voice, "The wind this morning is in our favor. We'll go up through here to a big beech tree. Deer feed on the nuts at night and we might be able to start one into the wind towards you. We'll give you five minutes to get situated."

Even Jarvis had to marvel at Rascal's ability to guide and know how to move deer and where they are likely to go.

Rascal and the prime minister started up through the trees. When they came to the beech tree, it was obvious several deer had been there during the night. Their tracks, he pointed out were going just where he wanted, toward the valley.

As they reached the edge of the tree line and the valley Rascal pointed towards two white flags moving away from them towards the road. They went out in the middle of the swamp and he had the prime minister follow the deer trail and he usually would stay on the left of the hunter, but this morning he changed and stayed on the prime minister's right. And within sight of him.

They started down through the swamp going at a slow pace. Rascal didn't want to start the deer running. There were plenty of fresh tracks in the swamp and they were now more than halfway to the old road. Rascal kept telling himself, *Any minute now.* He took one more step and one high power rifle shot. He turned to look at the prime minister and he was smiling as happily as if he had just shot his deer.

Rascal gave him a thumbs up and they continued, still going at a slow pace. Just in case the president happened to miss. But when they were closer to the road they both could hear excited conversations. By the time they reached the downed buck, Jarvis had it cleaned.

"Look at this, Rascal," and he turned the head so he could see the rack. "It's identical to the prime minister's buck. Do you suppose these two were twins?"

"It sure is possible." The president was as excited about shooting his trophy buck as if he were a child on Christmas morning. "Well, let's get this to the lodge."

It weighed exactly what the other buck weighed and the rack was identical. Jarvis and the president skun and put the head and cape in another wooden box to be taken out later.

After eating an early lunch, Emma said, "After lunch until supper is ready, I want you men to stay out of the kitchen and cafeteria. Anita and I are fixing something special for supper, and we want it to be a surprise. This includes you also, Rascal."

Cutlidge and Kingsley retired to the log cabin and Jarvis and Francois remained outside to secure the premises.

"Mr. President, let's say both countries agree to this unification where will the capital be? Ottawa is too far out of reach for the states as Washington is for the Provinces. Any idea?"

"My first thought would have been Minneapolis, Minnesota, but since talking with you I have had a change of ideas. I am thinking about where the capital would be situated so that part of it would be in the old United States and part of it in the old Canada."

"Good idea, as long as there is good access. What did you have in mind, Mr. President?"

"What about the area of Upper and Lower Michigan Peninsula, across the river including Sault Ste. Marie? There would be room for expansion as needed in all three directions."

The prime minister was silent, thinking about this. He started walking back and forth the length of the cabin. Finally he said, "I like it. Its accessibility, defense and I think this really might help sway the French in Quebec as this new capital would be in their back door. I think this would be an excellent location. I'm quite familiar with that whole area and the more I think about it, the more I like it."

"Okay, let's get to something else."

"What have you in mind?"

"We both have a democratic form of government. There are differences and I think if we can get the popular vote on this, a committee from both sides should be established to iron out any wrinkles."

"Canada leans more towards social systems than we do, but maybe it would be good to integrate both systems."

"I understand what you're saying, Mr. President, and I think comprises on both sides—well, then I think we'd have the best economic and form of democracy in the world. You know I think we may have something here. Now if we can sell it to our people and if I can get our parliament to petition England for complete autonomy. If parliament can obtain that, then the rest will be simple."

"It'll take time to make the transition," President Cutlidge said.

"What about a flag, a national anthem?"

"I think that would have to be left to the committee or a subcommittee."

"This is exciting, Mr. President. Any idea what we would call our new country?"

"I have a couple of ideas, but I'd like to wait and see what our new friends come up with."

The prime minister started laughing and said, "I wonder what Emma and Anita are planning for a surprise supper?"

"I don't know, but you can bet it'll be fantastic."

"You know Mr. President, I don't see that we have too much more to discuss, I'd like to lay down right here and maybe get an hour or so of sleep before supper."

"That's a good idea. I can't remember when I have gotten so much exercise."

Meanwhile Francois and Jarvis remained outside on security. "I don't think this is a job I would want every day," Jarvis said.

"The pay is good. They are very quiet inside now."

Francois was very interested with Jarvis' life as a game warden. "In Canada, or better in Quebec, a game warden would be called garde-chasse. I couldn't even begin to imagine coming out here to work for days and as I understand, you did just that and much of the time you slept in the woods and at times you had very little to eat. And I can't imagine your wife putting up with a life like that."

"It wasn't always easy for her or me. I missed out on a lot of my kids growing up. We were married after I became a game warden, so she knew what she was getting into. But it was a great way of life. And I'd be lying if I were to say I didn't miss it some."

* * *

An hour before supper the four men walked back to the lodge and were not allowed inside. They had to sit out on the platform until Emma unlocked the door. Rascal came back from feeding the chickens and closing up the house for the night and he joined the others. Emma had set out glasses and a bottle of brandy that she had been saving for a special occasion. And this was good a time as any.

No one questioned where the brandy had come from or any offhand remarks. Rascal poured the brandy and they each took a glass and sat down to tell stories.

With the brandy glasses empty Emma allowed the men upstairs to clean up and that meant for Rascal also. "And put on the clothes I laid out on the bed for you." She and Anita had already changed into their evening attire.

Anita finished filling each glass with wine while Emma made the finishing touches to their smorgasbord of:

> Canned beaver meat
> Frog legs
> Smoked fish
> Canned deer meat
> Fresh potatoes and gravy
> Spiced crabapples
> Fried green peppers, onions and tomatoes
> Fresh sliced tomatoes
> Fresh cucumbers
> Pickled fiddleheads
> Biscuits

Emma hollered upstairs, "You can come to the cafeteria now."

"A smorgasbord gentlemen. Pick up your plates and serve yourself."

Everyone was sampling a little of everything. Suddenly Prime Minister William Kingsley stopped and exclaimed, "Holy Mother of Mary! Francois look at this *les jumbo d'grenouille.* Oh, Madame, you have touched my heart. How we Canadians, *I,* love the frog legs. They are such a *délicatesse.* "

After everyone sat down, including Emma and Anita, there was still plenty of food left.

"I can't remember when I have eaten such delicious food. I mean everything, not just this smorgasbord. Fishermen and hunters alike will return if only for your food," the president said.

"Emma, what are these two types of red meat. They each are very delicious, but I cannot place them," the prime minister said.

"What you have on your fork now is beaver meat. The other is deer. Both canned."

"Rascal, I'm surprised you don't weigh three hundred pounds," the prime minister added.

All of the dishes were so good no one wanted to stop eating. Then finally, one by one, they pushed their plates away from them, and pushed their chairs back some. "I bet I will have gained ten pounds by the time I get back to Washington."

Emma and Anita cleared the food and put it away and when they started to do the dishes, the prime minister said, "No, ladies, you both have done enough. Go sit in the living room. The president and I will do the dishes."

* * *

The dishes were done and put away and they all sat in the living room enjoying the soft glow from the fireplace and conversations.

"Have any of you come up with a new name?" the president asked.

There was North America, Can-Am, The United Provinces of America, United Canada and States and finally the prime minister said, "What about simply America. As the president pointed out we all are actually Americans."

They all seemed to like that one the best.

"If you'll excuse us for a minute," and the two gentlemen went upstairs and were gone for several minutes and when they returned they were carrying several plaques. Rascal's, Emma's and Anita's name were on one plaque thanking them for being excellent hosts. Another for Jarvis Page for coming out of retirement to aid in the president's service and the prime minister gave each a similar plaque. Then both men gave another to Francois Dubois for his services.

"Our business has been fruitful and neither of us can justify staying any longer. So we both have decided to take our leave tomorrow," the president said.

"Jarvis, you'll take both crated heads and cape back with you. Would you like the rest of my deer? I'm afraid the meat would spoil before we got back to Washington."

"Yes, Mr. President, I surely would."

"And what about the rest of my deer, Rascal and Emma? I would have the same problem."

Emma spoke up, "We would be glad to accept it, Mr. Prime Minister."

"Now if I may I must telephone my security chief in Beech Tree to have the train stop here in the morning and again in the afternoon."

Mr. Butler went down to the train station right after the president's telephone call and he talked with Sam Grindle the Canadian-Atlantic supervisor and all arrangements were made.

"In all honesty, Mr. Prime Minister, I didn't think we would come to such a complete agreement so soon."

* * *

The next morning Emma had planned for breakfast,

apple pie, sharp cheese and plenty of coffee.

The prime minister said, "Mrs. Antony, Anita, if I may, how would you like to come and work for me? Be the chief of the culinary staff."

"Oh, Mr. Prime Minister, that is an awful tempting offer and I want to thank you, but I'll have to say no. Rascal and Emma are like family to me. And I really enjoy living here. I'd be lost in a big city. But thank you."

"I had to try."

Rascal had already set the red flag and he had the prime minister's luggage on the platform.

"Last night the president and I talked for a while and we decided to give each of you a $100.00 tip or bonus, however you want to call it. And you also, Francois. This only partly pays for your services and friendship and hospitality."

The president added, "We cannot express enough our thanks."

"There's the half mile signal," Rascal said.

The prime minister shook Rascal's hand, and Emma and Anita—he kissed both sides of their cheeks.

Before the prime minister boarded the train, Francois checked out the passenger and freight cars. As the train pulled out, Anita had tears in her eyes.

"Would you men like another pot of coffee?" Emma asked.

Rascal looked at the president and Jarvis and they both nodded their head. "That would be good, Em, and join us with a cup."

It was a nice day, a bit cool, but nice. They all had heavy shirts or jackets on and they chose to sit out on the platform.

Emma came back shortly with a pot and poured each of them another cup. She sat down beside Rascal. She could not imagine being happier. In a few minutes, Anita joined them also. Her eyes were still red.

What Jarvis said next surprised everyone, particularly

Rascal. "Marcel Cyr? He and his wife Arlene are moving on."

"Where are they going?" Rascal asked.

"Somewhere in central Maine. It seems as though Arlene doesn't like being left alone so much. She said she worries too much about him when he's away for days at a time. And I don't think he ever felt comfortable out here in the wilderness."

"I don't think he did either," Rascal said. "So now, Em, it looks like we have to break-in another new game warden."

"Not necessarily," Jarvis said.

"What do you mean, Jarvis? You coming out of retirement?"

"No, I wasn't talking about me. You, Rascal. I don't know a better man for the job. You already know this country better than anyone else."

"You know, Jarvis, I used to poach some," everyone burst out laughing.

"All that has been taken into consideration. You wouldn't hire a doctor to build you a house would you?"

"No."

"Well, a reformed poacher makes the best game warden."

"Gee, Jarvis, I don't know. We have just gotten started with the lodge and it wouldn't be fair to Em and Anita. Besides, I probably make a better living here. And what about my leg, Jarvis? Right now I don't let it slow me down too much. But as I get older, it'll probably start giving me more trouble. Would the warden service hire someone who has a 100% disability from the Army?"

"You were wounded twice in France weren't you, Rascal?" the president asked.

"Yes, shrapnel in the stomach first and then as we were retreating downhill someone behind me shot me in the butt. That's the wound that bothers my leg."

"Have you ever seen a doctor since being discharged from the Army?" the president asked.

"No."

"You know, Rascal, medicine has come a long ways since the war. I wouldn't be surprised but what a specialist could fix your leg for good. And without a limp."

"A doctor could do that?"

"A specialized surgeon I'm sure could."

He turned to look at Emma, "What do you think?"

"If it could help you, let's go for it."

"Okay, now what do I do?"

"Let me take care of that. When I get back to Washington I'll have my personal physician contact the right people at the Walter Reed Army Hospital is Bethesda, Maryland. Just as a guess, I would say probably not until after the first of next year."

"That would be fine."

"Okay, then when Dr. Rollin can set up something I'll have him contact you personally. I have your address and telephone number."

"Gee, Rascal, just think not having to limp with a sore leg anymore," Emma said.

"That would be nice."

They stayed on the platform enjoying the nice weather and each other until it was time for lunch.

For lunch they had warmed smoked fish, cheese, milk and biscuits. When they had finished the president excused himself and went up to his room and put on his hunting traveling clothes, his wig and mustache. When he came back down, at first no one recognized him. Then they all began to laugh. "I'll bring down the rest of your luggage, Mr. President," Rascal said.

"Ah, from here it's Mr. David Elliot."

The train engineer blew the steam whistle warning of the approach. "Rascal, I can't thank you enough. I'd like to come back some time."

"Anytime, Mr. Elliot."

Jarvis loaded the luggage and the two crates and like Francois, he had to check out the passenger and freight cars. "All is clear, Mr. Elliot."

The president hugged Emma and Anita and gave them each a kiss on the cheek. "Goodbye, friends," he said and disappeared inside the car.

The train left for Beech Tree, and Rascal, Emma and Anita were left on the platform.

"Imagine that, Emma, we were both kissed by Prime Minister William Kingsley and President Kevin Cutlidge." Anita went inside where it was warm.

"What do you think, Em?"

"Two world leaders right here in our home. Unbelievable, Rascal."

"It would be a nice story to pass down to our grandchildren, if we had any, wouldn't it?"

"Yes it would. And who's to say we won't have any. I think it's time we got started on making a family, Rascal. Come on. I mean now."

The End

About the Author

Randall Probert lived and was raised in Strong, a small town in the western mountains of Maine. Six months after graduating from high school, he left the small town behind for Baltimore, Maryland, and a Marine Engineering school, situated downtown near what was then called "The Block." Because of bad weather, the flight from Portland to New York was canceled and this made him late for the connecting flight to Baltimore. A young kid, alone, from the backwoods of Maine, finally found his way to Washington, D.C., and boarded a bus from there to Baltimore. After leaving the Merchant Marines, he went to an aviation school in Lexington, Massachusetts.

During his interview for Maine Game Warden, he was asked, "You have gone from the high seas to the air. . .are you sure you want to be a game warden?"

Mr. Probert retired from Warden Service in 1997 and started writing historical novels about the history in the areas where he patrolled as a game warden, with his own experiences as a game warden as those of the wardens in his books. Mr. Probert has since expanded his purview and has written two science fiction books, *Paradigm* and *Paradigm II*, and has written two mystical adventures, *An Esoteric Journey*, and *Ekani's Journey.*

Made in the USA
Columbia, SC
27 February 2025

54502671R00154